Praise for Alison Paige's
Little Red and the Wolf

"Alison Paige pulled me into the story from the first pages. I loved the rapport between Maizie and her elderly grandmother, Ester. The descriptions of their love, devotion and loyalty were nicely done...Despite the fact Maize and Gray fight their attraction to each from the beginning, they're perfect for each other...and the sex...get a fan, because it's sizzling hot and intense."

~ *Literary Nymphs Reviews*

"Alison Paige has created an indulgent & salacious read that will make you rethink the old take of Little Red Riding Hood. I always knew there was a much deeper story, and the author lured me into a truly magical and paranormal world of shifters that I can truly never get enough of."

~ *Book Junkies Reviews*

Look for these titles by
Alison Paige

Now Available:

Tame Horses Wild Hearts

Little Red and
the Wolf

Alison Paige

A SAMHAIN PUBLISHING, LTD. publication.

Samhain Publishing, Ltd.
577 Mulberry Street, Suite 1520
Macon, GA 31201
www.samhainpublishing.com

Little Red and the Wolf
Copyright © 2010 by Alison Paige
Print ISBN: 978-1-60504-929-8
Digital ISBN: 978-1-60504-902-1

Editing by Anne Scott
Cover by Kanaxa

First Samhain Publishing, Ltd. electronic publication: February 2010
First Samhain Publishing, Ltd. print publication: September 2010

Dedication

A special thanks to the wonderful people at Samhain who make their authors feel like part of a great family. Thanks to Anne Scott for all her hard work and patience, and thanks to my family who understand it's not a competition between them and my writing, it's proof of a deep love of both.

Chapter One

"Wolf." Granny leaned into the table, her liver-spotted hand resting on Maizie's. "You hear me, Little Red? The man's a beast."

"I hear ya, Gran." Maizie glanced over her shoulder at the Armani suit strolling toward the front doors of the Green Acres Nursing Home. "He's a wolf. Got it."

The word iced through her brain. Maizie didn't like wolves or dogs or pretty much anything four legged and furry. But pushing the nightmare images of fur and fangs from her mind wasn't hard when her brain had better things to entertain it.

Salt-and-pepper hair curling over his collar had Maizie guessing Granny's wolf-in-an-Italian-suit was about forty-five, maybe fifty. No rings or tan lines on his fingers, and the sprinkle of dark hair over sun-kissed skin contrasted nicely with the stark white of his shirt cuffs.

Smoother, taut skin on his hands bounced his age down to forty-five, maybe forty-two. The expensive suit jacket hid the details of his ass—not that she was checking him out, strictly diagnostic. Although if she were checking him out, she'd be intrigued by the way his slacks cut a fine line down to the gray shine of his shoes.

He stretched a hand toward the push-bar on the door, looked back as though he felt her watching.

"Whoof." Her reaction was purely chemical, instinct, no higher brain function needed. Heat flushed through her, burning her cheeks, wetting her panties.

The man couldn't be a day over thirty-five with ice-blue eyes that found hers as though he'd known exactly where to look before he'd turned. He paused, his hand resting on the push-bar, and stared at her.

Reflex nagged her to break the eye contact. She didn't. There was something about the way he stared at her, as though daring her to shy away. Shy was so not Maizie's thing. She lifted her chin, feeling her expression turn hard, confident.

Nostrils flared, making the trim shape of his nose seem more delicate. His face was all sharp angles and hard lines, a squarish jaw and a gently rounded chin to match his nose. His brows were black, thick, just like his lashes, and set off the contrast with those pale blue eyes.

He was clean-shaven, although he'd probably look just as good with day-old beard stubble. From this angle his hair appeared more silvery-gray than speckled, with thick waves that rolled back from a scowl-wrinkled forehead.

Just when she thought she might have pushed her bold stare a second too long, his brow smoothed and a faint, lopsided smile dimpled his right cheek.

Great googly-moogly, his mouth was too perfect. If he was a wolf, she'd let him gobble her up. Maizie stiffened, worrying her thoughts might show on her face. She turned around, ending the sex-charged staring contest. The back of her neck tingled like thrumming fingers rippling across her shoulders and down her back.

He was still watching her, she knew it, but she'd had enough. No sense toying with the idea of something she didn't have the time to finish. There were only so many hours in a day and she'd already wasted more seconds than she could spare on Gran's sexy silver-haired wolf-man.

Every minute was accounted for, a half-hour visit with Gran then back to the shop. And her neglected libido would not steal another second of it.

Maizie knew the moment he left, the warm tingle of his stare vanishing from her skin. *Good.* What'd a man like that even want with her grandmother? "So why's he a wolf?"

She hated eating up their time together discussing him, but Gran was getting up there in age and it wouldn't take much to confuse her, take advantage. Maizie wouldn't let that happen, no matter how sexy the guy was.

"Because he's after the cottage, of course." Granny nudged Maizie's plate closer. She'd been feeding her peanut butter sandwiches since she was seven. Now she made sure the nursing home staff had one ready the moment Maizie walked in the door.

Didn't matter that she wasn't hungry and the things were like a gazillion calories. Gran said eat, she ate. Old habit from an obedient childhood. Maizie picked up a triangle half and took a bite. Besides, peanut butter sandwiches had always been her comfort food.

"No one wants the cottage, Gran." The two-bedroom hovel had only been one good storm away from being a pile of rubble when she was a kid. It hadn't gotten any better since they'd both moved out.

"Bah, course not. It's the land. He wants the dang land. Gonna tear down all my trees and build one of them malls. You hear me?"

"Uh, sure, Gran. I hear you. The big bad wolf is after your land." Maizie swallowed the knot of emotion in her throat and shifted her attention to the wicker basket she'd set on the table beside her, pretending to sift through its contents. She didn't want Granny to see the tears welling in her eyes. The cottage was in the middle of nowhere. No one would want to build a mall there.

As good days and bad days went, this was still one of the better days for Granny. She called them "spells" when she described them to Maizie. Days when the world was a whole different place where everyday things got twisted in her head and memories, real or imagined, mixed with the reality of present day. The worst part was when the spells passed and Granny remembered—everything.

"I brought you some of my chocolate-chip cookies," Maizie said, hoping to pull Granny out of her fantasy world. "The ones mixed with white chocolate and almonds. You still bribing Nurse Ron for extra time on the back veranda?"

Granny's face wrinkled, her bright eyes wider, confused. She nodded. Did she know she was locked inside one of her spells right then? Maizie didn't want to think about it. She owed this woman everything. Making her feel as comfortable as possible was the least she could do.

"I brought some of those cinnamon sugar twists Clare at the front desk likes. And two boxes of the gingerbread cookies so you have something to offer your room guests." Maizie busied herself unloading everything she'd brought from her Pittsburgh bakery onto the table.

"He said I should sell him the land. I remember..." Granny's voice wobbled. "He said I was being selfish holding on to it. That you needed the money."

Maizie snapped her attention to Granny. "Who said that?"

"I...I'm not sure. Riddly? I think it was my Riddly."

"No, Gran. It wasn't Dad. Riddly Hood's been dead for twenty-one years. He died in a car accident when I was seven.

Both him and Mom. You remember that, don't you?"

Granny blinked, the droopy skin of her eyelids making her confused expression painfully adorable.

"It's okay, Gran. I forget things sometimes too." Maizie reached over and smoothed the white wisps of hair framing Granny's face toward the neat little bun at the top of her head. She straightened the edges of her cardigan and fastened the top pearl button.

Everything about Granny seemed so fragile, so unlike the woman who'd taken her in, raised her, given her everything. Granny should've had the last twenty-one years to focus on herself. She'd raised her son. But she'd set her own needs aside and raised Maizie anyway. By the time Maizie could fend for herself, age had begun toying with Granny's mind. It wasn't fair.

Confusion vanished, Granny's bright-blue eyes turned steely with determination. "You need money, dear? Tell Granny. I've got a little something in the coffee can on top of the fridge. Take what you need, Little Red. That's why it's there."

Maizie squeezed Granny's hand, gently, careful not to harm her brittle bones or bruise the velvet soft skin. "No, Gran. I'm good. The bakery's finally turning a profit this year."

It was half true. The bakery she'd opened two years ago, Red Hood Bakery, a play on her flaming hair color and nickname, was in the black for the first time, mostly. Maizie's personal finances, however, were a brighter red than her hair. Nursing homes, good ones, weren't cheap.

In a perfect world Maizie would've kept Granny with her and cared for her on her own. The world is far from perfect though, and Granny's medical needs, her hatred of the city and the time demands of a new business made a nursing home the best and only option for both of them.

Of course that didn't stop Maizie from brutalizing herself with guilt. She'd bankrupt herself, and the bakery if she had to, to make sure Granny had the best care. With any luck, the bank would approve her loan application and none of it would be a concern anymore. The truth was, selling the cottage she'd grown up in and the hundred and three acres it sat on would solve so many problems.

"When's the last time anyone checked on the cottage?" Maizie asked.

"Oh, my handsome silver wolf checked in on it just the other day. Everything's fine. He said he put fresh violets in the vase on the sill. They're my favorite, you know?" Granny's smile bunched the extra skin on her cheeks, a flush of color making her look ten years younger.

Maizie hissed an oath under her breath. Just like that, Granny was lost to one of her spells again. At least this one Maizie knew. This wolf, Granny's big silver wolf, had been a part of her childhood, a character in her bedtime stories. Granny seemed to forget he was make-believe sometimes. Maizie could play along though and still have a relatively sane visit with her grandmother.

"What else did your silver wolf say? He didn't air out the place by any chance? Maybe check the gutters and the cellar, make sure no critters had moved in."

Maizie hadn't had time to stop by and check on the old place for months. Surrounded by Granny's hundred acres and the neighbor's four hundred acres, the little house was nestled chimney deep in dense forest. All manner of wild things tended to take over in no time.

Granny nodded, her smile never faltering. "Yes, dear. He checked everything. My big silver wolf knows how important that place is to me. Says he's keeping it just how I left it for when I move back."

Maizie swallowed the sudden knot in her throat. She'd had no idea Granny believed she'd return to the cottage one day. "Gran…"

"Relax, dear. You'll blow a fuse. We both know living in that cottage is too much for me like this. I can barely take a tinkle on my own. He's just a tease, is all. Tempting me. I like it. Makes me laugh."

"Makes you laugh, huh? You always told me he was a big *bad* wolf. Gave me nightmares with those stories about how he'd eat me up if I went playing too deep into the forest. Told me all about his great big ears and razor-sharp teeth…"

"Oh, that. Well I suppose he could've mistaken you for a tasty fawn or a fox or something, but mostly I just didn't want you wandering off too far and pestering the poor thing."

"So it was a parenting tactic? Nice." Maizie squeezed a playful wink at Granny. "Maybe I'll go out there and see what's so special about this handsome silver wolf that you'd terrorize my childhood to protect him."

"No, no, I don't think that's wise. He's decent and polite, but there's still a wild beast in him. Don't ever forget that, Little Red. No. It's best you just leave him be. Besides, you hardly lived your childhood in terror. You were the most fearless little thing I'd ever seen. Worse than your father. I can't think of anything that could shake you, except…"

Maizie's heart stuttered. The two of them fell silent. She knew where Granny's thoughts had gone, same as her own. The night of her parents' death. The car accident. The haunting eyes a luminous green through the windshield. There and then not. It was too dark, too much rain. Her father couldn't see, couldn't stop in time. He swerved, but it was too late. The vicious roll down the embankment was inevitable, unstoppable.

How had she survived? She didn't know. Couldn't remember. But she remembered those eyes.

Maizie still saw them long after the image of the aftermath had faded, the broken body of a wolf pinned beneath the car, her parents in the front seat, their faces and bodies cut and battered beyond recognition, glass everywhere, twisted metal, the smell of burnt rubber and gasoline, the coppery taste of her own blood in her mouth. Wild green eyes had tormented her for years. God, she hated that wolf.

"Yeah, well. That was a long time ago." Maizie didn't want to remember anymore.

"Yes, it was dear. You've come so far since then."

Maizie forced a smile and steered the topic away from those dark memories. "And here you are still talking about that mysterious silver wolf coming around here, making you laugh, tempting you. C'mon, Gran, what's he tempting you with? Is it something that'll make me blush?"

Granny didn't bat an eye. "With becoming one of them, of course. That's the only way this old body would ever make it back to the cottage, isn't it?"

"One of them?"

"Yes, sweetheart, a lycanthrope. A shape shifter." She sighed at Maizie's continued confusion. "A werewolf, child. A werewolf."

"Annette, it's Mr. Lupo." Gray adjusted the BlackBerry against his ear.

"Yes, Mr. Lupo?"

"Get me everything there is on a Maizie Hood. And I mean everything, business and personal. I want it all. We should have her numbers on file with her grandmother Ester's." Hell, he'd helped Ester file for the kid's social security number when she'd realized Maizie's parents hadn't. Back then it hadn't been automatic.

"Maizie? The little girl from the—"

"Everything, Annette."

"Yes, Mr. Lupo."

Gray punched the disconnect button with his thumb and slipped the wide phone into his breast pocket. He stared out the darkened privacy window of his limo at nothing as they pulled from the driveway of the Green Acres Nursing Home.

Jeezus, he still couldn't believe it was her. She'd changed so much, matured...beautifully. But her scent was the same, exactly the same, despite having taken a second to place it. Twenty-one years was a long time, even for him.

Gray shook his head, rubbed the weariness from his eyes with both hands. Maybe he was imagining it, the smell of broken trees, of sap, of gasoline and burnt rubber. He could still smell the blood in the air around her, the earth and rain. He could still taste the tears, hers, and his.

He had to be imagining it. His enhanced olfactory sense was good, but not twenty-one years good. Still, seeing Maizie Hood just now proved he'd made the right decision all those years ago. The memories swamped over him like quicksand, pulling him under so he could hardly breathe.

Back then, it would've killed him. He was right to ask her grandmother, Ester, to keep her away, at least keep her from venturing into his part of the forest. He just couldn't bear her scent, the scent of death. She was told to stick to the paths, and he avoided them. It'd worked. Until today.

Gray snatched the newspaper from the pocket on the car wall. He leaned back, unfolded and refolded it with noisy crisp snaps. The ink was still moist, not so much that humans could

17

smell, but they felt it on their fingers just as he did. It was a good feeling, a good smell, mundane. Innocuous.

He turned to the real-estate section first—who's buying, what's selling. Business foremost in his thoughts, Maizie Hood would fade away into the dark recesses of his mind where he wanted her. He scanned the listings.

Cinnamon. The other scents were there, or not, but he'd smelled cinnamon on her for sure. *And chocolate.* Ester always had a peanut butter sandwich waiting for him, his favorite, or rather his compulsion. But then she'd offer some sort of delicious pastry or cookie for dessert.

He'd noticed Maizie had one of those quaint wicker baskets with the double handle and red-and-white-checkered lining. Was she Ester's pastry supplier? Ester had never mentioned Maizie's visits, what she'd brought.

Why would she? Ester knew how he felt. He'd made it perfectly clear all those years ago and Ester was a true, understanding friend.

What he'd sampled of the sugary confections, though, was heavenly. Better than most professional chefs he knew. Did Maizie bake for fun or profit? He wanted to know.

Sweet peat moss, what's taking Annette so long?

The wall of trees along the country road broke for a wide open field and drew his gaze. He stared, only half noticing the huddle of cows, the barn and corn silos in the distance. His mind wandered too quickly to red hair and long silken legs.

Maizie looked good enough to eat. He'd known her hair was red. He'd remembered that much. But the luminousness, the thickness. Jeezus, he'd had no idea. The color reminded him of autumn leaves, the ones that made the forest seem ablaze with cool fire. And with those thick locks tumbling all the way down to the top curve of her ass, it seemed more a cloak than hair.

Gray tried to blink the vision from his mind and focused again on the paper. He found the name he'd been scanning for in seconds.

"Anthony Cadwick, you old prick." The man certainly was busy. Harassing Ester in the morning and closing a major real-estate deal in the afternoon. Strong-arming homeowners and manipulating eminent domain laws was his specialty.

Cadwick was every bit the stereotypical wolf Ester had called him. Gray just hoped Ester could keep her wits about her when he came around again. He couldn't let Cadwick get his hands on the Hood land. Just the thought of housing developments or discount supermarkets so close to his forest made his balls shrink.

Gray knew without looking the moment they turned onto the highway. The limo's suspension was superior, but the difference between country roads and smooth highway was like cobblestone and glass.

No. Ester had Cadwick's number, and Gray had her back just in case. Convincing her to sell would be like pushing water uphill for Cadwick. The wildcard was Maizie. Blanking her from his reality had knocked her off his radar completely. She was an "in" for Cadwick that Gray hadn't considered.

No doubt she held a lot of sway with her grandmother. That alone was a danger he couldn't tolerate. How easily could Maizie be manipulated? Did she need money? Was she easily seduced? Was she smart or gullible? Did she have skeletons to be exploited, dreams and goals Cadwick could hand to her on a platter?

Gray checked his watch. "Jeezus, Annette."

Cadwick would do anything to turn a profit and with the kind of Fortune-500 clientele he dealt with, he had a lot of play room. Of course with Maizie's looks it wasn't hard to guess which tactic he'd try first.

At seventy-eight Gray looked the same age as Cadwick who was in his midforties. Though Gray was as fit as a man in his twenties. But Cadwick could still turn a pretty head or two. He had Romanesque features, larger nose, broader shoulders, stockier build.

His eyes were a dull brown, his hair as black as Gray's, once upon a time. But where Gray's had turned a silvery color, speckled with hints of black, Cadwick's still held the dark tones, only turning a dirty ash at the temples. He wore it shorter than Gray, neatly trimmed over the ears and a half inch above the collar.

Which one of them was more Maizie's type? Which one of them could seduce her best? Gray didn't have a clue. But what if it came to that—to seduction? Could Gray do what needed to be done to keep the Hood land from being sold? Could he seduce Maizie Hood?

His gaze drifted out the window, to the cars falling back as his limo cruised past them. But it was a vision of fiery red hair and shapely long legs that filled his mind.

She'd looked like sinful innocence, if such a thing existed. The nubile body of a woman cloaked in a snow-white sundress spotted with daisies and a contrasting forest-green apron. Her full breasts had strained the dress's low rounded collar, pressing against the apron so he'd been utterly incapable of shifting his attention enough to read the white lettering on the front pocket.

He'd noticed the sexy little sandals she wore though, and her painted toenails, a shade of red that paled in comparison to her hair. And he'd sure as hell noticed her lips. A ripe hue that had nothing to do with waxy makeup and everything to do with a woman in full bloom.

But beyond all that, it was her eyes that captured him. Green, the color of new alder leaves, they'd looked on him unabashed. He could still feel the heat of her gaze vibrating down his chest to his groin. Sweet peat moss, he'd almost come in his pants at the thrill of it.

Of course she couldn't know what she was doing. The rules were different in her world, but the challenge had felt just the same. Without a word, she'd questioned his authority, defied it, demanded he prove his place otherwise she'd stand as his equal or dominant. And perhaps she was his equal. Certainly no one else had dared challenge him since he'd been bitten forty-three years ago.

He'd had no idea how much he missed it, how much a part of what he was needed that challenge. The beast in him craved the battle, ached to *win* his place, to win the female. Maizie's bold defiance touched the very core of what he was, charged him with adrenaline and a primal lust he was only now fully absorbing.

A growl rumbled in his chest of its own accord, his hands fisted the paper, his eyes squeezed shut fighting the growing need. Blood surged through his body, hot tingling through his skin, pooling in his groin.

His cock grew heavy and thick, straining inside his slacks. He shifted in his seat, but the rub of his clothes against his sex only made the need worse.

"Fuckit." After a haphazard fold to the paper, he tossed it across the compartment to the opposite seat. The limo was roomy, plenty of space to stretch, but Gray wouldn't need much to find at least a small taste of relief.

Jeezus, he felt like a hormonal teenager. Couldn't remember the last time he'd taken advantage of the privacy barrier between him and the driver, the dark windows to the outside world. Had to be more than a year, but this would be the first time he'd indulged alone. The beast in him had simple needs, but when those needs arose they could be all-consuming.

The swirl of emotion that surrounded Maizie in his mind—resentment, anger and pain—mixed with the desires she stirred in him as a man—lust, loneliness and attraction. He had to do something or lose all control.

He leaned back against the thick leather seat, tugging his slacks, trying to loosen the growing tightness. That helped, but his hard cock was still squeezed inside his briefs, and he wanted to do more than just give the Big Guy some room.

He closed his eyes and allowed the image of Maizie's plump breasts, swelling over the edge of her sundress, to consume his thoughts. He could imagine the full ripe flesh filling his hands, her nipples puckering hard as cherry pits against his palms. God, he wanted to squeeze them, to twist and tease the little nubs with his fingers, with his teeth.

Gray stroked his cock through his slacks, the taut fabric almost providing enough of a barrier to trick his mind into believing it could be someone else's hand. Her hand. The sensation rippled electric tingles through his balls, along his thighs. The muscles tugged, pressing his cock harder against his slacks, against the stroke of his hand.

He worked his belt and button, unzipping, freeing himself. He wiggled, holding his shaft firm in his right hand, his left hand freeing his tight, way-too-sensitive balls. *Jeezus, that feels good.* The ache was like he hadn't come in years.

His fingers shifted, collecting his sac and sending a jolt of pleasure through him so fast a bead of white cream peeked at the head of his cock. He smoothed his hand up the solid trunk, his thumb darting over the head, wiping away the wetness. He gasped when his fingers caressed over the ridge of its head and moaned out loud when he stroked over it again.

"Fuck...me."

Another long stroke and then another, the velvet skin warmed against his palm, a building need dizzying his head. His right hand worked on instinct, fondling his sac, feeling his balls rolling over his fingers, squeezing, tugging gently and then not so gently.

He couldn't help it, images of Maizie flashed through his mind. Her long fiery hair brushing his belly while those sweet lips wrapped around his cock, sucked him dry. He could almost feel her tits squeezed between his thighs, bouncing against his balls.

"Maizie...yeah...fuc—"

"Sir?"

"Shit..." Gray let go of his balls to punch the intercom overhead to his driver.

"What?" He barely sounded human, but then again he barely felt human at the moment.

"We've arrived at the Cadwick building, sir."

"Fine." Gray's right hand kept a steady stroke, his hips rocking with the rhythm. "Give me...a minute."

He poked the intercom button and returned his left hand to its previous duties.

His mind zeroed in on thoughts of the fiery woman again. "Maizie...mmm." Her sexy curves, those daring green eyes.

Gray stroked his cock faster, squeezed his balls. He pictured Maizie sprawled between his legs, her pink tongue teasing the tip of his penis before she took the full length of him between those luscious lips.

Hot and tight, wet and slick, he could almost feel his cock

ramming hard into that sexy mouth, her tongue firm against his shaft...

The cell phone buzzed.

"Fuck!" Gray yanked the phone from his breast pocket. "Speak."

A moment of silence passed, just enough for Gray to regret his harsh tone with his dear Annette. He'd known it was her. The phone only buzzed like that when the call came from the office.

"Mr. Lupo, I have some of the information you requested. I...I thought you'd want it as quickly as—"

"Yes. I'm sorry, Annette. You assumed correctly as usual. What've you got?"

Annette cleared her throat, banishing the previously timid tone. "Ms. Maizie Hood has a C+ credit rating while maintaining minimum monthly payments on a sizeable business loan and mounting fees to a Green Acres Nursing Home in Glide, Pennsylvania. She recently applied for a personal loan."

"Approved?"

"No official word yet, but it doesn't look good."

"Hmm... Go on," Gray said.

"Yes, sir. She has a small one-bedroom apartment forty-five minutes away from the nursing home on the South Side of Pittsburgh for which she pays four-hundred-fifty dollars per month."

"Extortion." Gray's cock softened in his hand.

"Yes, sir. She's received three traffic citations and two speeding tickets in the last six months. She has a regular gynecologist but not a general doctor. She has fillings in both her lower molars and a prescription for birth-control pills. Her credit-card statements show a good deal of grocery purchases."

"Interesting."

"I thought you'd say that. The, ah, business loan is for a small bakery, also on the South Side. Ms. Maizie Hood is listed as sole proprietor. She has two employees. A young woman named Cherri Pi fresh out of the culinary institute and a high school dropout with a commercial driver's license named—"

"Chocolate Cake?"

"No. Bob."

"Bob. No last name?"

"Smith, sir. Bob Smith."

"Perfect. Anything else?"

"No, sir. I'm still waiting to hear back from my sources on her personal affairs. This is all I could find on public record."

"You said minimum monthly payments on the loan? Is she making the nursing-home payments on time?"

"Yes, sir. But she's cut it close a few times. Same with the business loan."

"The business turning a profit?"

"If she doesn't list her salary, just barely."

Damn, it was worse than he'd thought. Cadwick wouldn't even break a sweat buying her. Hell, maybe he'd already charmed her out of hearth and home.

"Call Chuck Woodsmen."

"Judge Woodsmen?" she asked.

"Yes. Tell him I'm going to need that information we discussed. It looks like we may have to use our last resort after all."

"Yes, sir."

"Get back to me."

"Of course, sir."

The phone went dead before Gray pushed the disconnect button and shoved it into his jacket pocket. His hard-on completely evaporated, Gray tucked all his precious bits back in place and fastened his slacks. Maizie Hood had officially become business and Gray Lupo didn't fuck around with his business.

He'd known Anthony Cadwick for twenty-four years. He was a competitive, backstabbing, envious prick who thought he was a lot smarter, a lot better looking, and a lot more deserving than he ever was. Which basically meant that outside of himself, Gray didn't know anyone more dangerous.

If Gray wanted a chance in hell of protecting everything that he cared about, he'd have to play this on the sly. Find out how far Cadwick had already weaseled his way into the Hoods' good graces, which meant Gray would have to do a little competitive weaseling of his own.

He punched the intercom button to his driver. "I'm getting out."

Chapter Two

"Mr. Cadwick, please."

The too-thin model-esque secretary pursed her lips, her gaze taking him in as though he was the main course at an all-you-can-eat buffet. "And you are?"

"Gray Lupo."

She straightened, doe-brown eyes widened. "Oh. I'll let him know right away, Mr. Lupo."

Her skinny brows wrinkled when she glanced at the appointment book in front of her. "Oh, shoot. He's, uhmm, in a meeting. It might take a few minutes, maybe—"

"I'll wait." Gray ended the exchange with a curt bow of his chin and turned to the plush leather seating arrangement filling the far side of the outer office.

Cadwick's personal office was located on the top floor of the Cadwick Enterprises building. The lower floors were filled with various divisions of his company, several thousand employees all owing their daily bread to Anthony Cadwick. *Astonishing.*

Gray was not without a bit of clout himself. He had no problem gaining admittance to the exclusive floor with the simple mention of his name.

If you didn't know who Gray Lupo was, you were in over your head. He settled into one of the high-back leather chairs.

The room was like any office waiting room, the obligatory ficus plants and ferns—all fake—providing a splash of color.

He snagged the *Forbes* magazine from the dark wood coffee table in front of him. There were two other magazines on the table, both the same issue as the one he held. He glanced at the magazine's thick front cover and Anthony Cadwick's middle-aged face grinned back at him. Red block letters stamped across his forehead.

"Top twenty companies to watch." Gray snorted and wondered if by watch they meant, keep a suspicious eye. He flipped through the pages to find the lead story. Cadwick had scored a two-page spread. Nice chunk of free advertisement. The prick was doing pretty well for himself.

"Mr. Lupo, Mr. Cadwick can see you now."

Gray angled his gaze up to the tall secretary standing next to the coffee table. Her endless legs were hidden to the knee by a filmy brown and blue dress that revealed too much of her nonexistent cleavage and long pale arms. Her nut-brown hair hung in waves to an inch past her shoulders. He watched her face, the stillness of it. Not at all unappealing.

"Forgive my rudeness," he said. "I didn't ask your name."

Her shoulders shifted back, a genuine smile stretched her cheeks. Her teeth were too big, grin too wide, face too large. She was pretty up-close but from a distance she could be stunning. Perfect runway looks. "Alicia. Alicia Sanders. And can I say it's an honor to meet you, sir. I mean, I've seen your name like everywhere. In the Fortune 500 and *Time* and *Newsweek* and—"

"Yes. Thank you, Alicia." Gray pushed to his feet, ending the fan-girl gush. He pulled a business card from the breast pocket of his jacket and pressed it into her palm, holding her hand in both of his.

"Go here Monday. I'll see what I can do."

"Seriously? I mean... Thank you. Really. I do some modeling and I'd die to snag a contract with the agency your company owns—"

"Read the card, Alicia."

She flipped the card over. "No shit? You are awesome, Mr. Lupo. Thank you, thank you."

"I didn't hand you a contract, Alicia, just a shot at one." Gray straightened his tie. "That's the CEO of Bad Wolf Modeling. He'll know the card came from me. Take it in Monday morning. Be prepared for anything they may want you to do, photo shoot, go-see, interview."

"You bet. I'll be there, for sure." She was literally bouncing on her toes, cradling the card as though it was the golden ticket to the chocolate factory.

"Alicia? Shall we go see Mr. Cadwick now?"

"Oh, shoot. Yeah." She cleared her throat, all signs of giddy fan-girl vanishing. "This way, Mr. Lupo."

Rock stars had women throwing their panties at them. Men like Gray got résumés and head shots. He rarely guaranteed a job, but always allowed for the chance at one. Bad Wolf Inc. was twice the size of Cadwick Enterprises and far more diverse. The odds were pretty good he had openings if a person had the balls to ask him.

Alicia pushed open *both* thick wood doors as she led the way, no doubt on orders from Cadwick. It was much more of a grand reveal that way.

Four of the outer offices could fit easily inside this one and have room to spare. Cadwick sat at his desk, reminiscent of something you'd find in the Oval Office, a wall of windows and the Pittsburgh cityscape as his backdrop. Nice, if you liked that kind of thing.

"Lupo," Cadwick said, looking up from some paperwork as though he'd been caught totally by surprise.

"Cadwick."

The overacting businessman stood and made the effort to come around his desk, hand out, to meet Gray halfway. Their hands rammed together like the couplings on a train, Cadwick adding a manly slap to Gray's arm. "Do I still have a secretary?"

Gray gave the compulsory laugh. "We'll see Monday."

"I knew it. I knew it." Cadwick returned the gentlemanly chuckle.

He led Gray to the two leather bucket chairs in front of his desk. "What can I do for you, old man?"

Tension rippled across Gray's shoulders and right down his spine. *Old man.* Gray wouldn't dignify the dig with a response. He smiled, ate the irritation and waited until Cadwick had settled into his ergonomic chair on the opposite side.

"I've got some livestock coming in about eighteen months," Gray said. "Moose. A mating couple. Thinking of expanding the preserve."

Cadwick shook his head, a canary-eating grin stretching his stout face. Elbows on the chair arms he leaned back, hands steepled in front of him. "You and those animals. You got what, three-fifty, four-hundred acres tied up in it already and you're looking to add more? Money to burn, huh?"

Gray cleared his throat, allowed his discomfort and growing irritation to show by the hard crease of his brow. He shifted in his seat, leaned forward. "Word is your company's been buying up a good chunk of land around my place. Land that wasn't previously for sale."

Cadwick's smile didn't so much as flicker. "A good

businessman makes his own opportunities. Wasn't that what you kept telling us?"

Gray sighed. Some things never changed. "I'm glad you found my class so...beneficial, Anthony. However, I don't recall teaching extortion, intimidation or political backwashing as part of a good business plan."

Cadwick opened his hands and shrugged. "I always said I should've taught the class."

"I taught that business course at the university twenty-four years ago. Yours was my last class. Go apply for the job."

"Those that can, do. Those that can't..."

"Umm, touché." Huge tension knots kinked along Gray's shoulders and stabbed the small of his back. Playing nice guy was going to cost him a fortune in Chinese massages. Airfare was outrageous.

Gray rolled his head on his shoulders. Loud snaps and crackles helped hide the low growl vibrating his chest.

Cadwick leaned forward, bracing his forearms on his desk. "Twenty-four years ago and you don't look a day older. How is that, Lupo? I mean, I've kicked your ass in business every which way from Sunday, and I've got the gray hairs to prove it. But you...I swear to God, you actually look fuckin' younger."

Gray smiled, a quick flash of teeth. "Clean living."

Cadwick snorted, but held Gray's stare, waiting. After a few pregnant seconds, it was clear there'd be no further explanation. "You're a card, Lupo, I'll give you that. Shoulda been a comedian."

Hardly. "I'm buying the land edging my property from you, Cadwick. Name your price."

Cadwick barked a laugh, his dull brown eyes wide. "You don't say? Name my price, huh? Damn, you got balls."

"The size of coconuts. Now how much?"

Cadwick raised his hand, his pinky, ring and middle fingers standing at crooked attention. "Three. Count'em. Three major dick-swinging companies I got lined up. You can't outbid them by yourself. Are you nuts?"

Cadwick didn't have a clue how big Bad Wolf Inc was. No one did. Gray hadn't spent the extra years his werewolf blood had given him chasing rabbits. He'd kept his holdings like the *Titanic*'s iceberg. What people saw on the surface was impressive, but the real spread of his power lay underneath, buried under oceans of puppet companies and subsidiaries. Some of them were nearly impossible to trace back to the mother company.

"You're selling to me and you'll leave the remaining land owners unaccosted. Clear?"

Cadwick's dark brows bunched, sarcastic humor vanishing under the weight of Gray's orders. "Listen, you old fart, you don't have the kind of muscle to come in here and try to push me around. I squash people like you and spread'em on toast for breakfast. Got it?"

The tangy scent of sweat wafted from Cadwick's suit collar, his heart rate ratcheted up several beats and a ropey purple vein bulged the side of his neck to his temple. The spike of his prey's emotion worked like Valium on Gray. He had him. The rabbit didn't know it yet, but he was already dead.

"Fight or flight," Gray said, his eyes closing, enjoying the adrenaline-soaked air like sweet brandy. "Fight or flight. Listen to your instincts, Anthony. Run. This isn't a fight you can win."

"What the fuck are you talking about? Run from what?" Cadwick burst from his seat, jabbing his finger at Gray across the desk. "You wanna fight? You got it. After I get old lady Hood to sign, I'm goin' after your place."

Gray remained unflinchingly calm, lacing his hands together in his lap. "Ester Hood? She's a dear friend, but I'm afraid she won't be selling."

"Oh yeah? Well her hot little granddaughter might say otherwise. I'm getting that land, Lupo. In two years' time there'll be a hundred and fifty acres of shopping mall and concrete surrounding your shitty little animal sanctuary. And there ain't a damn thing you can do to stop it."

A spark of doubt shot through Gray's veins. He didn't like it. Maizie Hood was a loose end, an unknown he couldn't tolerate. On paper she was a liability but he'd need to meet the woman to know for sure. What were her priorities? Where did her loyalties lie? He couldn't find out anything sitting in Anthony Cadwick's high-rise office.

A skin-crawling silence settled over the room. Gray slid his gaze slowly up to Cadwick. "This is your final decision on the matter?"

"Yeah. Ya'damn right it is."

"Very well. Excuse me." Gray pushed to his feet and headed for the door.

"Hey. Is that it? Where ya going?"

Gray opened the right-side door then paused to look back over his shoulder. "To prepare for battle, of course."

"Eww, that's bad. Here, smell." Maizie held the half-gallon milk container under Cherri's nose.

"No way. Why would I smell it after that face?"

Maizie shrugged. "Morbid curiosity. C'mon, make sure I'm right."

"Fine, but if you wanna test your other senses, trust me, the oven *is* hot, Asian women really *are* this beautiful, nails on a chalkboard *will* make you cringe and my devil's food cake is the only piece of heaven you'll find on earth."

"Yeah, yeah, funny. Whatever, Whoopi, just take a whiff."

Cherri poked a finger against the bridge of her wire-frame glasses then leaned in. "Oh yeah, jeezy-peezy that's bad. That's about two days past bad. That's so far gone it can hardly see bad in the rearview mirror. It's so bad—"

"Enough. Got it. Thank you." Maizie flicked the switch on the garbage disposal and dumped the chunky remains.

"Just makin' sure you don't ask me to check again." Cherri's pretty brown eyes narrowed with her smile, her round face seeming more so as she pulled her shoulder-length black hair into a tail then tucked it under a white hairnet.

She reached around Maizie and twisted open the cold water. "You're gonna ruin that thing. You're supposed to have water running when you use the disposal."

"That's an urban myth."

"No, the married guy who left his family for his nagging lover is an urban myth. This is just common sense."

The cowbell over the front door to Red Hood Bakery stopped Maizie's retort. Both she and Cherri turned to see who'd entered.

"Whoof."

Maizie elbowed Cherri. "That's exactly what I said when I first saw him."

Granny's Armani-wearing wolf guided the glass door to a close behind him, stopping the spring hinge from slamming it shut.

Pale blue eyes swung around to meet Maizie, connecting with an impact she felt all the way down to her toes. He smiled. Sort of. The very corners of his perfect lips curled ever so slightly, just enough to soften his face but not so much she could be sure of the expression. He looked away, scanning her small showroom.

The shop wasn't much, but Maizie was damn proud of the little place. She could still remember the day they'd finished the script on the tall front windows, *Sweets & Breads* scrawled in white script on one and *Red Hood Bakery* on the other. She'd hung red-and-white-striped valances on either side and a matching one on the door.

Display cases made an "L" counter along the side and back wall. They were filled with cakes, cookies, cupcakes, scones, pies, confections and almost everything else Maizie and Cherri made. An enormous wood hutch she'd found at a garage sale took up the other side, displaying two three-tier wedding cakes, a huge bread bowl filled with different kinds of bread, a couple of cheesecakes, a few decorative plates of various cookies and a silver-framed picture of her and her parents.

Mr. Armani Suit paused for a moment staring at the photo. His hand lifted like he might pick it up, but then stopped. He turned away, noticing the small guestbook table below the far front window, with the basket of business cards and flyers stacked on top and went to it. Using the pen next to the open guestbook, he signed.

"Afternoon," Cherri said.

Maizie elbowed her.

Cherri scowled and rubbed her side. She mouthed, "What?"

Maizie mouthed back, "I'll tell you later."

To which Cherri crinkled her brow. "Huh?"

"She said she'll tell you later."

Both women jumped at the masculine voice, snapping their attention to Granny's wolf.

"I'm sorry. You are?" Maizie said.

"Lupo. Gray Lupo."

"Get. Out." Maizie almost snorted. She stopped herself.

"Pardon?"

"Oh. No. Sorry. It's just, Lupo, that's Italian for wolf, right?"

"I wouldn't know."

"I think it is."

He frowned. "Interesting."

"You have no idea."

"My thought exactly." Gray's cool blue eyes swung up to meet hers. Their gazes locked and Maizie had to remember to breathe. Her hands went hot and moist in a second, her body warming fast. His gaze dropped to her mouth so she couldn't help the urge to wet her lips. He tracked the sweep of her tongue, his long lashes flicking up, revealing a flash of masculine hunger that sent a delicious tingle tripping all the way down to her sex.

Cherri's elbow poked her side. "Shake your head, your eyes are stuck."

Maizie snapped her mouth shut, straightened, drying her hands down her apron. "I'm sorry. Welcome to Red Hood Bakery. How can I help you?"

Gray smiled, and not one of those maybe I-think-it-could-be-a-smile, but a real cheek-pinching grin. He even laughed a little, his gaze dropping away for a minute, face flushing. *Perfect.*

When he looked back to her, his laughing grin had faded to a sexy, easy smile. He tilted his head to the side, just right, so the sun, streaming through the front windows, glinted off his pale eyes and sparked in the silver of his hair.

"Great shop. Yours?" He had a radio voice, smooth and

sexy—the late-night jazz hour by candlelight.

Then Maizie remembered this DJ was trying to swindle Gran out of her land. "I think you know the answer. Is there something I can get for you?"

His familiar scowl returned, the same one he'd worn at the nursing home. Her bitchy tone was better than cold water.

He went all businessman-stiff. "Ms. Hood, I'd like to speak to you about a matter concerning your grandmother."

Oh, she should've seen this coming. Couldn't charm the old lady out of her land so let's try seducing the granddaughter. Okay, so he wasn't actually seducing her, more like smiling really sexy and looking at her with those pretty eyes and using that perfect mouth and those big hands... *Semantics.*

"Why am I not surprised?"

"You shouldn't be. Ester and I have been friends for years. I care for her and, quite frankly, I'm worried."

"Worried about what? That she'll sell her place to someone else?"

"Yes. Well, in a manner of speaking. Is there somewhere we can talk privately?"

Maizie followed his nod over her shoulder to Cherri and then farther back to Bob standing in the doorway to the back prep-room. Damn, Bob was wearing his blind-guy glasses again instead of the eye patch. Always freaked out the other drivers, but the missing eye was just bad for business.

"Bob, where's your hairnet?" His long, stringy blond hair was a health violation waiting to happen.

"Van."

"How 'bout you go put it on? Cherri, give'im a hand, okay?"

Cherri glanced at Bob then back to Maizie, mouth drooping. "Seriously?"

"No. Just make sure it's a hairnet this time and not an old onion bag."

Bob gave his trademark hemp-boy chuckle. "Ya. Gettin' those flaky onion peels outta my hair was a bitch, man."

Cherri put a hand on Bob's thin shoulder and turned him back toward the prep-room. "Explain to me again how you got that CDL license."

Maizie crossed her arms over her belly and looked Mr. Gray Lupo right in his pretty blue eyes. "Private enough for you? You better hurry though. My evening crowd will be rolling in any minute now."

Evening crowd at a bakery. That was almost funny. Good thing Maizie was too ticked to laugh.

"That man's your delivery driver?"

"Bob? Yeah. Why?"

"Your insurance covers him?"

"Yes. Not that it's any of your business."

Gray shook his head, caught his suit jacket behind his hands on his hips. Very disapproving daddy. "Jeezus, it must cost you a small fortune to keep that half-wit behind the wheel."

"Bob's a three-quarters-wit, thank you. And again, it's none of your business."

"You're a goddamn walking liability."

"Excuse me? Okay, either get to the point or hit the bricks." She had well-paid employees to insult her. She didn't need it from this guy.

"The point? Do you have any idea what your irresponsible financial decisions are doing to your grandmother?"

"Let me guess," Maizie said. "She's worried sick I've stretched myself too thin trying to keep this bakery from going bankrupt while I'm paying for her to stay at Green Acres. And if

I cared about her at all I'd sell the land to *you* so my grandmother can stop worrying."

"Yes. No. I mean... What?"

"Well, forget it. I won't do it."

Gray's brows jumped to his hairline. "You won't?"

"I'd rather let the bank take the shop and move back to the cottage with Gran and cut my expenses than sell it to you, or anyone."

"Why not?" He sounded genuinely surprised. "Selling could take care of everything, your business, your grandmother's medical expenses."

"Yeah, at the rock-bottom price of my grandmother's happiness. No, thank you. If you were really Gran's friend you'd know how much she loves her little cottage in the woods. Yeah, she'd sell it to help me, but not because she wanted to get rid of it. I won't do it. Ever. She's already given up too much for me."

"Fascinating."

"Not to mention she'd kick my butt for breaking her promise to her make-believe silver wolf." Maizie rolled her eyes.

"What's that?"

"Nothing. You wouldn't understand. Old bedtime stories Gran told me when I was a kid. She used them to keep me in line and scare me out of my skin."

"Sounds awful."

"Yeah, and now the wolf needs me to protect *him*. Talk about irony."

Chapter Three

Maizie found the spare key right where it had been when she was a kid, in the front window box. The primrose and baby's breath helped hide the three-inch "I love bingo" key chain, but anyone who took the time to look would find it.

Her grandmother had hid it from the animals more than people. She'd tell Maizie that anybody desperate enough to break in probably needed whatever they'd find more than she did. The animals though, they'd just make a mess.

The philosophy wasn't exactly one Maizie agreed with and she hesitated a minute before leaving the key among the flowers. Seventy some years in the cottage and Gran had never lost anything she valued. She must have known what she was doing.

She slipped the key in the lock. The door creaked open, already unlocked. The key was one thing, but leaving the door unlocked was just asking for trouble.

Maizie peeked through the opening. "Hello? Anyone here? It's just me...Little Red...with a loaded three-fifty-seven magnum in her demure little hand." It would've been a much better threat if she'd actually had a three-fifty-seven magnum.

She listened. Nothing. "Well then clearly no one's here, 'cause a thief would answer back." Maizie rolled her eyes at her stupidity and slipped inside.

"Gawd, this place never changes." Maizie scanned the small living room to her right, tossed her backpack on the plump white sofa, almost knocking the lamp off the end table beside her.

On the far wall, next to the stone fireplace, one side of the French doors to the all-season room was ajar. She could see the corner of the outer room. The warm rays of the evening sun gave the terracotta floor tiles a fiery hue and set off the colors in the brick walls under the windows.

The living room, despite the buttercup-yellow walls and white airy curtains, was already cast in evening shadows. She reached down and flicked on the lamp next to her.

Light filtered through the curtained window at the top of the narrow staircase in front of her. The dark wood steps gleamed against white walls. To her left the kitchen windows behind the sink and counters stretched the full length of the room. She leaned forward, noticing the small vase of fresh violets on the sill behind the sink. No one had been here in months. *Weird.*

The kitchen was the size of a shoebox, a straight narrow room with the sink, an old-style gas stove and oven on one side and a shallow pantry next to the refrigerator on the other. Staring into it brought back warm childhood memories. It'd been more than big enough for her and Gran.

Maizie turned from the kitchen and the memories, and crossed the living room to the open door of the all-season room. Before she reached the fireplace, a familiar scent tickled her nose. Smelled like...like men's cologne. An icy chill shook across her shoulders, her heart picked up pace and her muscles tensed.

The aroma was fading, but she recognized it. She knew who wore that cologne. Who was it? She tried to click through the faces of possibilities in her mind, but her brain was too freaked on the fact that someone had been in her home. They might still be there.

Something moved in the all-season room, a scuffling noise against the tile floor, and Maizie's heart was in her throat. She froze, her mind flashing all sorts of horrific images of what could've made the sound.

Every slasher movie she'd ever seen flickered through her head in high-definition. Images of aliens eating their way out of people's stomachs, leather-faced men wielding chainsaws, hockey masks glowing in the dark, her twisted imagination kept her rooted to the spot.

Minutes ticked by with only the chirps of birds and the rustle of wind through the trees to listen to. Sanity began to seep back into her petrified brain. Clearly someone had been there and left the flowers. Nothing looked out of place, so they hadn't robbed her. If Gran did have someone checking on the cottage, maybe they'd left the back door open like they'd done to the front and some woodland critters had decided to check out the new digs.

"Idiot. It's just a raccoon or a mouse or something." She kept her voice to a whisper though, in case it *was* a big scary guy with a hockey mask and chainsaw.

The cushy carpeting made her stealthy advance toward the French doors all the more silent. She grabbed the fire poker from the cast-iron set by the fireplace and slowly opened the door far enough that she'd be able to slip through.

One, two...three. Maizie jumped over the threshold, turning to land facing the far wall to the left, feet spread wide, knees bent, poker double fisted and cocked over her shoulder like a baseball bat.

"Ah-ha!" *Oh crap. Not a mouse.* "Nice doggy."

A flash of silvery fur and a low growl caught Maizie's attention. Her gaze zeroed in on the large wolf just as he flinched, crouching, ready to bolt. The two of them froze, taking the other's measure.

The thing was huge, its big ears twitching, listening to more than her words. Cool blue eyes watched her as though waiting for the right moment to attack or run. A rumbling growl filled the space between them, though its face remained deceptively calm and curious. Its head low, eyes peering up beneath the shelf of its furry brow, it watched Maizie tentatively.

"Shoo, go away," she said, though she was still whispering. No sense upsetting the great big huge enormous wolf.

It tilted its head, ears pivoting forward, and straightened. Whatever fear it'd felt a second before seemed to vanish, bold curiosity taking its place. The wolf sniffed the air, its shiny black nose twitching.

"Go on. Out the door." Maizie wiggled the poker at the animal, edged forward, hoping it would back out the open screen door behind it.

A hard snort and shake of its head seemed a firm answer before the wolf moved toward her. Maizie backed up as many steps, keeping the distance equal. At this rate, the wolf would be shooing her out of the house instead of the other way around.

It was a beautiful animal though, hypnotic pale blue eyes and thick silvery fur.

A proverbial light went on in Maizie's brain. "Are you Gran's big silver wolf?"

The big animal perked its ears, head up. No wonder it was acting so bold. "I can't believe you're real. What's she been doing, feeding you?"

Maizie exhaled, finally, and lowered the poker. "Poor thing.

Probably miss her, huh?"

The wolf stepped closer, nose out, sniffing. She lifted her hand, the rest of her body still tight with caution. Just because Gran had gotten close enough to this thing to make it feel comfortable strolling into her house didn't make it any less wild.

"Please don't eat me."

Hot breath washed over her skin, as the animal took in her scent. Then it licked her.

Maizie jumped at the sensation, which gave the poor wolf a start. She laughed, the animal staring up at her crouched, waiting for a clue to her next move.

"Sorry. Your tongue tickles." Not that she thought it could understand, although clearly Granny believed it could.

The wolf straightened, startled fear melting into cool fire in its eyes. He stretched toward her and licked along her knuckles. Its rough tongue massaged against her skin, made her breath catch. He stepped closer. Licked again, and the sensation set loose a wave of goose bumps up her arm, spilling out all over her body.

The big animal lowered its head and a warm snort of breath touched her knee followed by the hot rasp of his tongue. He sniffed her, then licked, catching her below the knee and pressing up and over to the bottom of her thigh. God, she hoped he wasn't hungry.

The rough pulling sensation on her flesh felt nice in a weird way. He did it again, this time his long tongue wrapped around her knee and caught the sensitive little dimple behind. Maizie gasped, her breath shuddered, not sure if she was being tasted or titillated. ·

Exactly what had Granny been teaching this thing?

Emboldened or hungry, the wolf stepped closer. Maizie's fingers brushed the silky fur on his neck and head as he sniffed the hem of her dress. He raised his head, pressing his nose against her groin.

She flinched away. "Bad dog—I mean, wolf. At least buy me dinner first."

His cool nose nudged under the hem of her dress, lifting it as his tongue lapped at her inner thigh. The feel of it was a mix of embarrassment, fear and pleasure. The first two emotions far outweighed the last.

"Right. That's enough of that." Maizie dropped the poker to push both hands against the wolf's massive head, trying to hold him back and scoot away at the same time. But the wolf followed her step for step, licking when it could, until her back hit the wall. Trapped, his long tongue lapped at her inner thigh, skin tingling, muscles stiff. She closed her eyes, praying he wouldn't take a bite.

The long teasing licks moved higher, the wolf's big head raising her dress as he went. "Oh shit."

This wasn't happening. *What kind of wild animal does this?* With her hands fisting his ears and thick clumps of fur around them she pulled at his head, tried to raise a knee, push it into his neck. The wolf paid her efforts little mind.

His zeal for her taste intensified, his big body pressing in more and more. What was going through its mind, hunger or sex? She didn't like either possibility.

Her heart hammered against her chest, her breaths little more than frantic pants. Her knees trembled, elbows locked, pushing against the animal's head with every ounce of her strength. Another lick brought his tongue so high on her inner thigh, she gasped at the quick conflict of pleasure and disgust.

"No. Stop it, you stupid mutt." She pushed at him but his

tongue darted out anyway, tracing the crease of flesh between her leg and her sex. "Fuck."

His cool nose nudged against her panties and the wolf's whole body trembled with a sound like a low feral purr.

"No." Maizie twisted her leg, angled the heel of her shoe and stomped.

The wolf yelped and jumped away. It held its front paw off the ground, favoring it. The pain in its eyes was almost...human. Regret knotted through Maizie's belly. Dumb wolf didn't know any better. "Sorry, but I'm just not that kind of girl."

The silvery furred wolf shook his head, the twist traveling down his back and up his tail. His pool-water blue eyes swung up to her. He blinked. Barked once, loud enough to make her flinch, then turned and trotted out the open screen door.

"Hey. Wait. Let me check your paw at least." She jogged after it and nearly fell on her face when her shoe caught on a pile of rags near the door. She looked. Shredded pants, a shirt, even a pair of shoes poking out underneath the mess.

"Why shoes?" Maizie kept moving. She'd figure it out later.

Beyond the brick patio, the vine-covered arbor and the stepping-stone path winding through Granny's flower garden, a space of about fifteen feet separated the backyard from the acres and acres of forest. Maizie stopped at the very edge of dark woods. No sign of her nosey wolf.

She'd played in these woods most of her life, knew them like her own bedroom, though she'd never, in all her years, followed the path to its end.

The dirt trail wound and twisted for several miles through the woods, branching off at crucial sections to lead one way or another.

In one direction the narrow path led off to the local coal mines, with industrial-type buildings, and the hum of machinery and trucks rumbling day and night. Another section deep, deep into the woods branched off toward the game preserve. Beyond that another led to a crystal-clear quarry lake where teens were rumored to go skinny-dip. But the main path trailed through to a housing plan on the far side of the forest.

She hadn't traveled that path in years. The beautiful little housing development it led to was her old neighborhood. Where she'd lived before the accident, before her world had changed.

Granny had forbidden her from wandering that deep into the forest, frightening her into obedience with tales of vicious, hungry wolves. But she hadn't needed Granny's warnings to obey. Nothing but painful memories were at the other end of the overgrown route. A perfect life stripped away on a rainy night by a beast.

She had no desire to trudge through those memories. Besides, it was more likely that Granny's big silver wolf had headed back to the game preserve. There were supposed to be fences to keep the preserve animals in and humans out. If the wolf was part of the preserve, there was probably a problem with the fence. She'd check it out, maybe find the not-so-scary silver wolf and the hole he'd squeezed through to get out.

Maizie started on her way. Three steps in, and thick foliage gobbled up the last twinkles of sunlight. A cool blue-black illumination was the only sign full night had not yet fallen. She kept walking, finding her way almost on reflex. These woods were home for her, no matter how citified she'd become.

Within seconds Granny's backyard haven disappeared from sight and the forest sank in around her. She kept walking.

Minutes passed, five, twelve, before she found the faint remnants of the old trail to the game preserve. With her first step off the main path the thrum of invisible fingers tickled up her back. Instincts trembled. She wasn't alone. Her belly fluttered, leg muscles twitched, eager to take flight.

She kept walking, scanning the forest on either side. The high canopy of trees kept the undergrowth low. She could see for some distance although the dwindling light was making it increasingly difficult.

Between the trees, the highs and lows of small hills, the odd thicket of briers and clumps of vegetation over fallen trees, there were plenty of places to hide.

Maizie fought her instinct and came to a stop. Someone was near. She could feel it. Was it the wolf or something worse? Her pulse raced, hands fisting at her sides. She'd never been frightened of these woods before. But then she'd never wandered this far in.

The hairs at her nape tickled, her belly quivered. She narrowed her eyes, trying to see clearly. A flash of movement at the corner of her vision made her look. Maizie snapped her attention to her left. *Nothing there.* Another stir a little farther to the right.

She looked, but a half second too late. Again, several yards deeper, something stirred the low branches of a bush. She didn't see what it was. And then she caught a glimpse. Fur, brown, a shade lighter than dirt.

She squinted, tried to narrow her vision on a patch of briers where she thought whatever it was had hidden. Growls rumbled along the forest floor, vibrating through her chest. The sound sent ice chilling through her veins.

Darkness was falling fast. She couldn't see anything clearly and the shadows were growing thicker, closing in. The low rumble surrounded her, changing pitch, altering cadence until it was less like a growl and more like...a moan.

Curiosity and the fast rush of adrenaline that replaced her fear pushed her forward. A smacking noise echoed off the trees, accompanied by a stranger, wetter-sounding slosh, softer, but there. The sounds coming from just ahead of her, on the other side of a cluster of tree trunks, were too out of place to ignore.

She moved closer, careful to tread softly. Her hands on the nearest of the tree trunks, Maizie peered around and everything she'd been hearing made sense. And didn't.

Right there in the middle of the dense forest was a man, maybe late forties, on his knees, naked, his face tense with restraint and effort. Muscles defined across his flat belly, his thick upper thighs flexing, his hands clamped on the hips of a stunning woman. The man's hips rocked a hard, steady rhythm, his legs smacking against the ass of the woman on all fours in front of him, driving his sex deep again and again.

Maizie stood, mesmerized, watching the two lost in the sensations of their bodies. The woman's long curling blonde hair parted at her neck, revealing the smooth line of her back. Her eyes were closed, her body rocking, driving herself harder, faster against her lover's cock.

The woman spread her knees wider, taking more of the long hard cock into her body. Maizie caught glimpses of the man's shaft glistening each time he drew back. His powerful muscles tensed his ass, firm and round, thrusting himself so hard his lover's supple body jerked with the impact.

The sound of their sex thundered through Maizie's ears, her body suddenly warm, muscles low inside her going slick, flexing with a growing need. She should look away. Give them their privacy. But the instant the decision to turn entered her mind, the man glanced over his shoulder at her.

Maizie gasped, surprised he'd known she was there, embarrassed at having been caught watching, and horrified at how strong the urge to join them gripped her. She held her breath, waiting for him to scream at her, to curse her for her rudeness. The sound of her heart was so loud in her ears she couldn't hear the smack of their flesh.

A strange smile trembled at the corners of the man's mouth. He licked his lips, turned his head a fraction of an inch and a flash of color on his neck caught her attention. There was something there, red and lumpy. Maizie concentrated, fighting the luring distraction of love-making.

It took a moment, but she finally realized what it was—torn flesh. Something had bitten him. Blood had dried around the wound, crusting into dark, nearly black chunks and trailing in a long messy flow down his chest. Raw meat and blood glistened in the dim moonlight, but it looked as though the wound was healing. It certainly hadn't stopped him from indulging his carnal needs with this woman.

The man's position shifted, drawing Maizie's attention at the exact moment he, still staring at her, dropped his hand. She could see his cock perfectly now, wet and hard driving in and out of the woman's slick pussy. The sounds of their sex echoed in her head.

Maizie swallowed the thick ball of lust in her throat, her face hot, her thighs moist, her sex flooding with need. A sudden cry cracked through the hazy fog of her brain. The woman's rhythmic motions became frantic, ruthless with need.

Her ass tensed, toes curling, wrapping her ankles around her lover's calves, locking their bodies together as she rode her orgasm. He drove a counter rhythm, working his body with hers, pushing himself over the edge of orgasm a second later.

Maizie stepped away, sensing the time to flee was quickly escaping her. Her heel caught against an exposed root and she stumbled, suddenly drawing the attention of the woman. There was no hint of a smile from her.

"What the fuck?"

Maizie ran—because she'd been caught watching a private moment, because the look in the woman's eyes was both surprised and murderous, because too much of Maizie still wanted to find a way to join them. She ran. And they chased her.

Maizie knew the way, even in a blind panic she could find her way back to Granny's house. But she was so far from home and the sound of footfalls behind her was growing closer. In the back of her head, she heard every step, every long stride and then the strides changed, the rhythm doubled, lightened.

She glanced over her shoulder and realized the couple wasn't chasing her. A wolf was. Not the wolf from Granny's house. Another wolf must've escaped the preserve. God, how many of them were out here?

Its long powerful body gained on her easily, chocolate-brown fur tipped with blonde rolling over its muscles. In a blur it passed her, spun and blocked her path. It'd moved so quickly, Maizie hadn't had time to change course. She slid to a stop, staring down the long trembling muzzle of the snarling wolf.

"Easy, boy," she said, though her voice was almost too shaky to understand. "Just let me get past. I'll be out of your woods in a few minutes. Good, boy. Gooood, boy."

The wolf's snarls grew louder. This close Maizie realized it wasn't a boy. It was female. The wolf edged closer and everything inside Maizie screamed for her to run. She didn't. Despite there being no love lost between her and furry four-legged canines, Maizie knew enough not to run and trigger their chase instinct.

She stood her ground, fear boiling into resentment, anger. She didn't have a weapon and couldn't outrun it. If the beast decided it wanted her dead, there was nothing she could do about it, just like her parents.

She'd had enough. "Fine. Whatever. Kill me or leave me the fuck alone. I'm done with wolves haunting my dreams, haunting my life. Get it over with already." It was an animal. She knew it couldn't possibly understand, but yet it backed away.

And then she heard it. A distant howl. Another wolf's call. After a hard snort, her pursuer turned and darted back the way it'd come.

Maizie didn't even pause to think about it. She just turned and ran home.

His body stretched and contoured, pulling muscle and meat, reforming bones. The shift was painful as hell, but it let him know he was alive. Gray lay for several seconds staring up through the green needles of the pine tree. Above was the ink black of the night sky, the moon barely a slit of yellow, the stars few enough to count.

Old needles, brown and decaying, cushioned beneath him. He breathed deep, taking the cool air into his lungs, washing away her scent. Jeezus, he could still taste her, sweet and salty. The smell of her pussy so maddening his cock had gone from wolf to man without losing the rock-hard erection for a second.

Maizie. What was it about her that made him lose all control? Hell, he couldn't remember the last time a woman made him so damn hot the retractable wall between the seats in his limo constituted enough privacy for him to jack off. But never had this kind of crazed need transcended forms so even the beast in him craved her scent, her taste.

He couldn't believe what he'd thought about doing tonight, what he'd almost done. As wolf, some things became more complicated, almost impossible to understand, and other things crystallized with the sharpness of black and white. She was female to his male. He smelled her, the sweet musk of her sex. He tasted her. He wanted her. There was nothing else that mattered.

Two more seconds and he would have had her on her knees, humping over her back, ramming his dick into her juicy pussy. Gray licked his lips, tasted the hint of her there. He wanted more. As a wolf his tongue was so long he could've fucked her with it. He almost had.

He shook his head, tried to banish the thought and only then noticed his hand stroking the hard shaft of his cock. Fuck, he was losing his mind.

Gray didn't know how long he'd lain there, thirty minutes, an hour. Who knew? Thoughts of Maizie both relaxed and excited him but it was time to get back to reality. He pushed to his feet and strode toward the edge of the forest, his dick bouncing back and forth, practically pointing the way. This thing with Maizie was scaring the hell out of him and still his cock wanted what it wanted.

He wasn't a damn animal. He could control himself, choose when he'd give in to carnal demands and when he wouldn't. Unfortunately if he didn't give in soon, he risked doing something really stupid like screwing the first female who offered.

"Mmmm, need help with that?" His sister-in-law, the precise *something stupid* he worried about. She lounged naked on the chaise patio chair, eyeing his bouncing dick. One leg stretched straight, she bent the other and let it fall to the side so he could see the wet glimmer of her sex.

"Get dressed, Lynn." He may not have known how long he'd lain under the trees thinking of Maizie. But he knew it'd been at least an hour since he'd called his sister-in-law back to the house from her private run.

What the hell had she been doing out there so late on her own anyway? His human brain told him it wasn't any of his business, but the alpha in him growled, wanting to know the goings-on of his pack members. He pushed the overbearing urge from his thoughts.

Gray stomped up the stone steps onto the patio, his gaze glancing over her svelte body, he was a man after all and horny as hell. She looked damn good too, breasts high and firm, small waist and a gentle curve of womanly hips. She was a brunette, despite the sandy blonde hair curling over her shoulders. Her little pussy thatch didn't lie.

"Not till you tell me why you're playing cat and mouse with a human when you've got this nice piece of ass waiting for you." She grabbed his wrist as he passed, yanking his hand to her breast.

She arched into his palm, her hard nipple poking between his fingers. The strong flowery fragrance of her perfume filled his nose so he could barely smell anything else. His fingers squeezed before he could stop himself, feeling the supple flesh mold to his hand. Her little nipple pinched between his fingers, the feel of it sending a quick jolt through his veins to his cock. Self-disgust rolled over him like cold lead and he pulled away.

"You're my wife's sister. It's never gonna happen. Accept it. And get dressed."

"Your dead wife, you mean. You're pack, Gray. Not human. Their moral rules don't apply to us." She swiveled her hips around, moving her feet to the floor and stood. She stepped up beside him, pressing her naked body into his side so his arm nestled between her soft breasts, pressed down her belly and his fingers brushed the moist hair of her sex.

"Before Donna turned you she told you what we were, what you'd become. You knew being her mate would make you our alpha. You knew what that meant, what it still means."

Gray let his head fall forward, hating how much he liked the feel of her feminine curves against him. It'd been too long. Too damn long. His fingers curled, fondling through her hairs without him realizing he'd made them. She pushed her hips forward, gave him free access.

"I know what it means," he said.

The lips of her pussy were swollen, wet, like she'd just had sex. He knew she hadn't. Lynn didn't have a mate, hadn't since he'd refused to allow her to turn the father of her children. For that reason alone he'd be responsible to see to her needs, being alpha only obligated him more. He pressed a finger between her outer lips, found her clit engorged.

Lynn's hand clamped around his forearm, held him to her, she pumped her hips. His finger was drenched in seconds, slipping in and out of her pussy so easy he added another, then another.

Lynn threw her head back. "Yes. Oh God. Don't stop. Please, Gray...just...don't stop."

She slid her free arm under his, over his tight stomach to his stiff cock, her wild gyrations making it bounce all the more. Her hand clamped on, stroked the sensitive flesh. It felt good. Too good. *Dammit.*

He grabbed her hand on his dick. Held it still. She'd make him come. To hell with pack code, pack obligations, he didn't want that. He couldn't let his late wife's sister get him off. What little he did for Lynn was pity, guilt, not desire. The next time she found a suitable mate, human or otherwise, he wouldn't stop her. So said his human-half, his wolf-half wasn't so sure.

"Fuck yes!" She pressed into him, and Gray pushed his

fingers deep into her, held them there, feeling her soft wet walls squeeze and release with her orgasm. He waited for her hold on his arm to relax, then he pulled away.

"Mmmm. Will you still do that after you've tasted your new little bitch?" She gripped her hand around his wet fingers, stroking them like she'd tried to stroke his cock, using her cream to lube the way. His dick twitched, a bead of come pearling at the tip.

He clenched his jaw. Resolute. "No. Find a mate, Lynn. It's time."

"I did. You wouldn't let me have him." She practically threw his hand away, her voice a wicked hiss.

"He was married. He's still married. You broke it off with him before the twins were born and he never left her."

"Shawn would've left her for me. He wouldn't have had a choice if you had let me turn him."

"That's how you wanted him? By taking away all other options? He was cheating on his wife, Lynn. He would've cheated on you." Gray cupped her face. She tried to pull away but he snagged her around the waist. Their bellies pressed together, his dick finally softening against her.

"I want you to be happy," he said. "You and the kids deserve a good man. Someone your mom won't worry about. As your brother-in-law it's the most I can hope for. As your alpha it's the least I can demand."

She snorted and pushed from his embrace. "Shelly and Ricky are twenty-nine. They know who their father is and they don't need him. Mom wants her alpha to be part of a mating pair, like it should be. If it's not going to be me and you, then I'll find a man who'll fight for me, and the pack. Mark my words, Gray, you'll lose us all."

Chapter Four

The quarry lake was bathwater warm. Maizie slipped deeper, enjoying the silky feel of the water hugging around her thighs, wetting the tight red curls between her legs.

No. Wait. That wasn't right. The quarry lake was never warm and her thighs looked absolutely fabulous. *Ah. Dreaming.* Satisfied, Maizie's subconscious took control.

Careful not to slip on the stones beneath the blue-green water, Maizie strolled deeper and deeper until she was only dry from her breasts up. The fine hairs at the back of her neck prickled. She stopped, scanned the high quarry wall on one side, the shoreline and forest beyond on the other.

A cool wind swept across the lake, carrying the scents of the forest, and something else. There was a sweetness to the scent, but not of nature. It was definitely masculine, like men's cologne only more earthy, more rich, but nothing she'd ever smelled from a bottle.

Goose bumps blanketed her skin, and Maizie folded her arms over her naked breasts against the chill. Her puckered nipples tingled at the brush of her own skin, but she pushed the sensation from her thoughts. Someone was out there, hiding among the fallen trees and shadows. She could feel it in her bones.

Maizie squinted, looking for the odd form or out-of-place

color. It was nothing. There was no one in sight. She was just being paranoid. She turned back to enjoy her swim, ignoring her worry.

She opened her arms so when she bent her knees, tiny waves lapped at her pebbled nipples. The air left her breasts wonderfully chilled. The dirty little thrill of skinny-dipping had her entire body humming with forbidden excitement.

Invisible fingers thrummed down her back again. Dammit, someone *was* watching. She could feel their focused attention like hands groping her body. Maizie turned her chin to her shoulder, staring back into the forest. Nothing had changed, no sign of anyone, but he was there. She was sure of it this time.

He'd watched her undress and wade into the water. He was watching her now, confident, cocky, knowing he wasn't seen. "Probably have your dick in your hand right now, jackin' off."

She gave her back to the kinky voyeur and dove into the water. Currents massaged her naked body as she swam, fluttering over her breasts, warming between her thighs. She came to the surface and swam to the other side where the shoreline was three feet of jagged rocks and then a five-story limestone wall.

Maizie looked back to the other side where the forest edged the shore and her sundress and panties lay draped over a crooked log. He was still there—somewhere. Even at this distance she could feel him watching. A smile tugged the corner of her mouth.

Why was she smiling? He could be anyone, a rapist, a psychopath, a tax collector. She should be scared, alarmed, or wondering about receipts. She wasn't. In her dream Maizie was fearless, and horny. She was so turned on she could feel the hot juices creaming her pussy even under the water. She liked being watched...by him. Who knew?

Him? Did she know who it was? Yes. She realized she did, but her subconscious wasn't tellin'.

Maizie dove back under the water, swimming as far as her lungs would allow. When she came up again she was close enough to touch bottom and walk up the gradual slope to the edge. The water grew shallower with each step and Maizie rocked her hips for a sexier slow reveal. With both hands she smoothed the water from her face, over her forehead and through her hair. If her secret admirer wanted a show? She'd give him one.

She headed for the crooked log, but got a better idea when she noticed the huge slab of rock ten feet beyond, tilted on a gentle angle. It was wide and flat, a perfect stage.

Water tickled down her back from her hair, over her ass, streaming between her legs. Maizie bit her lip on a smile, her muscles tight, breasts heavy, cool air breezing over her skin.

There was no sexy way to climb onto the rock, but she managed with only a minimum amount of humiliating angles. She stretched out, lifting her long wet hair so it fanned out above her head as she lay down.

A rustle of leaves, the snap of twigs, her voyeur was moving around for a better angle. *Good.* This time she did smile. Maizie closed her eyes, opened herself to the feel of his gaze, touching herself where his hands couldn't reach.

The rock was warm against her back, the sun fighting the chill of a breeze over beads of water on her chest and belly. She rubbed her hands over herself, spreading the water, helping the sun dry her body. Her skin tingled under her touch, her breasts aching for stimulation, nipples hard and erect.

Her belly tightened with the feel of his gaze on her, her sex muscles pulsed, body going wet and ready. She rubbed her hand over her ribs, brushing up to cup a breast in her palm.

Her back arched. She imagined it was his hand, his fingers pinching her tender nipple, twisting, teasing.

Maizie smoothed her free hand down her belly, pretending they were his fingers slipping through the coarse red curls of her mons, caressing down to part the outer labia, teasing her swollen clit.

She moaned at the touch, the thought, her sex opening, aching to be filled. Her two fingers slid between her inner lips, pushing into her sex so her palm pressed against her sensitive clit.

Sensation hummed through her body, her sex muscles clenching, slicking, smoothing the rhythmic strokes. She held her breath, a soft build of pressure welling up from her center.

She imagined him there, next to her, above her, his fingers moving in and out of her sex, his focused stare watching her respond to his touch. He'd grow hard at the sight of her pleasure, wanting her, but wanting to watch too. Ripples of liquid heat tingled over her skin as though she could feel his breath hovering above her, almost kissing her, but not. She bent her knees, spread her legs, wanting him there inside her.

Maizie writhed against the hard rock, forgetting her audience, losing herself in the fast swirl of sensation building inside her. She bit her lip, concentrating on the delicious pressure, the release just a few seconds away. She lifted her hips, his fingers, her fingers, pumping her sex, driving her orgasm closer, faster. Almost there.

Something moved beside the rock. Maizie wanted to look, but didn't. She couldn't lose this feeling, this coming bliss. She clenched her teeth. Just another second then she'd look. Her hand kept the rhythm, her sex so wet, her thighs felt the chill of a breeze.

A swish of movement, the click, click, click of claws along

the flat rock, her voyeur had come to her. *Gray.* He was there, next to her. She opened her eyes, just a slit, caught a flash of silver fur and then it was gone.

Maizie tipped her head back, so close to release she held her breath. A hand squeezed above her knee. Not a paw, a hand, Gray's hand—distracting her just enough to knock her orgasm back a level, rebuilding it, making it more intense, more undeniable.

A second hand pressed against her other leg, both squeezing, massaging, up her thighs. She didn't stop masturbating. He was watching, just like she'd imagined. Her chest squeezed, need humming beneath her skin.

Warm lips pressed a kiss to her inner thigh, her hand brushing against the beard stubble on his cheek. A heated tingle rushed through her body from the spot, leaving a heated imprint of his lips in her mind. Gray's firm tongue traced the flesh where her leg met her sex, her thighs trembled with the feel of it, then he bit her there. Just a nibble but it made her jump and sent a sharp jolt of pleasure ricocheting through her body.

She gasped, head back, eyes closed. "Yes."

She raised her hips from the rock and felt Gray's silky hair brush her thigh as he leaned down and flicked his tongue over her anus.

Maizie sucked a breath, the sensation tripling the intensity in her pussy. Then he did it again, this time pushing at the opening.

"Yes."

His tongue pressed again, firm enough to spread the tight muscles but soft and moist enough that it didn't hurt. Her breath caught in her chest, muscles snapping tight, coiling, sensation building...building, and then just like that her release swelled over her restraint and every nerve ending in her body trembled in its wake.

Gray stayed there toying with the virginal opening while her fingers pumped her sex, her palm stroking her clit. Her body clenched around her, milking her for more.

She was drenched, creamed from thigh to thigh, and she was coming. Really coming. She held her breath. *Yes. Gray. Yes.*

"What's that knocking?" Gray said in that the sexy radio voice from between her thighs.

"Anyone home? Hello?" The voice wasn't as sexy anymore and sounded farther away.

Maizie opened her eyes. Scanned the room. Her room. In Granny's cottage. She looked down. Her spaghetti-strap nightgown was pushed below her breasts, both her hands were in her panties, knees wide, sheets a tangled mess around her feet.

"Shoot." She dropped her head back into her pillow. The world's most mind-blowing orgasm was gone. "Today already sucks and I haven't even gotten out of bed yet."

"Hello? Last chance. Anyone home?"

Maizie jackknifed in bed. That was a man's voice. Coming from inside the house. She kicked her feet free of the sheets and scrambled toward her bedroom door, straightening her nightgown, grabbing her robe.

Pounding down the stairs, she shoved her arms through the sleeves. Who was it? Some squatter who'd found Granny's cleverly hidden key, a vacuum salesman, a born-again something-or-other? Whatever.

Whoa, Nelly, did they pick the wrong house to break-and-enter. Well, enter. Hell hath no fury like a sexually frustrated woman. The first time she'd spent the night at the cottage in months and she caught someone taking advantage of Granny's down-home trust. They had it coming.

The front door was open. Maizie raced down the last few steps and grabbed the corner wall to help swing herself into the kitchen. She reached across the counter and snagged one of the big cleaver-style knives from the woodblock holder and headed back toward the living room.

"Hey. What the hell do you think you're doing?" She rested the cleaver against her shoulder, her weight on one hip.

Yeah, she wouldn't kill him. Didn't have it in her. But he didn't know that.

The man—tall, probably six-one, six-two—spun to face her from just past the threshold to the all-season room. He was older, around forty-five with thick black hair graying at the temples. He was kind of stocky, but very debonair with his coal-black suit, powder-blue shirt and matching tie.

"Oh. Sorry. Didn't think anyone was home." His brown eyes raked down her body, pausing a little too long at her breasts. A lopsided grin blossomed over his clean-shaven face. "You must be Maizie."

There was a leer in his voice, if a voice could leer, that made a cold chill settle at the base of her spine. Maizie straightened, suddenly feeling vulnerable despite the six-inch cleaver in her hand. She pulled the edges of her robe together, holding them shut rather than setting the knife down to tie the belt.

"You're trespassing," she said. "I already called the cops." Great idea, too bad she hadn't thought of it before she raced down half-dressed to shoo away the criminal. *Ugh.* Her brain was oversexed, frustrated mush.

"Really? How awkward. You see, I'm here at your

grandmother's behest." He stepped into the living room.

"Stay back." Maizie brandished the cleaver in both hands.

The man stopped instantly, his cocky smile melting away along with all the color in his skin. He held up his hands in surrender. "Hold on, Maizie. Relax. I told you. I'm a friend of Ester's. Call her. Check it out."

"Yeah, right. How do I know you're not some serial killer here to chop me into little pieces as soon as I turn my back to use the phone?"

His smile returned, minus the cockiness. "Well, you're the one waving the meat cleaver around. And this isn't my people-chopping suit."

Okay, good point. Most serial killers probably didn't wear Versace on the job. She recognized the style. "Who are you? Gran didn't mention anyone was coming. I just saw her yesterday."

He dropped his gaze, looked away for a moment then back, his eyes suddenly sad. "Ester doesn't always remember things clearly. I'm sure she would've told you, but, you know."

Shit. She knew exactly what he meant.

His smile warmed. It was a nice smile that lit his eyes and sharpened the roundness of his jaw. He was kind of handsome, in a stiff, businessman sort of way, with a thin nose, thick brows and short wavy hair, cut just above the collar.

"The name's Anthony. Anthony Cadwick." He stretched one hand toward her, very slowly. "I don't bite and I only chop people into little pieces figuratively."

Okay, so now she felt kind of stupid holding the cleaver like a hatchet ready to chop off a limb. She lowered it to her side, then set it on the end table next to the front door.

"Hi, Tony. I'm Maizie, the crazy granddaughter."

"It's, um, *Anthony*, actually. Nice to finally meet you. Your grandmother speaks of you often." He stepped forward.

They shook hands. His skin was warm and soft, his handshake firm not wimpy like he worried he'd hurt her. She liked that.

"Anthony. Sorry. Nice outfit."

"Same to you." His gaze dropped to her open robe and then to her bare legs from above her knees. "I woke you?"

Maizie tied her robe, made a knot. She shoved her bed-hair back from her face, the other hand holding her collar together. "Actually you interrupted a really great dream."

"Mm, sorry about that. Ester said you lived in the city. Didn't think anyone was here." He checked his watch. "Afternoon, someone's got a great work schedule."

"I stopped by last night to check on things. Took a walk in the woods. It got pretty late, so I just stayed. The place is more comforting than I remember. Particularly the wildlife."

"Umm..."

"Wait. What time did you say?"

He checked his watch again. "Twelve twenty-five, now."

"Oh, crap. I don't even have time to shower." She spun around and headed for the stairs. "Uh, listen, I have to be at work, like now, so if you can see yourself out... Lock the door behind you. Thanks."

She'd already turned the landing when she heard him start up the stairs. "Actually, it's quite a propitious circumstance. Your being late for work notwithstanding, of course."

She stopped and leaned over the banister. "Okay, maybe I was too vague before. I have to change clothes and haul ass. You need to leave."

"But I've been wanting to speak with you. It's about your

grandmother. I'm really quite concerned."

"Yeah? Maybe it's something in the water." She didn't have time for this. Maizie took the last two steps at once and raced to her room. She slammed the door and twisted the cheapy knob lock. Better than nothing. Maybe he'd see the closed door and get the idea.

Maizie jerked out of her robe and ripped her little nightgown over her head. Her gaze fell on her sundress from yesterday. Not only had she worn it to work the day before, but her escape from the pissed-off wolf had left a nice long tear in the hem. There had to be something better.

She went to the closet. Maybe some scrap of her old clothes had hidden out in there. She started digging and realized her old room closet had apparently become the place where out-of-date coats went to die.

"Y'know...Maizie?"

Sheezz, the guy couldn't take a hint. Or a simple direct order. She rolled her eyes and kept searching through the plastic-covered garments. "Yeah?"

"Oh. Uh, your grandmother cares for you a great deal. Talks about you all the time."

"That right?" *Bingo.* Right between a maroon tweed jacket and the overstuffed winter coat, she found an old wraparound denim skirt. "Gawd, were these things ever in style?"

"What's that?" Anthony's voice sounded louder, like he leaned against the door. Was he listening to her change clothes? *Creepy.*

"Nothing. So, you were saying Gran talks to you about me?" If he was yackin' away out there, she knew he wasn't listening to her being naked in here.

"Yes. Yes, she does. All the time."

Maizie rolled her eyes again. She needed a top. She'd reached the end of the closet and found nothing in there that would do. She turned and raced across the room to her old dresser.

Top drawer...junk, playing cards, pens, rubber bands. She shoved it closed. Next drawer...books.

"I don't think there's anything on the planet she cares about more than you," Anthony said.

Maizie slammed the book drawer closed then moved to the next...more books, same as the last. She yanked open the bottom drawer.

"Clothes, thank gawd." Double-D boulder-holder bras, enormous granny-panties, and...*eureka!* A nice little stack of old T-shirts.

"The only thing she might care about half as much is her big silver wolf." Anthony laughed, but Maizie's blood ran cold. She froze.

Until last night the silver wolf had been a figment of an old woman's imagination, a character in a fairy tale. But he was real now.

He was real and beautiful and... She didn't want to think about the rest of it. About his strange cameo in her dream. What was that? There'd been a moment, after she'd caught the animal in Granny's house, that she'd been afraid. Not afraid of being killed, but afraid she couldn't stop him if his embarrassingly bold licks intensified, morphing into something more, something worse. Maybe that fear, that weird possibility had tainted her dreams.

"Maizie?"

She shook her head, snapping out of the odd train of thought and grabbed the top T-shirt. Taking it to the bed, she dressed.

"What did Gran say about the wolf, exactly?" she asked.

"I'm sure you've heard it before. She said she has to protect it and she promised never to sell the land so he always has a place to run. Same as always."

The T-shirt was tight, but it'd do. She'd throw an apron on when she got to the shop. Maizie dug her brush out of her purse and grabbed her hair ring from the nightstand.

"If you ask me," Anthony said, "I think the wolf is you. Metaphorically speaking."

"What? Uh, no." Okay, given last night and her dream, that was just too twisted.

"Think about it. She made a promise to protect it, to keep the land so it'd always have a place to live. There's nothing she loves more. Sound familiar? Like the promises she made to care for you?"

"Yeah, but..." He was missing a few vital bits of information, like there really was a big silver wolf running around the forest. Maizie had no intention of setting Anthony Cadwick straight. She found her sandals and plopped down on the bed to strap them on.

"I think it's a real burden on her, mentally and physically. No matter how you look at it, she's holding on to this place because of you, and I think it's costing her."

"Costing *her*? Ha." Maizie snapped her big mouth shut. Her finances were none of this guy's business.

"Yeah, I know it's costing you, too. So does Ester."

Okay, maybe her finances were his business, and apparently anyone else's who'd had a chat with Gran. "I'm good. The land's good. The nursing home fees are good. The shop's good. We're all good."

"You sound convincing, but I'm not buying it. And neither

is your grandmother. She's not a stupid woman, Maizie. How do you think she feels knowing you're struggling and not knowing why? Not knowing how to help?"

She knew exactly how Granny felt. She wanted to protect Maizie, to help her with anything and everything she could. It made her nuts seeing the worry on Maizie's face, worry Maizie couldn't hide from Gran, worry Maizie wouldn't talk about.

Granny had always hoped Maizie would move back to the cottage one day, but if she knew how hard things were money-wise she'd sell in a heartbeat to give her the cash. Of course Granny *didn't* know, so she wouldn't sell. Maybe Anthony was right. Granny was holding on to the land because of her and it was hurting them both.

Maizie grabbed her purse and opened the door. Anthony stumbled into the room. Ha! She'd been right. She *knew* he'd been leaning against the door. "Sorry."

He straightened. "My fault."

"I really have to run, but I'll think about what you said."

Anthony gave her his card. "I understand if you want to tough it out and hold on to the place. I mean, Ester loves it here even if she'll probably never see it again. But if you decide you want to clue her in. Let her know how she can help. Give me a call. I know some people who'd be interested."

His gaze dropped to her breasts, brown eyes sparking. That cocky, I'm-picturing-you-naked grin pinched one cheek again and he chuckled, low and suggestive.

She shifted her weight to one hip, propped her hand on her side. "Maybe you'd like to take a picture."

He laughed. "If only. You going to wear that to work?"

Maizie looked down at her shirt. "Oh, perfect."

She'd grabbed a T-shirt from her youthful rebellious days,

her salute to the environment. A cartoon of a fuzzy, flat-tailed beaver and beside it, *Save a tree, eat a beaver.*

"I knew this day was just gonna get worse."

"How's Maizie?" Gray could've toppled Ester with a good sneeze. She blinked at him across the table, mouth lax.

"My Little Red? She's good. Fine. She's just fine. I thought..."

"I know." Gray knew what she was thinking. He'd made it clear he wanted to forget the girl even existed. No mention of her—ever. That was the rule. But she wasn't a little girl anymore and his brain couldn't seem to let her go. He hadn't seen her for days, since that night in the woods, but he could still smell the sugary sweetness of her body, taste her tangy skin.

He shrugged. "It's been a long time."

Granny nodded, pushing the box of gingerbread cookies closer to his plate. "Too long. It wasn't her fault—"

"Ester." It was a warning, but he didn't mean to growl. He just wasn't ready to go there. He chewed the last bite of peanut butter sandwich and snatched up two of the cookies.

Gray chuckled, looking the tiny little man over, front and back. "She made these. All these years it was her baking I was eating."

"Sure was," Granny said. "Her mama taught her. I think they remind Maizie of better days. She's been baking them since she was a little girl. Same length of time you've been eating them."

"Strange."

"Or fate," Granny said. "You both lost a piece of yourselves that night. Stands to reason you'd each have what the other needs to make up for it."

Gray tossed the cookies back into the box. "Enough, Ester. They're cookies."

"I just meant—"

"I lost my wife." He lowered his voice. "My mate. You know about me, about us, what we are. We mate for life. She's gone. Nothing can make up for that."

"Humph." Granny snatched one of the gingerbread cookies and bit off its head. A heavy silence settled between them. Gray let his gaze drift over the room.

Green Acres' social hall was bright and inviting. Soft yellow walls decorated with country crafts and vintage pictures. Round white tables with matching chairs filled the largest part of the room. The smaller areas were busy with comfortable green couches and upholstered chairs.

People visited with relatives, watching television and playing games, even rippling out a tune on the grand piano.

Gray's attention focused across the room to the wall of open glass doors, the patio outside and the forest far beyond. He tried to imagine himself trapped in a place like this. As nice as it was, it wasn't freedom.

"Stop scowling, Gray. I'm happy here. I've got friends and I see more of you and Maizie than I ever did at the cottage."

He swung his gaze to her. She knew him well. "Don't you miss it? The cottage? The forest?"

Ester shrugged. "Sure. Sometimes. But I'm an old woman, not a beautiful wolf. This is where I belong."

He reached over and took her hands in his. "I could change that, Ester. One nip. A small bit of blood. You'd feel years younger, have years and years left to live."

Granny laughed, a sweet-old-lady laugh. "No, dear. This is my life. I'm happy. Soon I'll be seeing my Frank again. I don't want to put that off any longer. Maizie is the one I'm worried about. And you."

Gray shifted in his seat, taking back his hands and rubbing his palms on his thighs. "I'm fine. And Maizie's...Maizie is..."

"A wonderful young lady who's too gosh-darn busy trying to make her life perfect she's missing out on the best part. Love. And you—"

"Ester." He tried to stop the lecture he knew was coming.

"Hush, and let an old lady have her say for once. You're so busy mourning what you've lost you can't see all that's slipping through your fingers."

She leaned forward and rested her soft withered hand on his arm. "I know you mate for life, dear, and the woman who died was your wife. You loved her. But that doesn't mean she was your life's mate. The heart wants what it wants. Tell me, Mr. Lupo, what is that wolf heart of yours whispering to you about my Little Red?"

Chapter Five

"It's not Lilly, Gran, it's Maizie. Lilly was my mom." During one of her spells, it was almost impossible to talk to Gran.

"I know that," Granny huffed. "Haven't gone completely off my rocker. You *sound* like her, is all."

"Okay." Maizie would have to try to be more sensitive next time. No one liked being reminded that their mind was slipping.

"Can't blame me for hearing Lilly's voice. I always think of her when I've spent the day with Riddly."

Silence settled through the phone connection while Granny's explanation sunk in. "Umm..." How to put this? "Did Daddy visit you today?"

"He didn't tell you he was coming?"

"No, he didn't. I haven't talked to him in a long time." The back of her throat dried, made it hard to swallow and her eyes stung. She wouldn't cry.

"Well, don't be angry with him, Little Red. He's so busy these days. Doesn't even have time to play a round of Kings." She tsked, and Maizie could picture her shaking her head. "He's just so wrapped up in work. Not good for the boy. He didn't used to work so much. And now he's worried about you."

"Me?" A bitter smile trembled across her lips and she swiped at a runaway tear. "Why's he worried?"

"Same as always. Thinks you've spread your finances too thin. Worried you'll sacrifice the bakery to keep the cottage for me." Granny stopped talking, but it didn't feel like she'd finished her thought.

"Gran?"

"He thinks I should sell the land, Maizie. I told him you said the business was doing fine, but..."

What if Anthony Cadwick was right and Gran was holding on to the land for Maizie because she didn't know what else to do for her? Why else would she keep having these delusions about Riddly coaxing her to sell?

"Gran, you know you can't live in the cottage alone anymore, right?"

"Of course, dear. Don't get around as well as I used to."

"And you know I want to live here. In the city. Near the bakery?"

"Yes, Little Red, I know how much you think you love the city."

Think? Maizie smiled at that. Gran always believed she knew Maizie better than she knew herself. "That means no one will live in the cottage."

"Yes, dear. I understand."

"Then tell me the truth. Why is it so important to hold on to the land?"

"Because I made a promise, of course."

"To who? To Dad?" Maizie asked.

"Your father? No. Riddly never understood. He still doesn't believe. No, dear. I promised the wolf. My beautiful silver wolf. Our land stands as a buffer between his world and ours. I promised he'd always have that buffer."

Maizie's breath caught, memories swamped her brain, that

silky fur, those hypnotic eyes, the erotic dream. She pushed the distracting thoughts away.

The wolf didn't want her to sell. A few weeks ago she would've rolled her eyes at the statement, but having met the mysterious beast it didn't seem so farfetched.

Maizie didn't care why Granny wanted to keep the cottage. She didn't want to sell. Maizie wouldn't allow it to be sold. Simple as that. It was the very least she could do for a woman who'd given her the last good years of her life.

"Maizie?"

"Yeah, Gran. I'm still here."

"He said you've been late on your loan payments. Next week will make you a full month behind. Is that true?"

An uneasy weight sank to the bottom of her belly, sat there like bad seafood. How could Gran know her payment history? "Who told you that?"

"Is it true?"

Yeah, it was true. She'd make the payment, but there'd be a late fee, which would only make finances tighter. There was no way Gran could've known though. Someone must have told her. Someone not made of twisted memories and wishful thinking. Someone real.

"I'm making the payments. Everything is fine. Now who've you been talking to?"

"Riddly. It was Riddly. He said..." Her voice was soft, unsure. And when her words trailed off, Maizie knew she was realizing her mind must have been playing tricks.

"Gran, Dad's dead. He couldn't have told you what's going on with my loan. Think. Who was it?"

Whoever was feeding her personal financial information about Maizie was obviously after the land. He'd use whatever means necessary, including making an old woman feel guilty for aging. But impersonating her dead son? That was beyond low.

"He said he was Riddly. I didn't believe him at first. But I get confused sometimes. He looks like Riddly...a little. I just miss my boy."

"I know. I miss Dad too. But it's not him. Someone's trying to trick you into selling the land and I think I know who it is. I'll talk to Clare, at the front desk. We'll figure it out."

Thoughts of Gray Lupo pulled Maizie in two different directions. Her belly soured. Gawd, she'd always considered herself a pretty good judge of character. How could her instincts and libido be so off?

Maybe Gran meant someone else. Gray had seemed happy when Maizie told him she wouldn't let anyone get their hands on Granny's land. If she didn't know better she'd swear he really cared about Granny.

Ugh. I'm grasping at straws.

"You're sure you don't need the money, Little Red?" Granny sounded suddenly lucid. "I promised the wolf, but he'd understand my granddaughter's needs come first."

"I'm sure. The wolf can relax. I won't allow the land to be sold either."

"Ah, what a strange twist of fate," Granny said.

"What's that?"

"All those years protecting the two of you from each other and here you are. Each protecting the other from the world."

"Yeah. Twisted alright." Maizie couldn't help thinking her life would've been a lot easier if the big, bad wolf had stayed in the misty world of bedtime stories where he belonged.

"You have any idea who Mr. Gray Lupo is?" Cherri paused mid-sift to look at Maizie, half the tray of cream danishes speckled in powdered sugar.

Maizie shrugged. She glanced at Cherri then looked back to her apple pie crust, pinching perfect dents around the rim. "Doesn't matter."

"Bullshit. You're telling me you didn't google him?"

Maizie shrugged, the queen of indifference. Of course she'd googled him. But admitting that meant admitting she had a thing, a heavy-breathing, panty-creaming, forget-her-own-name thing, for the guy trying to con her sweet little Granny. She didn't want to admit that. Not even to herself.

"Well, *I* googled him," Cherri said. "And he is The Shit. I mean it. He's The Man. The Big Guy. Mr. Monopoly. Boardwalk, Park Place, the man owns the whole damn board."

"Impressive. I'm still not letting him in to see Granny anymore. I talked to Clare. It's a done deal."

"Clare? The toothpick at the front desk? I know kindergarten teachers tougher than her. You really think she can stop a man like Gray Lupo?"

"It's a private facility. He's not above the law."

"Uh, hello?" Cherri pushed at her glasses with the back of her sugarcoated hand. "A guy with that kind of money and power? Yeah. He is."

"He doesn't intimidate me."

"He should. He's dated some of the most beautiful women in the world—movie stars, models, even a princess. Does that intimidate you?"

"No." *It's just depressing.*

"He was married once."

"Really?" Now that was news to Maizie.

"She left him. Vanished."

"It happens."

"He can buy and sell Donald Trump. The man doesn't own a pair of shoes, belt or briefcase that wasn't once an actual living thing. When he eats Chinese food, he does it...in China."

"I don't care."

"He doesn't wash his underwear. He just buys new ones."

"Cherri."

"And they're tailored."

"Enough." She couldn't keep a straight face much longer.

"Fine. How about this one? He's also your neighbor."

"What?" Maizie snapped her gaze to Cherri, pie in one hand, oven door in the other.

"You really didn't google him, did you? Can't believe it." Cherri turned and finished sifting powdered sugar over danishes.

"Okay, okay. I stopped reading after the princess thing. Happy? Now tell me about him being my neighbor." Maizie shoved the pie in the oven and set the timer, then took the empty stool at Cherri's prep-table.

"Well he's not physically your neighbor, unless he lives somewhere on that Wild Game Preserve next to your grandmother's land."

"The preserve?"

"Yeah. He owns it."

Maizie always figured the preserve was some government project. She'd never seen anything remotely exotic...except for the big silver wolf. She certainly hadn't seen any signs of a house.

"He owns it?"

"Yeah."

So why was he trying to get Granny to sell her land?

The cowbell over the front door clanked. "Hello?"

Maizie snapped straight. She knew that radio voice. "That's him."

"Him, who?" Cherri leaned back, trying to see through the doorway into the showroom.

Maizie scrambled out of her apron, tossing it over the stool. She twisted the hair at her temples around her fingers. Corkscrew curls bounced back, revitalized. She groped the swirl of hair at the crown of her head. *Messy bun, still messy.*

A smudge of flour on the hem of her tan sleeveless dress caught her notice and she hurried to brush it away before checking her dull reflection in one of the metal pots hanging over the table. *Still redheaded. Still freckled. Nothing to be done about it.*

Maizie took a breath and headed through the doorway. "Stay here."

"Okay. But him who?" Cherri said after her.

Maizie came around the display cases. "Mr. Lupo. What can I do for you?"

He looked confidently casual in reddish-brown pants, a black jersey-knit T-shirt that hugged his chest, and a lighter brown plaid jacket, worn fashionably open. He even wore sneakers, leather lace-up track shoes, probably cost an easy hundred bucks.

Maizie thought about the underwear. Tailored? And then she thought about the package inside the underwear. All natural. Her cheeks flushed hot. *Thanks a lot, Cherri.* She tried to think of something else.

"Ms. Hood, you look..." He exhaled. "Lovely." He said "lovely" like it was an understatement. *Nicely done.* She fought her smile while his gaze traveled down her body and back again. Not the slightest bit lecherous or ogling, but very male. A quick shudder raced across her shoulders.

"If this is about my grandmother and Green Acres there's really nothing to discuss."

Those pale blue eyes met hers, brows tight. "Sorry?"

"Oh." Maybe he didn't know about the no-admittance she'd set at Green Acres. "Why are you here, Mr. Lupo?"

Judging by his tiny flinch, she must've sounded ruder than she'd intended. "It's Gray. Please. Mr. Lupo sounds so... I'd be honored if you called me Gray."

"Fine. Gray." She waited for an answer although the way he looked at her, as though he was fighting the urge to reach out and touch her, it really didn't seem so important why he was there. She was just glad he was.

No. He's an ass.

He smiled, one of his lopsided almost-smiles that made her think he could read her mind. "Have lunch with me," he said.

"Lunch?" *Didn't see that one coming.*

"Yes."

She'd thought he'd come to issue warnings, relay the dangers of defying a man of his considerable power and wealth. *That*, she could've handled. But this? "I can't have lunch with you."

"Why not? You haven't eaten already, have you?"

"No."

"You do eat, don't you?"

Maizie scoffed. "Yes." *When I remember.*

"Good. Then come with me."

"It's the middle of the day. I have a shop to run. Y'know, some of us still have to get our hands dirty in order to keep our business going. I can't just—"

"I got it covered," Cherri yelled from the back prep-room. "Go. Take the day off. Won't even miss you here."

Maizie could tell by the closeness of her voice that Cherri was leaning against the wall next to the doorway, listening. "She's joking. I'm absolutely essential here. They can't run the place—"

"Yes I can," Cherri called. "Done it before. A bunch of times. Go. Have lunch. No reason to be *intimidated.*"

That's it, first chance she got, she'd fire that neb-nose. And this time she'd mean it. Probably. Okay, probably not, but she'd make her think she did.

Maizie looked back to Gray in time to catch him rake one of his big guy hands through his hair. What a nice contrast, tan skin, parting through silky silver and black. The gesture hiked his jacket sleeve, showing off a muscled forearm brushed with dark hairs. So purely male.

She couldn't help tracking his hand back to the front pocket of his pants, his thumb hooking at the corner just like the other. When he stopped moving, her gaze jumped to his.

He'd been watching her, watching him. That half grin tugging the corner of his mouth again. Maizie's body warmed, a wash of heat rippling down to her core, readying her body for what it wanted, never mind her brain's protests.

"Why?" she said.

His brows pinched, cocky grin fading. "Pardon?"

"Why do you want to have lunch with me?" He could date anyone. He'd dated everyone. Why her?

"I thought we could talk."

Ah-ha! Talk. About Granny and her land, no doubt. She was right all along. Cut off from the old lady, he'd come to use those pretty eyes and that sexy voice on her.

Finally.

How many deals had he done this way? How many of those women he'd been photographed with had fallen prey to his charm and palpable sex appeal?

Would he jet her off to some exotic location? Ply her with expensive wines and three-hundred-dollar caviar? Would he buy her jewelry and a designer dress just to take her to a sold-out ballet or maybe an opera? Would he try to buy her help to turn her against Granny?

"Just talk, huh?" she asked. He was sexy as hell, but the whirlwind date wouldn't make her forget the cruel tricks he'd played on Granny.

"Yes. Just talk. And eat."

Gawd, it would be great to let him throw all his money around, flashing that sexy almost-there grin, thinking he was being sly, manipulating her. And then at the end of the day she'd tell him "bite me", watch his jaw hit the floor. *It'd serve 'im right.*

"Fine. Take me to lunch."

Gray figured Maizie would be surprised when his driver turned onto the gravel road next to the Wild Game Preserve sign, but she looked almost mystified.

"Is there a private airstrip somewhere in the forest? Maybe a helipad?" She searched through the car window, scanning between the trees, squinting into the shadows. Her hands tensed around the pastry box on her lap, denting the edges.

"Uh, no. No airstrip. No helipad." Jeezus, where'd she expect him to take her for lunch? He'd dated plenty of women who expected over-the-top outings, but he hadn't pegged Maizie as the type. Being raised by Ester, he thought she'd be more down to earth, more...real.

Several minutes along the gravel road into the forest, the car came to a stop. Gray reached down and pulled a shoebox from under the driver's seat.

He held it out to Maizie. "Here. You might want to put these on."

She turned, her gaze dropping to the box. A strange grin curled her lips. "You bought me shoes, huh?"

"Actually, I—"

"What are they, Manolo Blahnik? Jimmy Choo? Prada?" She handed him the pastries and threw off the shoe lid as though she was exposing some guilty payoff.

"They're Timberlands," Gray said. "My niece's boots. I wasn't sure of your size, but you look about as small as Shelly. It's kind of a hike. Not muddy, but not exactly a high-heeled-sandal trail." He opened his door. "You wanted designer shoes?"

She paled, practically shrank back into her seat. "No. No, I just thought... Never mind. These are fine, perfect."

Dave, the driver, had gotten them as close to the picnic site as he could. Still, the quarry lake was a good distance from the road. Gray hadn't been there in years, but he'd had a strange dream the other night about Maizie and him at the lake. She'd come up out of the water—naked.

Gray shook the erotic memory from his brain. He wanted to keep a tight rein on everything today, his actions as well as his thoughts. He didn't want to risk losing control like he had in his wolf form. Jeezus, she brought the animal out in him.

Carrying the pastry box for her, he heard Maizie's muffled oath and glanced back in time to see her recover from a stumble over a tree root. He grabbed her hand without thinking. She flinched, but then held his hand tight. It felt good. He tried to ignore it.

Gray watched her step high over the jutting root, her shapely leg stretching the limits of her form-fitting dress.

The idea was to ingratiate himself with Maizie, get to know her, let her know him somewhat. Yeah, he'd use seduction enough to influence her. He'd use her already budding attraction to gain her loyalty. When Cadwick made his move he wanted Maizie to have every reason to refuse him.

Nothing more. No matter what Ester hoped, there'd be nothing *real* between him and Maizie. There couldn't be. There was too much between them already. The fact she couldn't remember didn't change anything.

They stepped into the narrow clearing along the shoreline.

"Ohmygod." Maizie exhaled the words. "The quarry." She'd gone pale.

"You don't like it?" He gestured to the low table set atop a large Oriental rug. Big colorful cushions lined two sides of the table while the sun sparked off several silver dish covers.

Maizie's gaze skittered over the table, her lips parted. "No. It's...it's beautiful. Surprising. I never would've guessed. I..." She glanced in the opposite direction and Gray followed her gaze.

When he saw the huge flat rock tilted gently toward the water, his sudden hard-on made him light-headed for a second. The memory of what she'd done in his dream. *Good God*, he'd come just thinking about it. He turned away, scrambling to rein in his thoughts. But then her hand trembled in his, her palm moistened. She was flushed, her breathing shallow. She was as turned on as he was, just as quickly affected. Why?

"Should we eat?" She dropped his hand and headed for the table. "Can't wait to see what's under those covers."

He followed, but his mind was a chaotic mess with a million thoughts, a thousand questions. Something was happening between them, something he couldn't explain but he could feel, like the forest around him. The pulse of life beating beneath the surface, touching the primal nature within him, he was connected to the forest and he was connected to Maizie.

His jaw stiffened. "No." *It's not right.*

"What?"

His gaze snapped to Maizie's, her eyes questioning, a touch of hurt wrinkling the corners.

"We're not eating here?" she asked.

"Yes. I'm sorry, I was... Excuse me. Please." He gestured to the oversized purple cushion closest to them.

They toed off their boots and shoes, handing the pastry box back and forth, careful to step barefooted onto the rug.

Those greener than green eyes were staring at his feet, a look of utter female appreciation shading her face. "Nice feet."

This was definitely a bad idea.

Gray ignored his semi-hard-on. He moved them to the table, guiding Maizie with his hand at the small of her back. She sat like a lady, knees together, legs curled to the side. The tight hug of her dress left her few options. She set the box between them on the table.

Annette had set the two entrées side by side. The other side of the table was filled with floral arrangements, a rather large bowl of fruit, and two flickering candelabras. With space limited and Maizie already seated, Gray had no choice but to take the cushion next to her.

After a second or two of fidgeting, they both accepted that her legs would press against his thigh. Gray did his best to ignore the sensation.

"So what's under the covers?" she asked, suspicious. "Lobster? Truffles? Or no, I bet it's steak tartare? Or maybe quail?"

Steak tartare? Rather than deny her bizarre guesses, Gray reached over and removed both covers at once. "Peanut butter sandwiches, chips, and a glass of milk. I was told it's your favorite."

She blinked, staring at the ordinary dish.

"You're disappointed. I'm sorry. I thought—"

"No." She grabbed his hand, smiled at him. "It's perfect. You're right. It is my favorite. But you...I'm sure you'd rather have, I don't know, soft-shell crabs or something."

Gray snorted, setting the covers off to the side. "No. Not a seafood lover. Besides, nothing's better than peanut butter sandwiches for nerves."

"I know." Her gaze snapped to his as though she'd just heard what he'd said. "You're nervous?"

"Oh. No. I meant..." He glanced at her. Something had changed in the way she looked at him. A softening of her eyes, the easy curve of her smile, as though he was suddenly more attractive to her. God help him, he liked the way she was looking at him.

"Yeah," he said. "A little. I guess. You?"

She laughed and the tiny curls tickling the sides of her face swayed against her blushing cheeks. "Yeah. Me too."

He could smell the lavender scent of her shampoo, but he'd love to feel her flaming red hair in his hands, press it against his nose, inhale her, the very essence of her.

Gray blinked. A quick shake of his head and he was out of the mental fantasy.

"You okay?"

He couldn't stop his scowl. "Yes. I was just... How's your sandwich?"

She laughed again, light and happy. "I haven't tried it yet, but it's peanut butter. Kinda hard to screw that up."

"Yes. That's true." He tried to laugh, but he knew it'd sound forced.

"It's beautiful here. Y'know, I've heard teenagers in the area like to sneak up here to skinny-dip."

His attention riveted on her. "Have you?"

"Me?" Her blush colored her face and raced down her neck beneath the round collar of her dress. Gray tracked the wash of color. Did it spread farther? Did it warm her breasts the way it did her cheeks? Did it warm between her thighs?

"Well, yeah. Once or twice. But it was ages ago. Back when I lived at the cottage with Gran."

He didn't want to think about it. He couldn't stop thinking about it. The memory of his dream, the reality of her swimming naked, the thoughts and images mixed like an erotic movie in his head.

She took a sip of milk, leaving a thin white mustache lining her top lip when she finished. She licked her lips, but a faint milk line remained. "So why'd you bring me here? This is about Gran's land, isn't it? I'm at least right about that."

"Yes." He swallowed, his gaze stuck on that line of milk tracing her lip. "I wanted you to see what's at risk if your grandmother sells."

"But aren't you the one trying to buy Granny's land?"

"No, Maizie. I don't want Ester to sell to anyone."

"So then you're not trying to seduce me?"

Gray opened his mouth but realized he didn't know the answer. He exhaled. Closed his mouth and looked away. His gaze landed on the pastry box, edges dented, still sitting between their plates.

"You ever going to show me what's in the box?" he asked. Not the smoothest topic switch, but it'd do.

Maizie blinked, catching up. She straightened. "Oh. It's...it's nothing really. I thought I'd bring dessert."

She opened the box and the heavenly scent of chocolate wafted out.

"Brownies?"

"I hope you like walnuts," she said.

He smiled, she couldn't know why. "I do. My mother used to make me brownies. She was a pretty fair baker in her own right. God, I loved helping her."

"You bake?"

Gray snorted. "Hell no. What I did could never be described as baking. I measured. Stirred the occasional batter. Set the oven temperature. My specialty. Mostly I just watched her."

"You were close?"

It'd been so long ago. Being a werewolf had extended his lifespan, which meant those memories were even further away. "Yes. We were very close. She passed away years ago, but I can still remember her gliding around the kitchen, gathering ingredients, preparing pans, mixing without ever looking at a recipe. She moved like she was drifting on a cloud. Never a mistake."

"Did your dad help too?"

Gray scoffed. "No. My father was of the belief that men were men and real men didn't enter a kitchen except to inform their wife what they wanted for dinner."

"Wow. How very nineteen fifties of him."

She was closer than she realized, but Gray kept the information to himself. "Right. A real men-don't-cry kind of guy. Didn't matter. I had her. Those hours spent alone with my mother while she baked set me free. I could tell her anything, my fears, my heartbreaks, my dreams, and she never thought less of me. Never made me feel ashamed for not being tough as steel all the time. I...miss that."

"I know what you mean. Used to bake with my mom too. She made the best chocolate cake. After she passed away, I used to sit in the kitchen for hours with my eyes closed, imagining I could still smell that sweet fresh-baked scent. It was like she was still with me."

An invisible band squeezed around Gray's chest. Memories of the night Maizie had lost her mother flashed through his mind. He pushed them away.

"It's stupid," she said. "But that's a big part of why I love baking. Makes me feel like she's still around. Twisted, huh?"

He reached out, brushed the milk, still a moist line above her lip, away with his thumb. Dear God, her lips were as soft as they looked. His hand slipped along her cheek. "No. It's incredibly loving. I'm sure she'd be proud of you."

Maizie's eyes darkened at his touch. She licked her lip, tracing where his thumb had been. "Maybe we could get together some time and you could, uh, measure for me."

She laughed and the sound tickled along his skin, made his heart skip.

"I'd like that."

"Yeah. It'd be nice to share that with someone who, y'know, gets it." Her smile flickered, her eyes suddenly glistening with unshed tears.

His heart squeezed, muscles going tight wanting to gather her into his arms. Without thinking, his hand slipped to the nape of her neck, pulled her to him. His gaze flicked from those soft lips to her eyes just in time to see them flutter closed, and he took her mouth with his.

Little Red. Jeezus, it wasn't just the wolf in him that wanted to gobble her up.

Chapter Six

She felt the kiss. *Everywhere.* Any fleeting thought she'd had of refusing him vanished. Emotions clogged her throat, thoughts of her mother, missing her, missing the comfort and safety of her parents, danced over her heart. Gray understood what she'd lost. He understood what she needed. She couldn't refuse him, even if she'd wanted to.

His lips were strong, but so soft. His tongue traced along her bottom lip, teased her tongue, coaxing it into his mouth. And when she slipped it through his lips, he actually made a noise like a purr. The sound vibrated through her body straight down to her sex.

His big hand cupped the back of her neck, kept her pressed to his lips. The position was awkward, leaning over her bent legs. She didn't care. This felt too wonderful. Tingles rippled over her skin from head to toe, her body warmed so fast she felt flushed.

One hand braced on the table, she reached the other to his cheek. He'd looked clean-shaven but she could still feel the coarse texture of fresh growth beneath her fingers. His cologne filled her nose, sweet, manly, mixed with the earthier scents of nature. *Intoxicating.* She breathed him in, let the smell of him make her dizzy.

She could taste a hint of scotch on his kiss. Together with

his scent and the fast rush of her pulse, it was all Maizie could do not to swoon in his arms.

She shifted, pushing up to her knees and he rewarded her with a harder, stronger kiss. It was so easy, the kiss, the desire. Her body seemed to recognize his touch, warm at the very possibility of it. On her knees, she was a bit taller than him and his hand slipped from her neck to her waist. Still he pulled her to him, as though she'd never be close enough.

Holding her, his free hand smoothed over her ribs to her breast. Maizie's breath caught even before his palm cupped her, before his fingers squeezed. Every muscle in her body worked for more, more pleasure, more sensation, more.

A quiver tickled through her belly. Her thighs trembled, the muscles in her sex pulsed, flexing wet and needy. She wanted to straddle him, to press her pussy against him, to make it clear what he did to her, what he made her want. What he made her need. The dress was too tight, she'd been lucky to get to her knees.

His hand massaged her breast, found her nipple hard and wanting. He toyed with it, coaxed it to harden more, to press undeniably through the fabric of her bra and dress. Maizie moaned and leaned into his touch, her hips pressing her groin against his chest. She didn't care where they were, who he was, what he'd done. She wanted him. Now. Filling the emptiness between her legs.

His fingers pinched hard so Maizie threw her head back, gasping. She arched her back and felt his mouth hot and wet through her dress, his teeth nipping the pebbled nub. Her body curved the other way, arms circling his neck, cradling his head against her chest.

Gray scrambled to his knees, gathering her into his arms, pressing her whole body to his. The hard line of his cock through his pants pushed against her thigh, teased her mercilessly. He took her mouth again, frantic, hungry. The finesse of his first kiss lost to an explosion of passion.

One arm around her back, he dropped the other hand to her ass. He squeezed, hard, lifted her, pressed her pussy against his cock. His want of her was clear, as clear as her own.

She tried to spread her legs wider, but the dress caught at her thighs. It wouldn't give and she couldn't get her hands down to hike it up.

"Too many damn clothes." She'd mumbled it into his mouth, though it barely registered in her brain. The next instant everything changed. Gray's whole body went stiff. His lips pulled from hers.

"Jeezus." He was breathless, still holding her flush to his body. "What the fuck am I doing?"

Maizie opened her eyes. He looked horrified, his pale eyes scanning her face, brow tight, as though searching for some shred of understanding. He released her and got to his feet so fast she nearly fell over from the force of it.

Gray paced the rug, wiped her kiss from his lips with the back of his hand, then roughly shoved his long waving bangs from his face. He held his hips, storming back and forth, eyes down, scowl set.

Was it something she'd said? What did she say? Maizie's lust-drunk mind raced to untangle the mystery. Bewildered, she sat back on her pillow, her hand wiping the wetness rimming her bottom lip. The brush of her finger tingled along her mouth, her whole body too sensitive for idle touches. What had happened?

"That's not why I brought you here." Gray didn't look at her. He kept pacing. "I'm...sorry."

"Sorry?" For what? Kissing her senseless or stopping?

He stopped, his angry eyes slamming into hers. "Yes. Of course I'm sorry. You didn't think I wanted that..."

He must have read something in her expression, disappointment, embarrassment, doubt. He seemed to rethink his words. "I didn't mean... Hell. Obviously, I wanted... I mean, I'm the one who... Dammit, Maizie, something about you makes me...mindless." His gaze softened, hoped.

Maizie forced a smile, not big, but the best she could muster. She could accept "mindless". It was better than "sorry".

Gray grunted at their unspoken truce and started pacing again. "This should've been a simple thing. Textbook. A picnic lunch. Seductively understated. All the women's favorites. A little harmless flirting to get her seeing things my way. I didn't expect to like..."

Maizie shrugged, feigning nonchalance. "Mission accomplished."

"What?" Gray stopped, looked to her.

"If all this was to try and convince me *not* to coax Granny to sell her land, then you've been seducing the willing. So to speak."

He blushed and looked away for a moment, but rallied quickly. "Easy enough to say, but everyone has a price, Maizie. What's yours?"

She tried not to feel insulted. Maizie knew the kind of man Gray Lupo was. A wheeler and dealer, a playboy, wealthy, powerful, he got what he wanted no matter the means, no matter the little redhead who got caught in his way. The glimpse of the tender-hearted Gray, the boy who loved spending time with his mother, the man who shared her pleasure, was gone.

She was insulted. She was hurt. And it was taking too much damn energy to deny. She stiffened, let her temper boil over her wounded pride. "My price? My grandmother's happiness. If she wants the land, wants to protect that pushy wolf that runs around up here, then I'll keep the land."

He blanched. She didn't care why. "If she wants to sell every last square foot, then I'll sell it all tomorrow. I'll do what I have to do to make her feel secure."

Maizie pushed to her feet, smoothing her dress. "I'll let my shop go bankrupt. I'll move back into that isolated cottage. I'll do whatever it takes to make sure you're not pretending to be my dead father, trying to convince Granny to sell the one thing that means the world to her."

She took a breath, tried to calm the anger and hurt that shook down her arms. She fisted her hands. "So you see, *Mr. Lupo*, my price is simple and nonnegotiable. Happy?"

She folded her arms under her chest, chin high. Her belly rolled and pitched, her knees were shaking and a flood of tears clogged at the back of her throat, but damn him if she'd let any of that show.

Gray met her gaze, his hands still propped on his hips, jacket snagged behind his wrists. Silence settled between them like a referee calling a time-out.

His nostrils flared with each breath, his muscled chest swelling and shrinking. A soft wind fluttered the ends of his hair over his collar as his gaze traveled down her body. The study was so intense she could almost feel its path. She'd swear he was pissed. Who wouldn't be after that tirade? But the look in his eyes, the heat, that wasn't anger.

He growled, his hands dropping from his hips. "Hell with it."

His long strides ate the ground between them in a blur. All at once she was in his arms, scooped up against his hard chest, one hand around her waist, the other behind her head. And

Alison Paige

then he froze.

His warm breath bathed her lips, so close she could imagine the feel of his kiss. But he didn't kiss her. He stood, holding her. After a heavy moment, pregnant with anticipation, Maizie squirmed.

Gray's arms tightened around her. "Sshh."

She met his gaze, his eyes distant for a moment before they focused on hers. He didn't say a word, but she understood the meaning in his look. He wanted her to listen. Something wasn't right. They weren't alone.

Maizie straightened, pushing from Gray's embrace. She kept her eyes on him, but her mind searched her senses, listening, smelling, tasting the air.

A snap of twig off to the left, then a rustle of leaves farther over. The hairs at the back of her neck bristled, invisible fingers thrumming down her back, icing her spine. "What is it?"

"The pack. Wolves. They think it's a game, but they're too upset. It's not safe. Things could get out of hand."

"Well, let's go back to the car." She turned to leave, but he caught her arm, pulled her back.

"We won't make it. My house is closer. They'll think clearer there."

"Who?"

Gray caught her chin between his fingers, brought her gaze to his. "Stay with me. You'll be fine. Don't look back. Don't look around."

"But—"

"Don't. Just...trust me." His voice was soft and steady, utterly confident. She let the sound of it wash over her, calm the jittery nerves tingling her muscles, edging an instinctive panic.

96

Without taking his eyes from hers, he reached down and took her hand, his big palm swallowing hers, his fingers holding tight and firm. The simple touch did more for her than any drug. She was safe. No matter what.

Without another word, he turned and used his full long stride to lead them into the forest. Barefoot, their pace never faltered, yet remarkably each step found soft pliable ground.

The paths she'd always been so aware of were nowhere to be seen. Gray made his own way, somehow slicing through low branches, tumbled trees and prickly brier patches without effort. Without pain. The forest floor should be rough against her feet. It wasn't. Why?

They were moving fast, Gray's strides a half step longer than hers, but she managed to keep up with little effort. Her body was light, easily pulled and turned like a kite on a string. On either side of her the trees blurred, the forest becoming a smear of green, flashes of light, a tangle of browns.

Wind hissed past her ears, raking through her hair so the loose bun tumbled free, strands snagging on branches. She kept moving. It wasn't hard. Like a drop of water tumbling down a river, a part of the whole but separate. The scents and sounds of the forest cascaded over her, honeysuckle, a crow's caw, pine sap, a burrowing rabbit. Everything mixed and melted into her, through her, around her. She was the forest, every bit of it, and the forest was her—one and the same.

And then they stopped.

She nearly rammed her nose into his shoulder. She held his arm for a moment, her head against his back, waiting for her mind, for the world, for time itself to catch up. She peered over his shoulder.

"What the hell was that?" she asked. "Felt like we were doing some low flying. That's not possible. Right?"

Gray glanced over his shoulder at her. "I'll explain later. Okay?"

He looked worried, or like he had bigger things to worry about at the moment and he hoped she wouldn't add to it by insisting on answers. She could do that. For now.

They both turned back to the *mansion?*

Maizie blinked, her brain struggling to reconcile what she thought possible and what her eyes were seeing before her. "No way. Cherri was right. You do have a mansion hidden in the forest."

Three stories tall, the size of a small hotel, the huge gray-stone monolith was nevertheless dwarfed by the surrounding forest. Maizie glanced behind them, the forest's edge was at least ten feet back, dense and shadowed. She could imagine walking within feet of the clearing to Gray's yard and not seeing the enormous mansion through the foliage.

Gray tugged her hand and Maizie stumbled after him up the cascade of stone stairs to his patio. Three enormous glass doors opened the lower portion of the house to the patio and offered a clear view into the room beyond.

At the back of the room, carpeted stairs filled the far wall. She could see a huge stone fireplace, a big sectional couch and a smoky mirrored bar. Maizie watched as three pairs of silky long legs descended the stairs into view.

The women were lovely, the second two a slightly younger version of the woman to her right. The oldest and youngest of the trio had hair the color of brown sugar while the woman in the center was a shimmering corn-silk blonde. They wore matching green kimono-style robes, with lapels and sash a complementing blush-pink, radiant against their tawny skin.

The women sauntered out in order, curvy feminine hips swaying. The middle woman turned toward the small patio bar in the corner the moment she passed the threshold. The other two walked a determined line toward Gray. Maizie tried to wiggle her hand free of his, but he held her.

"Gray, my sweet boy," the older woman said as she neared. "Back from your outing so soon? We missed you, dear."

"Mother Joy," Gray said, by way of greeting.

Clearly the oldest of the three, Joy still looked years younger than Gray. Her soft brown hair fell in long waves over her shoulders and down to midback. Her skin was flawless, her body tight, shapely. There was a thickness about her though, a way of walking, speaking, which comes with experience if not simply age.

She pressed her hands to his chest, pushed up to her toes and kissed his cheek. He stood as he was, body stiff, head straight, scowl firmly in place.

"She's my guest, Joy." He stared straight ahead at nothing, as though he didn't want to look at her. "I expected more from you. Couldn't you make the slightest effort to behave, set an example? At the very least dress...your age?"

The woman laughed, a soft chuckle, and playfully slapped his chest. "We were just curious, sweetheart, and Lynn had us convinced you were keeping secrets from us. Said you'd chosen a mate. You can imagine our disappointment."

"That's what had all of you worked up?" His gaze flicked to the woman at the bar. "You should know better than to go out in that state of mind. Could've gotten out of hand fast."

The older woman rolled a shoulder. "Yes, well, you could've told Lynn about your flavor of the week here and saved all of us the trouble." Her bright blue gaze shifted to Maizie. "No offense, dear. I'm sure you're perfectly pleasant."

Maizie shook her head, though she had no idea what they were talking about. The woman couldn't be more than forty-five and Maizie wasn't sure what about her dress or behavior Gray had taken issue with. If Maizie looked that good at forty-five, she'd wear skimpy silk robes too.

Joy turned away and found a seat on a wood chaise lounge. The youngest of the threesome sauntered across the stone patio to Gray, not as graceful, her pretty face marred by the pucker of skin between her furrowed brows.

"Save your breath, Uncle Gray. Totally don't need a lecture. It was Mom's idea. And we were just looking. Y'know this kind of thing wouldn't happen if you'd stop bringing these human skanks around."

"Enough, Shelly."

She looked at Gray's tense expression, his jaw muscles flexing with restrained anger.

Her gaze shifted to Maizie then to Gray and back again. "What? Was Mom right? Something different about this one? No. Of course not. Whatever."

The young beauty stretched to her toes, her hand smoothing up Gray's chest to his neck, forcing him closer. Her pretty pony-tailed hair swished across her back as she kissed Gray's cheek, leaving a fresh pink smear of lipstick behind.

The junior femme fatale stepped back, pouting. The silken robe slipped loose, flashing a flat belly to her navel. At least her breasts managed to stay hidden, nipples tenting the luxurious fabric like erect little soldiers. Maizie glanced at Gray. He stood as stiffly as before, his eyes focused straight ahead, lips a flat line.

Shelly joined Joy lounging on the wood patio furniture, their robes falling open as they may. Gray didn't seem to notice or care, his attention shifted to the third woman.

She stood next to the little cart, holding a glass and stirring the clear iced liquid with her finger. Obviously enjoying the attention, she pulled the finger from her drink and sucked it dry with long draws and red painted lips.

"Oh." Maizie swallowed her gasp. She knew this woman. This was the woman she'd seen having sex in the woods. Maizie's cheeks warmed. What'd happened to the man she was with? The bite mark she'd seen on his neck had looked bad, though it hadn't bothered him enough to keep him from screwing her brains out.

"Bad move, Lynn," Gray said. "You overstep your bounds."

She laughed, soft and pretty, her long blonde hair blanketing over her shoulders. In her midtwenties or so, Lynn's body was at its prime. She hadn't even gone to the trouble of tying her robe's sash. She strolled toward him, her curvy hips swaying, the edges of her robe flashing bare belly, brown thatch and firm thighs.

"Have a lovely day at the lake, Gray?" she said.

"If any harm had come to her— The smell of frightened prey, you know how easily that could've gone wrong, gotten out of hand. You led the rest out there knowing how upset they'd be when they saw she wasn't my mate."

"Just proving a point, dear *brother*, same as you." She snatched his shirt at the collar, fisting it in her grip. A hard yank pulled him to her, reflex opened his hold on Maizie. She let her hand drop to her side, watching.

Lynn took Gray's mouth with hers, her jaw stretched wide, tongue driving deep into his mouth. And Gray took it. Not a muscle on the rest of his body responded, but he didn't deny her the kiss. As deep and long as she wanted, he obliged.

She released him with a small shove, wiped her mouth with the back of her hand and took a sip of her drink. Her gaze drifted to Maizie. "Besides, if you were so worried we'd lost our senses and were truly hunting her, why'd you bring her here?

She's a liability, just like Shawn."

"Wrong. This was business," Gray said. "And why wouldn't I bring her here? This is my home. I expect my family to behave like civil human beings here, if nowhere else."

"But of course." Lynn slinked toward Joy and Shelly and the last unused chaise lounge. The fluid movement of her body was mesmerizing. "Business, you say? Really? Only if your business is seducing ignorant little girls. Or maybe she gets faxes through her ass and that's why your hand was on it."

Lynn laughed at her own wit, looking to the other women who smiled indulgently, though Joy seemed tired by the display. Lynn lay back, her robe slipping down the sides of her body, leaving her completely exposed. She raised one knee, shielding her trimmed bush and showing off the smooth round of her ass.

"This is Ester's granddaughter." He stepped toward them, growing the distance between himself and Maizie. "She has influence with her grandmother. I did what I had to. And the rest of you will not interfere."

"You did what you wanted. Like you always do." Lynn set her drink on the side table between her and Joy. "We're the only ones held to archaic rules and codes."

Gray took another step, his face flushing with anger. "There's reason behind our rules."

"Yes." Lynn sat straight, body rigid. "And we were just illustrating those reasons, like you did for me. You were vulnerable, Gray. She made you slow and stupid and vulnerable. You couldn't protect her in this form. You couldn't protect yourself. And your feelings for her, your fear of her reaction, stopped you from doing what you *should've* done. What you would've done without thinking if it weren't for her."

Gray glowered at her, his jaw muscles twitched. Then

suddenly a strange calm washed over him, as though he'd chosen the demeanor rather than achieving it. His hands slipped into the front pockets of his pants, deceptively casual.

"It is not for you to educate me. You were my wife's sister. But don't delude yourself. Push me on this and I will strike you down. Mind your place, Lynn, or I'll put you in it by force." His voice was low. His words were precise and the sound of it sent a chill racing down Maizie's spine.

"Her place, Uncle Gray?" All eyes turned to the stunning young man pushing through the far glass door onto the patio. "Oh good. Let's discuss places. Hierarchy."

His naked body, carved perfection, glistened with a thin sheen of moisture, his short spiked hair dappled with water. Each casual stride swung his cock, semi-hard, growing harder when he noticed Maizie's stare. A smile rippled across his lips, then he shut it down, attention shifting back to Gray.

Maizie blinked to stop her gawk, looked away at...anything. But Gray had noticed, saw her eyes widen on the young man. She could feel his muscles tense but he didn't say anything to her. "Don't start, Rick."

"Start? Uncle Gray, when I decide to, I won't just start, I'll damn well finish and there'll be nothing you can do about it. Trust me."

Gray growled his words through his teeth. "This is business, Rick. Stay out of it."

"Right. Business. Why am I not surprised?" Rick's blue eyes, an exact match to Shelly's, shifted to Maizie. "Did you bother to tell the girl? By the looks of her, I'd say she's just as hopeful as the rest of us were. The difference is, we know you. We're used to you playing at taking a mate and always falling short. Whatever. If you won't take her, maybe I will. She seems pretty open to the idea."

Gray glanced back at Maizie, caught her gaze stuck on Rick's cock before she flicked her attention to his face, her cheeks blazing red. Her mouth gaped in protest. "What? I was just... You're naked. I'm not dead. I'm also not an animal. I don't jump anything that crosses my path and looks ready and able."

Rick's brow rose, a smile lifting one cheek. "Not an animal? You hear that, Uncle Gray?"

It was obvious the young upstart was getting off on her attention, wrinkles smoothing, his cock growing as she watched. Dammit, why'd he trust his family would act human in front of Maizie if she met them here instead of in the woods? It was always a competition with Rick. He wanted to be alpha despite the worries and protests from the women in their lives.

Lynn, Joy and Shelly had begged Gray not to step aside, not to walk away and hand the pack over to Rick. As much as Rick might want it and as much as Gray would like to give it to him, he couldn't do that to the kid.

They were right. Rick was too young. He'd get himself killed by a stray mutt inside a week. Sooner, if he kept trying to use Maizie to get his way. Gray would see to it himself.

Gray straightened, not moving but blocking Rick's path to Maizie by sheer will. "This isn't a game, boy."

Rick stopped short, his gaze shifting from Maizie to Gray. "You're damn right. This is life, old man. You bring a prime female back to the den and think you won't have to fight for her? You're the one who's delusional."

He patted Gray's shoulder, chuckling, and stepped around him. There was no mistaking the challenge in his eyes, though Gray knew it had less to do with wanting Maizie as his mate than it did with wanting to lead the pack. He should've seen this coming. Bringing her to the house was a mistake. He hadn't realized things had gotten so unstable.

"Prime female? Really?" Maizie's tone was dripping with indignation and shock.

Gray also knew if by some miracle Rick managed to defeat him in a fight, Rick wouldn't pass on his right to take his opponent's mate. That wasn't going to happen. Not with Maizie. Not ever.

"You don't want to do this, kid. Not now. Not her," Gray warned.

Rick's conquering stare faltered, dimmed, but he battled back. "Tell me she's the one. Tell us you're ready to be the alpha this pack needs, and I won't try and take it from you. If she's not your wolf's choice, then why would you care if I took a little taste?"

Frustration itched across his shoulders, knotting his muscles. It was a simple thing. Announce that he had a romantic interest in Maizie, that he claimed her as his, and make everyone happy. Hell, his family would be thrilled. Having a mated alpha meant security for the pack.

The alpha mates alone proved the pack was vital and alive. A lone male alpha with no hope of producing strong male heirs told outside males the pack was dying. The viable females, Lynn and Shelly, would be pursued, encouraged to join healthy packs. Or killed. Gray wouldn't, couldn't, let that happen.

So why couldn't he claim Maizie as his? Because there *was* something about her, something different he'd never felt before, compelling, addictive. He wanted none of it. He'd been married once, had his chance at love. Donna was his wife, alive or dead, he'd made a commitment. His human-half wouldn't let him turn his back on that, not for the woman whose family had killed her.

"It's business," Gray insisted.

Rick looked to Maizie, intent renewed. "Is it true what they say about redheads?" He brushed past her shoulder, leaning in to whisper in her ear but loud enough Gray could hear. "Are you a wild and wicked hellcat in the sack?"

Gray's hands balled to fists. He told himself Rick was just a kid, young by werewolf standards. He didn't fully understand the danger, the instinct his actions triggered in Gray. But the battle between intellect and primal demands was faltering. Gray's nails dug deeper into his palms, a low growl rumbled in his chest.

Maizie held her expression, calm indifference, and slid her eyes to see him askew. She caught his gaze. "Do you kiss your mother with that mouth?"

Rick feigned a laugh. "Why don't you ask her? She's sitting right over there."

Maizie's gaze shifted to the three women. Gray knew none of them looked old enough to be Rick's mother. Lynn politely raised a hand, wiggling her fingers, and Maizie's eyes stretched, mouth gaping. "That's not...that's not possible."

He'd forgotten how shocking his family appeared to humans. "Ignore them, Maizie. My nephew likes to tease. He's a little insecure and thinks irritating his uncle will get him what he wants." Gray speared Rick with a withering glare. "He's wrong."

Rick threw back his head, barking a laugh. "You think? At least I'm willing to do what needs to be done to protect this pack. She's Ester's granddaughter. She already knows, or she would if she let herself believe. What more do you want? If you won't bite her and make her the alpha mate, I will. You can't expect to stay single and lead this pack."

"Bite me? You bite people?" Maizie's too-wide eyes swung to

Lynn. "You bit that man, didn't you? I thought...I thought it was one of the wolves. But it was you."

Gray glanced from Maizie to Lynn and back again. "What're you talking about? What did you see? What man?"

"Nothing," Rick answered for her. "She didn't see anything. You're both just trying to delay the inevitable." He reached for Maizie's arm.

Gray didn't know what he meant to do. Not that it mattered. His primal reflex took hold like the snap of an overstretched cord. He punched out, connecting solidly with Rick's chest so fast his own mind couldn't track it.

Rick sailed backward through the air. His young muscled body slammed against the stone wall of the patio at least eight feet away. His head and shoulders whipped back over the edge then forward, his hands clutching his chest as he slumped to the floor.

Gray stood between them, his shoulders heaving, his hands fisted at his sides fighting to rein in his anger, tamp down the pure male adrenaline humming through every muscle in his body. He'd been dreading this, fighting to avoid it, for a long time. Regret warred inside him.

If it'd been any other woman he could've kept his self-control. But not Maizie. Maizie was his, had been since the night he gave her back her life. He hadn't realized it until that singular moment. Gray had kept her at a distance, tried to ignore her existence, but all the while he'd seen her as his.

A replacement? Payment for what he'd lost? He wasn't sure. His wolf-half didn't care. With Maizie thrust into the mix of the growing tensions between him and the young male pack member, Gray's tightly leashed instinct broke free. The wolf's need to defend what was his ruled him mind and body.

Lynn jumped between them, shoving Gray hard enough at

the shoulders that he staggered back a step. "What was that? Huh? What was that? I asked you to keep him safe, and you practically break his neck."

She went to her son, pulling the edges of her robe together, kneeling beside him, cradling his head and shoulders to her chest. Rick pushed up the wall with his elbow, his legs still sprawled in front of him. He rubbed the back of his neck, a sideways smirk hiking the corner of his mouth.

"Maybe she is the one. Just make up your mind about it soon or I promise you, I will." He pushed away from his mother and got to his feet.

The kid thought he'd succeeded in distracting Gray. He had, but only for a minute. He turned to Maizie who stood stunned in silence. *Jeezus, she must think she's stumbled onto the set of* Deliverance *the way his family behaved.* He told himself it didn't matter what she thought. Never mind that he didn't believe that for a second.

"What did you see, Maizie?" he asked. "What did you see Lynn do?"

Maizie blinked those pretty green eyes at him as though restarting her brain. "They were in the woods. They were making love. The man's neck was torn, like he'd been bitten. It was covered in blood, his neck, his chest. I thought he'd been attacked by wolves, and I couldn't understand how he could make love right there in the woods after such a brutal attack."

"Who was it?" Gray pushed. "What did the man look like?"

Maizie shook her head as though she was still struggling with all she'd heard and seen. Then her gaze slid toward the house and she pointed a finger. "Him. It was him."

Gray turned and his heart nearly stopped. "Shawn."

He tugged Maizie behind him without thinking and took a menacing step. "What the hell's going on, Lynn?"

The father of Lynn's children, Shelly and Rick, the man who'd cheated on his wife, the man he'd forbidden Lynn to turn, stood bolder than he had any right to. Lynn was at her lover's side in a heartbeat, putting her body between her alpha and her certain ruin.

She held up a hand, as though she could ward off Gray's outrage. "I turned him. I needed someone, Gray, and you were too busy running around the woods with little Red Riding Hood there to do the job."

A menacing growl vibrated through Gray's chest and he edged forward. It was an excuse and they both knew it. The guy was no good for her. He could feel it.

"He left his wife," Lynn said in a rush.

"Before or after you made it impossible for him to stay with her?" Gray asked, teeth clenched.

"What difference does it make? He's mine," she said. "You told me to find a mate. He's the one. He's always been the one."

"He's a cheat. He's weak willed. And he smells like betrayal." Gray looked at his sister-in-law, a woman he'd sworn to protect—his family. "He's not good enough, Lynn. He'll hurt you and the pieces he'll leave behind won't be big enough to put back together."

"No. It doesn't always end that way, Gray." Joy moved between him and Lynn. "I know Donna's death destroyed a big part of you, but that doesn't make it a foregone conclusion. Sometimes love feels good."

Gray blanched at that, snapped his mouth shut. Did they really think his objections about Shawn were some sort of transference of his own hang-ups? They weren't.

Gray exhaled. None of them understood. Love was a fleeting untrustworthy emotion, never the same from one day to the next, twisting into something unrecognizable from where it'd begun. He knew better than anyone you can't base life decisions on love.

"It's not like I'm a stranger." Shawn edged forward, hand out as though he could wipe the tension and misunderstanding from the air. "I mean, I've known Lynn for years now, and the kids, well, I'm their father. She's told me everything about your family. Explained how it works. I...I love her."

Gray eyed the man. He looked older than Lynn by at least three decades, but Gray knew the difference was a lot less than that. "What about your other family? Your other kids?"

"When I learn enough control, I'll work out a custody arrangement with my ex. I didn't leave because Lynn made me one of you. I left because I realized I love her. I've been miserable without her all these years."

Gray scoffed. What better proof did he need that the guy wasn't good enough than a statement like that? "Made by a beta. He'll never be strong enough to make a challenge."

"I know," Lynn said. "I don't care. I just want...him."

"If you love him, if you'd already gone and claimed him as your mate, why have you been pushing so hard for me to take up the role?"

Lynn blushed, her cheeks bright red, and looked away. She shrugged. "Habit maybe. I've been angry with you so long it's hard to know how not to be. I don't know. I didn't want you to find out about Shawn too soon. I knew what you'd do, knew you'd kill him before he was strong enough to defend himself."

"I still might."

She looked at him, her expression hard. "And I wanted you to pay. All those years alone, all the heartache. I just...I just couldn't let the anger go."

"And now?" Gray asked.

"Obviously I've still got some things to work through where you're concerned. It's taking some time, but Shawn's helping me put it behind me. With his help I'll get there. I know it. Let me have him, please, Gray."

Gray huffed, too close to a wolf's snort. "It's done. He's pack or he dies. Show him his place, or I will." He headed for the closest door, his hand tight around Maizie's, tugging her away as fast as he could.

He didn't care anymore, about Lynn and her poor taste in men, about Rick and his drive to lead the pack. He didn't care about any of it.

All he cared about was getting Maizie away from any possible threat, getting her someplace safe. He led her up the stairs into the grand foyer, with its black marble floor and grand sweeping staircase. And no werewolves.

"Mr. Lupo." Annette breezed in from his home office to the left, her legs carrying her petite body faster than a person twice as tall. "I didn't realize you were back."

She held her ever-present notepad with a letter clipped to its envelope on top. She pushed at her brown-framed glasses, too big for her small face, but somehow fitting with her upswept hair, buttoned-up shirt and fitted skirt. Her gaze shifted to Maizie. The corners of her thin lips swept to a pretty smile. "Ms. Hood. You're here. How wonderful. Does this mean—"

"What is it, Annette?" He recognized that glint in her eye. She had an inconvenient tendency to romanticize things when it came to Gray. It wasn't hard to imagine the leaps she'd make having seen him and Maizie walking hand-in-hand.

"Yes. Of course, Mr. Lupo. Sorry." Annette stiffened, all business. She read from her notepad. "You received the information you've been waiting for from Judge Woodsmen."

"Thank you. Leave it on your desk and I'll get to it later."

Damn, he hoped he wouldn't need that information.

"Yes, sir. Also, Ms. Pi called from the bakery, for Ms. Hood. She said, and I quote, 'Smoky Joe finally kicked the bucket and took a chunk of firewall sheeting, the Pearlman bar-mitzvah cake and half the dirty-girl pastries for the Richmen bachelorette party with him.'"

Maizie whispered an oath then moved to Annette. She took her hands, leaning close. "Annette, is it? You have to get me out of..." She glanced back at Gray. "I mean, I need to get to my shop. Help me get out of here. *Please*. No. Wait. My shoes."

"Thank you, Annette," Gray said, stepping beside Maizie. He wrapped his arm around her shoulders, jerked her close. "I'll make sure Ms. Hood makes it out of the forest. Personally."

Chapter Seven

"It belonged to Maizie's mother," Gray said.

"Lilly's?"

"Found it a few weeks after the accident." He placed the gold quarter-sized locket in Granny's hand. "The clasp was broken. I had it cleaned and repaired."

Granny's sad blue eyes peered at him beneath the hood of her lids. "You kept it all this time?"

Gray shifted his focus out the glass doors to the open backyard of the Green Acres Nursing Home. His face warmed. "I'm not sure why I didn't return it sooner. Maybe because there was nothing left of Donna's to keep. Maybe because Riddly and Lilly had taken something of mine and I wanted to take something of theirs. Foolish. I don't know."

Granny reached her withered hand over to his. He could feel her tremors, age keeping her constantly off balance, unsteady. "You needed it more than us. Maizie was too young for a piece like this and I...I wouldn't have known what to do with it."

"Thank you, Ester." It was a poor excuse, but he'd take it. "You have it now and I believe you'll find the photos inside quite useful."

Granny looked to the locket, her thin fingers working its

tight seal. Her thumbnail wedged between the oval halves and the locket popped open. Seconds passed as her mind processed the images and a bright smile blossomed across her face.

Gray knew what she saw. He'd stared at the photo of the young Hood family and the one opposite of Riddly holding an infant Maizie a million times over the years. Such a photo didn't exist of his family. He and Donna never discussed children. Ironically, he hadn't realized how much he'd wanted a photo like that until the possibility of it was taken away beneath the crush of an SUV.

Gray forced his thoughts from old dreams and wishes. "Maizie mentioned you'd had a visitor. Someone pretending to be Riddly."

Granny's cheeks flushed apple red, a bashful smile flickering across her thin lips. "Oh, I know Riddly wouldn't want me to sell my little cottage. Not without a good reason. It was all my imagination. My mind plays tricks on me sometimes, y'know."

"I don't believe it was your mind playing tricks this time, Ester. I think someone is trying to take advantage, using whatever tactics he can, to get his hands on your property. And I'm fairly confident I know who's behind it."

The news brought a flash of relief to her eyes. An instant later resentment took its place. "Advantage, you say? Uhmph. We'll see about that. The next time that ol' dog comes around, I'll..." Her pledge died on the air, her gaze flicking to Gray.

He knew her thoughts without hearing them. She'd been tricked once, believing her deceased son was visiting, issuing orders, how would she know differently next time?

Gray cupped his hands around hers, still holding the open locket. "This will help. Wear Lilly's locket. Look at the pictures next time someone calls himself Riddly. Remember where it was found. That Riddly is gone. That Lilly and Donna are gone. Cadwick may resemble your son, but not enough to stand up to his photograph, or those kinds of potent memories."

He couldn't stay with Granny 24/7 and trying to ban Cadwick from the premises wouldn't work any better than Maizie's attempt had. Gray had used his werewolf-enhanced charm and familiarity with the staff to skirt around Maizie's restricted-visitors list, but Cadwick was a master at zeroing in on a person's pay-off point. He'd locate the weakest link in security and buy his way in.

No. Granny would have to use her mind and wits to protect herself. The locket would help.

"You never got to bury your wife, did you?"

Granny's question caught him utterly by surprise. He stuttered. His mind shifting gears so fast he didn't have time to throw up the barriers that would keep the most painful of the memories at bay.

"No. I...she... No. Donna died before she could shift back to human form. They disposed of her body as they would any *roadkill*." He winced at the term, his heart pinching.

"You couldn't request they leave her with you? The accident happened on your land."

Gray shook his head. If only it'd been that easy. If only he'd been able to think clearly, quickly, maybe he could've come up with a way. "Taking the...*carcass*...is procedure. There was nothing I could say that wouldn't seem strange. I had to think of the pack. Protect the rest from curiosity or suspicion."

Gray had given permission to the Hood family alone to use the shortcut through his forest from the housing subdivision on one side to the cottage on the other. He would never advance such trust again. The police arrived as fast as they did because Riddly and Lilly Hood had betrayed their agreement.

Another car, friends of the Hoods, was following behind when they'd hit his wife. Because of them, because of the police and ambulance and everyone else mulling around in his forest, he'd had to stand by, helpless as they thoughtlessly disengaged his wife's body from the mangle of metal. They tossed it in the back of the tow truck like it was so much debris. Carted his wife away to be burned to ash in a city furnace. Or God forbid, something worse.

His only consolation was that nothing like it would ever happen again. He'd closed the single-lane gravel road, technically just two tire paths with weeds growing between, immediately after the accident. He planted trees, encouraged undergrowth, so that by now there was barely any sign the road had ever existed.

Granny shifted the locket to one hand and wrapped the other around Gray's palm. "It was an accident, dear. I know you blame my Riddly, but he didn't have a mean bone in his body. He wouldn't have wished the kind of suffering you and Maizie have endured on his worst enemy."

"I don't blame him." Gray was surprised how easily he said it. He'd been thinking it from the start, but never out loud. "It was my fault. Donna and I were arguing...fighting. I accused her of cheating and she ran out. I didn't go after her."

He remembered the smell of another man on his wife, a man he recognized. There was no suspicion, no guessing. He knew she'd been with someone else. The rub was he wasn't as upset over her infidelity as he was with himself for not feeling more betrayed. He loved Donna, but there was something missing between them, something that only became truly perceptible after she'd turned him. Maybe children would've made a difference, filled that missing piece between them. He'd never know.

"I was happy for the distance between us," he said. "Until...Jeezus, I can still hear that sound, that crash, like an explosion. I knew before I started running. I knew Donna was gone. I could feel it."

"I heard it too." Granny shuddered. "What an awful sound. I knew my boy was gone. I'm just thankful my Little Red survived. Lord knows how she did."

Gray knew how she'd survived. He'd been the one rushing headlong down the hillside over the butchered swath of forest so fast no one saw him go by. With the family friends useless, gawking down at the ruin from the road through the rain and darkness, it was up to Gray to assess the damage.

The truck was on its roof. He'd recognized the unmistakable odor of death, a mix of bodily fluids and cold meat. The parents were dead. The smell told him before he'd reached in to check for a pulse. Neither had been wearing seatbelts. They were gone before the truck stopped.

Their little girl, Maizie, was buckled into the backseat, but the shoulder strap had slipped to strangle across her neck. She was unconscious, her little face turning blue. But she was alive—barely.

He tried to unbuckle her, but the lock had jammed in the roll. Breaking it was nothing for his enhanced strength. Her little body fell into his arms and for a strange moment, gazing down into her slowly pinking face, he could breathe. His mind didn't allow him respite for long, though. The sound, the thunderous explosion of metal and glass, the hideous thud, and the instinctive knowledge Donna was gone all came crashing in on him anew.

He laid Maizie in a soft patch of ferns and slowly made his way to the front of the truck. He couldn't see her at first, the way the truck was lying, the rain, the darkness, made seeing anything difficult. Then he crouched and peered under the front of the truck. Only her tail and hindquarters showed, soft brown fur, wet with rain, and blood.

Gray raced around the truck to the driver's side front wheel. Donna lay at an angle, pinned between the fender and the tree, her front paws, chest and head spared the crushing weight of the truck. She was dead. She was dead before the truck had stopped—God willing.

How long had he stood there? How much time passed? He wasn't sure. Maybe if he'd snapped out of it quicker, reacted faster, maybe he could've gotten Donna's body away before the police showed up. But once the first cop tripped and stumbled his way down the hill, it was too late. These people and their pretty little redheaded girl had altered his life irrevocably.

And now that pretty little redhead was poised to do it again.

"I'm not mad. I'm just curious." Yeah. If she said it out loud a few more times maybe she'd actually believe it. After all, what other emotion would make her do something this stupid. And, Maizie had to admit, walking deep into the forest at dusk, full moon rising or not, was stupid. Really stupid.

But she had to talk to him. She wanted to know why Gray had waited twenty-one years to give Granny the locket. "Twenty-one years. That's a long time to hold on to something that's not yours. Not that I'm mad about it."

She wasn't—really. It was just an excuse. More than anything she wanted to know about where he'd found it. Granny told her Gray had been there at the accident. But she was so pleased with having the locket back she didn't seem to care what his being there meant. He could answer questions no one else could.

What had he seen? What did he know? Had her parents said anything? Were they alive? Did he see the wolf that'd killed them? She had to know.

Anytime she'd asked those sorts of questions of Granny, or anyone else who might know, she'd gotten sad puppy-dog eyes staring back at her and no solid answers. "Just put it behind you, dear," Granny would say. "It won't bring them back. Consider yourself blessed that you can't remember."

This time she had a good excuse to broach the subject. She had a firsthand source to give her some answers. She wouldn't settle for puppy-dog eyes and placating clichés. This time she'd get her answers and that, more than anything else, pushed her into the forest to a place she hadn't been in years.

Maizie shined her flashlight off to the left. The path was clear, dirt covered, with tall weeds and brush kept at a distance. A small turn of her wrist to the right and the beam exposed a swath of low weeds cutting through the forest eight feet wide. Beneath were the remnants of a long-forgotten path. She could still see the twin ruts like old tire tracks through the weed stalks, though as far as she remembered there'd never been an actual road.

This path would lead to the housing subdivision, the place she'd once called home. She hoped it would also bring her closer to Gray's secret mansion in the forest. She had to find it again. She had to find him.

Maizie steeled her nerves and started walking. Her legs parted the weeds with each step. Green seeds and sticky leaves clung to her sweat pants and left dark stripes of dew along the gray fabric on her thighs and knees. Her mind raced, constantly analyzing sounds, shadows and strange movements.

This was a stupid risk considering she'd come face to face

with the big silver wolf once already. And she was pretty sure he'd chased her and Gray from the lake the other day. The wolf had been anything but deadly though. Of course his patient demeanor might've been dumb luck.

If she could just remember the path Gray had taken from the lake she wouldn't have to wander around trying to find the house by accident. She should've waited 'til morning. But she wanted answers and she didn't even care that she'd have to deal with his strange family. She'd already waited long enough.

Maizie had checked every map of the area she could find. Not one of them showed roads beyond the gravel driveway to the Wild Game Preserve. The forest was like a blank spot, the Bermuda Triangle of Pennsylvania.

This way, a straight path on foot, Maizie was convinced was faster. At least if she got lost she'd be in the right *part* of the forest.

Her pace quickened, though for no good reason she knew. It wasn't full dark yet, but she used the flashlight to scan the woods as she went, first one side then the other. Some small part of her brain realized the flashlight kept her at a disadvantage. The bright beam pinpointed her location for anyone or anything that might be tracking her.

She kept walking, body tight, eyes darting back and forth, hoping to accidentally shine the light on any attackers before they leapt. The odds were slim but that didn't stop her from hoping. The overgrown path traveled upward, and when she shined the light to her left she saw the tops of trees.

A better look made her realize the forest floor dropped off a few feet from the path. A fearless traveler venturing from the trail here could find themselves tumbling down a very steep, very long hillside. Maizie didn't want to think about it. Careening down hillsides was something she knew too much about already, even if she couldn't remember. She kept walking, resuming her flashlight scan to the right and left as the forest leveled off.

After more than an hour, full dark had fallen and above, the moon's soft white light barely penetrated the forest's thick canopy. Finally, Maizie strained to see a few small flickers of light through the trees up ahead.

"Wood Haven housing plan." She exhaled the words. Relieved.

It had to be the quaint streetlights of the neighborhood. Maizie allowed a little smile despite the pinch of disappointment.

She hadn't stumbled over Gray's house as she'd hoped, but she'd made it through the woods without being gobbled up by any big bad wolves.

Believing civilization was less than five hundred feet away, her confidence returned. Her shoulders relaxed, flashlight aimed in front of her. She trusted she'd make it to the nearest street and hopefully a convenience store where she could call a cab.

Three steps and Maizie's confidence evaporated with the rustle of movement off to her left. She froze, adrenaline tingles racing up her spine. She flicked the light to the left. A sapling and a cluster of tall ferns swayed. Had something brushed past them or were they moved by a breeze she only now noticed sifting through her hair?

Maizie dragged the light farther left, taking in all she could. There was nothing there but vegetation. She scanned the other way and found nothing out of the ordinary.

She forced a half laugh she didn't feel. "Paranoid much?"

No sooner had the words left her mouth than another movement, this time on her right side, iced her to the bone. She swung the light, trying to catch a glimpse of whatever was moving out there. Nothing.

She stared for several long minutes. Without moving her feet, she dragged the flashlight beam in a circle around her, her body twisting to cover as much area as possible.

She started to turn back and felt the familiar thrum of invisible fingers at the base of her neck.

The light swung fast in the direction she'd come and reflected off two glowing white eyes. "Oh shit!"

Her feet scrambled backward without benefit of thought or the shifting of balance to keep her upright. She landed hard on her ass, but didn't hesitate for even a second. Flashlight forgotten, her hands and feet dug at the ground, crab-walking as fast as humanly possible.

Without the reflection of the light, white eyes turned blue in the cool darkness and fixed on her. Maizie couldn't look away, didn't dare or risk the animal's inevitable attack catching her unaware. Somewhere in her brain a voice screamed *Get up! Get up!* But Maizie couldn't find a moment she was willing to spend on getting to her feet rather than moving away.

Watching those eyes, the same kind of wolf eyes from her childhood, the same frightening eyes from hundreds of nightmares and sleepless nights, meant she wasn't watching where she was going. The hard smack of a tree against her head stopped all progress.

She dropped to her ass with an oath. For one slim heartbeat she closed her eyes, her hand going to her head on reflex. She snapped her eyes open again and found the haunting blue orbs were still watching her—only closer. She could see the full body of the wolf now, big, muscled and...honey-brown.

This wasn't the same wolf Granny talked about. This wasn't

Maizie's naughty silver wolf. This wasn't even the wild beast that'd chased her the other night. This wolf was male and big, with a crazed look in his eyes.

The animal growled, its lips curling back from huge white teeth, its thick fur vibrating from the sound. Maizie pressed back against the tree, her sneakers digging at the ground as though she could push herself through the thick trunk to the other side.

"Nice doggy. Now, go away. Go home." It was worth a shot. But the massive wolf came nearer. Slow, deliberate steps, its eyes focused on her so intently she could feel the icy chill of it working to paralyze her body.

She had to get away. Maizie leaned to her right, pivoting against the tree trunk, ready to spin around to the other side. But just as she shifted her weight to her hip, a warm wash of air rippled over her shoulder and the side of her face.

She glanced sideways and caught the snarling jowls of a second wolf. Its coat was a light brown, the ends tipped with blonde. The female wolf that'd chased her the other day. It was close enough its saliva dribbled over her shoulder, the hot wetness soaking through her T-shirt.

Shit, how'd it get so close without her noticing? Maizie didn't waste time wondering. She spun the other way and got to her knees before a third brown-sugar wolf met her face to face—eye to eye. "Fuck!"

Maizie pushed back on reflex, landing on her ass again. She pressed her back to the tree, shoved herself up and managed to get her feet under her. The shortest of the three wolves came to her hip at its head. The tallest, the male with the honey-brown fur, was only a half inch shorter than her silver wolf had been.

The growls mixed and merged, uniting to become one low

rumbling sound that vibrated through her body like nothing she'd ever heard or felt before. They were too close, the larger wolf creeping nearer, snarling and drooling. Caged with wolves in front and on both sides, with the tree at her back, she was running out of escape routes fast.

Maizie rocked around the tree and ran. The soft fur of the wolf waiting at her left pressed against her leg, snagged through her fingers as it lunged to try and stop her escape. She got away.

No. They let her get away. On some level Maizie knew it was true. Why? *Screw it.* She didn't give a damn why they'd let her go.

She was free, running full-out toward the flicker of lights from Wood Haven. Maizie's panicked mind raced, trying to map the most direct route, but something was wrong.

She could only see one light now and it was fainter, as though a thick blanket of trees blocked it from sight. Where were the other lights? The dozen or so street lamps, the warm glow from living rooms and TV screens? There should be more lights. They should've been closer.

For a split second she shifted her attention from the hope of a single flickering light to the forest around her. The faint overgrown path she'd been following was gone. In her panic she must've run the wrong way. So what was the light she was running toward if not Wood Haven?

The soft thumping sound of padded feet crunching behind her chased the question from her brain. They were coming. The wolves had given chase. The hunt was on. Is that why they'd let her go? So they could chase her?

Maizie's heart thundered in her ears, her blood pumping adrenaline-rich oxygen through her body. Her lungs burned but she wouldn't slow up, couldn't, or risked being caught, eaten.

Oh God.

Up ahead a huge fallen tree blocked the way and she veered to the left to go around it. She barreled through the old limbs, cutting the distance she had to travel by several feet. The instant she broke through her whole world slammed to a halt.

A wolf. A fourth one, every bit as tall as her big silver wolf and only a few pounds lighter, stood before her. Its fur was the same brown-sugar color as the other two, its eyes a haunting luminous blue. Its lips hiked over its canines, trembling with a low menacing growl.

A trap. She'd been herded to the slaughter like a stupid sheep. The forest crunched and rustled as the other three wolves caught up and circled in. The brown, blonde-tipped wolf jumped to the fallen tree, towering over her right shoulder. The other smaller wolf stayed at her back and the last, the big darker-furred wolf, came around to her left.

Maizie's muscles trembled from the sprint, from fear and the overpowering urge to run. Her body tingled, flight instincts warring with common sense and odds of success. There had to be something she could do. Some way to get out of this, to get help. Only one glimmer of hope came to mind.

"Gray." She spoke just above a normal tone, unsure what the wolves' reaction would be. The growls rose in volume but otherwise they remained where they were, each a good four feet away.

"Gray, help! Help me! Someone hel—" The wolf in front of her stepped two feet closer then stopped. Maizie's breath caught. *Shut up. Shutup shutup shutup.* Self-preservation and fear screamed at her not to make another sound or risk the beasts' attack.

Intelligence told her, her voice was her only hope. She needed to use it while she still could. She breathed deep to get as much volume as she could. "Heeeellllp—"

The big dark wolf on her left lunged, slammed into her, knocking the remaining air from her lungs. Maizie opened her mouth with a silent, breathless scream as its sharp teeth snagged on the hem of her shirt, barely grazing the skin. The biggest wolf lurched toward her, but his massive body slammed into the darker wolf and they both tumbled into the weeds.

An instant later her shoulder stabbed with pain, as the smallest wolf drove sharp teeth through muscle and meat. In the next moment, Maizie gasped air and made the scream real and loud. But the wolf's powerful jaws clamped tighter.

Maizie writhed under the weight of its body, her hands frantic, pushing against its neck, fingers tearing out chunks of fur. The beast wouldn't let go. She looked around, searching for something, anything to use against her attacker, but all she saw was a quick blur of blonde-tipped fur racing toward her. She held her breath, braced herself for the next stab of pain, the next bite.

It came from the exact same spot on her shoulder, when the wolf's teeth ripped from its hold on her, its body flying off several feet away. The blonde-tipped wolf had knocked her loose. Who cared why?

The wound was deep and it hurt like hell. Even the slightest move sent a shower of pain pulsating out from the spot. It didn't matter. She had to get out of there. Maizie rolled to her hip, pushed up, trying to get to her knees and then hopefully her feet. She didn't make it to her knees before instinct told her things had suddenly turned from bad to fucked-up-beyond-all-recognition.

Her gaze shifted to the honey-brown wolf standing between her and the only manmade light she could see. He was creeping closer, low, as though stalking wounded prey. And he was.

She glanced behind her and saw the big brown-sugar wolf staring with unblinking blue eyes, recognizing her for what she was—food. Off to her right were the two wolves that had attacked and freed her. The latter still pinned the former to the ground, but both had their attention riveted on Maizie.

She was bleeding. The red smear of it was everywhere. There was enough blood the odor of it must have saturated the air, triggering instincts they had no reason to ignore. *Definitely FUBARed.*

The wolf in front, the darkest of the four, lunged first. Maizie saw it coming in time to spin away on her hip, but not fast enough to keep his huge white teeth from catching her calf and sinking in. She screamed and another set of powerful jaws snagged the back of her T-shirt. The fabric ripped just as a third nipped at her leg, catching her sweats in its teeth, scratching the skin beneath.

"Help me! Help! Heelllllppppp!"

Maizie tucked her head between her arms, protecting her face. Heavy paws scratched at her back, pushing against her, walking on her, fighting over her. She peered down her body at the enormous furry heads, nipping and snapping, tearing at her clothes, at each other. And then there was one less.

She blinked just in time to see another wolf sail backward into the woods. A big hand clamped around the neck-scruff of the third wolf, lifted, and sent it flying, its whole body squirming and twisting through the air. Finally two hands clamped on the muzzle of the fourth wolf, the wolf whose teeth were still deep in Maizie's calf.

One hand on top, the other underneath, he pried open the wolf's jaws. Maizie jerked her leg free, her gaze darting to the face behind the hands. "Gray."

Still holding those powerful jaws in his hands, Gray twisted the wolf's neck, forcing it away. The wolf's long legs stumbled back and Gray let him go. It shook its big head then snorted as if trying to realign its senses. It glowered at Gray, growling, its front shoulders lowering as though it would attack.

"She won't save you from this, Shawn. She can't. Push any further and you'll die here. Now," Gray said. "What'll it be, boy?"

The honey-brown wolf's growl stopped. It swayed back and forth on its front legs as though deciding on a course of action. A hard snort again, and then it turned and jogged off. Gray looked at Maizie, still sprawled on the ground.

"What are you doing in my forest?"

"Bleeding," she said. "Where'd you learn to speak wolf?"

Chapter Eight

"Holy Taj Mahal, Batman. You could fit the whole downstairs cottage in here." Maizie gazed over Gray's shoulder at the bedroom as he carried her into the master bath. "Including the sunroom."

The room was enormous, bigger than any bedroom needed to be. The king-sized bed, light wood color with thick, spiral-carved posts and matching swirl designs across the tall headboard, would've dwarfed her bedroom at the cottage, but in this room it was just a piece of furniture. It matched the armoire, dresser and chest of drawers, and the nightstands too.

The sitting room with its upholstered beige leather chair and matching ottoman, the classy fireplace, the small wooden minibar and compulsory floor globe was straight out of the decorating guide for rich-guy bachelors. The only thing that kept her from thinking she'd stepped onto a photoset for *Architecture Magazine* was the open masters chest with the gaming system and TV inside along with an impressive stash of games. One controller was stretched across the floor in front as though someone had been sitting on the leather-cushioned storage bench at the end of the bed, playing.

Gray sat Maizie on the counter. Her leg and shoulder throbbed dully, but a strange heat and excitement surging through her veins seemed to overpower the worst of the pain.

Adrenaline is a wonderful thing. "This is your bathroom? Seriously?" She'd stayed in hotel rooms smaller than this bathroom.

"Yes, Maizie. My bedroom suite is large."

"Very large."

"You've established that. Now answer my question. What were you doing out there? You've been told since you were a child to stay on the paths. To stay away from this part of the forest."

"How do you know that?"

"You know how." He squatted, reaching to the cabinet doors underneath. He tapped the inside of her knee, coaxing her to spread her legs. When she did he opened the door behind them. "Your grandmother and I have been friends for a very long time."

Maizie swallowed. Seeing that thick mane of silver and black hair bobbing between her thighs brought a rush of dirty-girl ideas to her head.

"You're too young to have been Granny's friend when I was a kid. You can't be more than ten, maybe twelve, years older than me."

He glanced up. "I'm older than I look."

His gaze dropped to the V of her legs. His expression melted from distraction to focused interest in an instant. He licked his lips then glanced to her face as though remembering she was watching. His cheeks warmed a shade then he went back to his search under the counter.

"There are things about my family, about me, you need to know. Especially after tonight. You see, we're not exactly *normal.*" Gray stood, his hands stuffed with gauze, tape, scissors, disinfectant and what looked like three different boxes of Band-Aids, one of them featuring the characters from *Scooby-Doo*.

"Not normal. Yeah, I got that the last time I was here." She scooched back, closed her legs, remembering the interplay between family members on the patio. "A real...close-knit family."

How could she forget? Power struggles with his nephew, battles with his sister-in-law, a niece who seemed pissed at the world and a mother-in-law apparently oblivious to it all. Gray was stuck in the middle, trying to make everyone happy, which to her mind was only making matters worse. She kept that opinion to herself.

"Close-knit. That's one way to describe us."

A deep breath felt warm in her chest. Her clothes squeezed her body, the air grew heavy, seemed to press in on her. "Why's it so hot in here?"

Gray set the medical supplies on either side of her and pressed the back of his hand to her forehead. His brow creased with the familiar scowl but he didn't comment.

Maizie closed her eyes. His hand was cool against her skin and brought the yummy scent of sweet male cologne and fresh forest closer to her nose. She tried not to enjoy it, but things were turning a little loopy in her head and the heat was making her body feel tingly, oversensitive.

The fact that she'd been considering every possible way to be alone with the ruggedly sexy man since she'd nearly jumped him by the quarry lake might have had something to do with it. A lot to do with it, actually. Not that it mattered. She was chicken when it came to letting a man know what she wanted. But tonight, somehow, she wasn't so chicken anymore.

He hooked his finger on the collar of her T-shirt and tugged enough to peer underneath.

"Looking for something?"

He let it go. "This shirt's ruined. And I need to get to the wound."

"Oh. Okay. So what do you want—"

A hard yank and he ripped along the seam from the collar to her shoulder before she finished the sentence. It jerked her whole body and made her heart leap into her throat.

The most provocative thing about her shoulder was her bra strap, but he stared at her exposed flesh like a man starved, male hunger flaring in his eyes. His hands held the torn edges of her shirt as though he struggled with conflicting thoughts, his chest rising and falling with deliberate breaths.

Excitement flooded through her system, tightening muscles, quivering through her belly and drenching the channel of her sex. "Far enough or are you planning on ripping it off me completely?"

Not that she'd have a problem with that.

Her hands fisted her sweats on her thighs. She held her breath. Tried not to imagine it. She met his gaze. Was he thinking the same thing? He hadn't answered, his face sober, brows furrowed in concentration.

After a deep breath he tore off a piece of gauze, dousing it with disinfectant. When he turned back to her, he was the picture of self-control. He dabbed the sopping pad against the torn flesh where she'd been bitten.

He could've stabbed her with a hot poker and made it hurt less. She hissed. "Son of a Cheech and Chong." So much for the adrenaline masking her pain.

He shrugged. "Yeah. This may sting a little."

"Y'think?"

"Sorry." He stepped toward her to see the backside of her

shoulder. His leg pressed against her knees so she opened them to allow him closer. The position pushed the bulge at his pants zipper against her knee and let her know his unaffected demeanor was only surface deep.

She swallowed hard, fighting the powerful urge to reach down and coax his semi-hard cock to rock hard and ready. She licked her lips, then bit the inside of her cheek. The need to touch him was nearly irresistible. What the hell was wrong with her?

Gray was sexy as hell, smelled like man-on-a-stick, with a voice that could melt butter and a body that could probably fuck her blind. But she'd never been this ripe and ready in her life. Besides, she barely knew him and what she did know about his life was twisted to say the least.

"It looks bad now, but it'll heal quick." He straightened, balling the bloodied gauze between his fingers. "I'm sorry about this. Really. But if you'd listened to your grandmother for once..."

"Hey. Let's not get into each other's family dynamics. Okay?"

He tossed the ball across the room toward the toilet and hit the wastebasket beside it without touching the rim. He stepped back and hooked his hands in the tears of her sweats at her calf. A quick yank and the material ripped. With no seam to follow the tear was uneven, ending well up over her knee.

"Confess. You like doing that, don't you?" She was trying to lighten an uncomfortable moment, but the rawness in her voice made it sound more like a come-on.

His small laugh was tight in his throat. "Yeah. Right," he said like he was joking—but not really. He took off her sneakers and socks then grabbed another wad of gauze soaked with disinfectant.

He knelt. His big hand smoothed soft as silk down her leg, careful to miss her wound. He felt over her heel and along the bottom of her foot then back to her ankle. The sensation sent a warm shiver to the top of her head and down to settle between her thighs.

He cleared his throat and started talking as though he hadn't just caressed her for no good reason. "Joy is my mother-in-law." He brought her foot to rest on his knee. Eyes alighting to hers he said, "It's going to sting again."

She nodded, clenching.

He cleaned the wound as he talked. "Lynn is my wife's sister. Rick and Shelly are Lynn's kids. Their father, Shawn, wasn't...one of us when the twins were conceived. They'd had an affair. He was married with no intention of ever leaving his wife and somehow in Lynn's mind that's my fault. He's not good enough for her. That's just the way I feel."

He shook his head and grabbed more gauze. "Anyway, after my father-in-law was killed by a rancher in Utah—"

"Killed? You mean murdered?"

Gray paused for a second to look at her. "Yeah. The guy caught my father-in-law killing his sheep. It's a common problem with wolves in that state. There were rumors. They couldn't prove any of them were werewolves. The fucking ranchers started using silver bullets just to be on the safe side anyway."

Werewolves? A chill raced down Maizie's spine despite the sweat sticking her T-shirt to her chest. The implication was pretty clear but too bizarre to accept. Combined with everything else—Granny's beloved silver wolf, more human than animal, and Gray's family, more animal than human and the wolf she'd met in the forest—maybe the bizarre was possible. Either Gray's father-in-law was mistaken for a wolf. Or he was one.

No. Werewolves don't exist.

Gray stood, tossing the balls of gauze. "His death left me as the oldest male. I kind of slipped into the alpha role without even realizing it. They're my responsibility now, Joy, Lynn, the kids. That's how it works. It's my job to see to their needs, food, shelter, clothes...sex. The last is really only an issue with Lynn, and then only because she knows the law and wants to make me pay for her disappointment."

He looked at her as though trying to gauge her reaction to the last. Maizie was still rolling around the word *alpha* in her head. "Sex? You have sex with them? All of them?"

"No. I could, but I haven't. Except...Lynn. Once." He looked to his hands, rubbing at the bloodstains along his fingers. "We have different instincts. It's not like a human family."

Human? "I have to go." To hell with her sexual fantasies about Gray and the first real chance she had of making them come true. This night had just shot into the red on her weird-O-meter. She tried to scoot off the counter but Gray stepped in front of her, his hands grabbing her hips, holding her to the spot.

"You can't, Maizie. It's not safe."

"Why not? Frankenstein and Dracula waiting somewhere out there for me too? Or is it just your family I have to worry about? That was them, wasn't it? They're the wolves that attacked me, almost killed me."

"Yes. But I don't think they meant to hurt you. Not really. The wolf in us is still a wild animal at heart. Unpredictable. Ruled by instinct." He sighed. "Listen, I know this seems strange—"

"Strange? No. We passed strange about three days ago." She squirmed, trying to break his grip, and trying not to feel the ripple of excitement at being so easily restrained by him.

135

"Okay. We won't talk about it anymore tonight. Promise. Just...stay. Please. I need you to stay here tonight." He sounded sincere, as though it meant everything to have her here with him. Why? What did he want from her?

Her mind filled with possibilities, the ripple of excitement grew. Her hands wrapped around his forearms, feeling the steel corded muscle under the gentlemanly dress shirt. Her breath shuddered, she closed her eyes.

As though he could hear her thoughts, smell her rising lust, Gray's fingers flexed on her hips, clenching the stretchy fabric of her sweats on either side. He stepped closer, wedging his hips between her legs. One easy yank and he pulled her to the edge of the counter, her groin flush with the full hardened shaft of his cock.

"Stay with me, Maizie." His voice was low, rumbling in his chest and vibrating through her body like distant thunder. "I want you here. You don't know how hard it is for me to admit that. I tried to pretend you didn't affect me, that I was making the choices. To convince myself the way I felt around you was controllable, ignorable. I was wrong. Stay, Maizie."

"You plan on keeping me here against my will?"

"No." He put his lips to her ear, her mouth to his chest. "But I'd love the chance to persuade your will to stay."

His breath was warm, soothing and erotic against her skin. She felt like a kitten on catnip. It'd been a strange night, scary and exhilarating. The over-hot room, the scent of him, the fight for her life, it all made her dizzy and left her body wanting. It was just too hard to fight. She didn't want to anymore. She wanted him, had from the start if she was being honest with herself. So she stopped fighting.

She breathed him in, her hands going to the belt loops of his slacks. Her legs wrapped around his. She pulled, pressing her wet needy sex against the hard length of him. "Convince me."

It was both an invitation and a challenge. Gray was good with both. Admittedly he wanted her to stay for her own safety, for her own sanity. The first shift was hard and scary as hell. But there was a part of him, a large part and growing larger by the second, that wanted her to stay for purely selfish reasons.

He liked how he felt with Maizie, comfortable, at home. He'd never felt like this before, not even with Donna. It wasn't fair. He should've been able to give her that, to fit with someone so perfectly like this. He hadn't. But he was so tired of punishing himself for the failure. For one night he'd accept that maybe he did deserve to feel happy.

Gray kissed Maizie's ear, then tasted her—just a quick flick of his tongue. *Sugar and spice.* Jeezus, he'd always thought that was just a nursery rhyme. Maizie's profession made it a distracting reality.

"Shower first."

She pulled back. "Oh. Sorry. I was running before and it's hot in here..." She bent her head down to her shoulder and sniffed.

"No. You smell...great." She smelled like dirt, cookies and sex, his three favorite things. "Your wounds, though... You'll be more resistant to infection, but I don't want to take any risks."

"Oh." She laughed, but there was a nervousness about it that came with first-time lovers. The sound made his muscles quake and sent the same nervous thrill through him.

He stepped to the side and scooped her up, carrying her to the glass-walled shower. The molded corner seat was wide enough for three but Gray had no intention of sitting beside her. He reached for the bottom of her T-shirt. She leaned back, clutching the hem.

"I can manage by myself."

He couldn't help the lopsided grin. "What fun is there in that?"

Understanding flashed in her eyes, lust warming the color of her cheeks. She dipped her chin, coy and sexy, peering up at him through the tousled red strands of her hair. "You first."

The virus was working through her system faster than he'd expected, enhancing her basic senses. He'd never seen anyone go through the initial stages besides himself and all he remembered from those days was pain...food...and sex. *Intense* was the catchword of the experience. The virus didn't make you do things you didn't want to, it just made everything taste, smell, feel *better*.

Gray snagged the edges of his shirt and pulled, sending the matching sea-foam green buttons tick-tacking off the glass and over the shower floor. The shirt was already ruined with Maizie's blood, but he'd have done it anyway just to see her eyes go wide like that again.

He pulled his arms free, tossed the shirt out of the shower and cocked a brow at her. He didn't say it, but he knew his look told her it was her turn.

Maizie grabbed the torn edges of her shirt and pulled. She widened the tear by an inch, but little else.

"May I?"

She nodded, catching her bottom lip between her teeth when he reached for the ragged edges. One quick pull and the cotton shirt opened across her body. She gasped, her breasts rocking in her pretty white-lace bra from the force. She was breathing heavy, and God help him, he couldn't look at anything else for three solid heartbeats.

"Stand. I'll help with the sweats."

She shook her head, a wicked grin teasing across her face. "Not my turn."

Gray didn't hesitate. He worked out of his slacks, pulling his underwear with them to save time. He wasn't wearing shoes or socks when he'd heard Maizie's screams, so after tossing his clothes to the bathroom floor, he was completely naked and harder than stone.

Maizie's wide green eyes stared at his cock wagging straight out from his body as though trying to reach her on its own. Her focused attention made his muscles coil, twitching the meaty shaft even more and pulling a bright hungry smile across her face.

Jeezus, he hated that they'd done this to her. But he couldn't help his excitement at her awakening senses and the enhanced need that would come with them. He wanted her. He had from the moment he'd seen her at Green Acres.

His wolf had known all along, and he'd tried to ignore it. But now with the virus pumping through her veins, the wild scent of the pack rising through her skin, he couldn't deny it, couldn't resist her. He was helpless. His wolf wanted its mate.

Maizie reached for him. Her long slender fingers lightly feeling over the smooth head of his cock, the ropey veins bulging along the shaft. Even seeing it coming, Gray's lungs seized at her touch, his body tightening. Her gaze flicked to his, her smile a permanent fixture on her face. She held him, not a firm palmed grip but enough that when she tugged he followed.

Three steps was all it took and Maizie's soft red lips parted over him. Her tongue explored the textures, swirling and flicking, making him lean into the feel of it. He pushed deeper into her, her right hand loose around the base, stroking what she had left to take. Her mouth pulled on him, sweet, wet suction that drew sensation from every part of his body like strings on a puppet.

She went down on him farther, and back with greater suction. Down and back and then again to the hilt. Gray's hips pumped with each draw, until he was fucking her mouth, as hard and fast as she could take him. Every thrust he went deeper, and Maizie took it, grabbed his balls, his ass and demanded more.

He held her head with both hands, his fingers digging into her thick fiery hair. His hips rocked, thrusting his shaft between her lips, feeling the sharp scrape of teeth, the hard pull of suction. He'd come like this if he wasn't careful.

Fuck. Sensation thrummed through his veins, swirling, building in his groin, feeling better and better by the second. He wanted to come. It felt so damn good. No. He could hold off a few seconds longer, enjoy it just a little more. Maizie's hands began a wicked tease. She rolled his balls through her fingers, caressed, and tugged. Her other hand slipped around his ass, traced the line of his cheeks, teasing, searching for his anus.

The sensation stormed through his body faster than he'd expected, a wash of heat and delicious pleasure crashing through his tenuous control—a flash of release.

He came before he could stop himself. He pulled out, holding her back before he lost any more of his load. Jeezus, it'd been decades since anyone had out-fucked him. He controlled his body. He couldn't remember the last time someone had managed to seduce that control away, even a little.

Maizie licked her lips, tasting him, eyes questioning. "What's wrong?"

"Your turn." The wolf growled in him, panting. She'd awakened the beast as she'd been doing for days, only this time he'd have his fill.

Gray pulled her to her feet, held her until he was sure she'd found her balance. She kept most of her weight on one leg, her hands braced, one on the back tiled wall, the other on the glass wall.

Arms out, her breasts seemed gifted to him, and he couldn't resist a quick caress, feeling the roundness, the supple give when he squeezed, the hard nipples straining beneath the lace. Her back arched, pressing into his palms and Gray gave a final squeeze, a quick pinch, a gentle tug.

He knelt, hooked his fingers on the waistband of her sweats, catching her panties as well, and drew them down over her hips.

He teased them both, pulling slow over the round of her hips until the first reddish curls peeked over the edge. A little lower and he could see the top slit of her pussy. He stopped, leaned in and flicked his tongue in the crease.

She gasped. He pushed his tongue firmer between the lips, tasting her cream even as he found her clit. She moaned, tried to open her legs further, but her sweats held her. She curved her hips, pressing her sex into his face and Gray breathed her in.

No sugar here, but plenty of spice and the heady scent of woman. Sweet Jeezus, he could live in that scent. His teasing, slow reveal had suddenly become a torture. He yanked her sweats to her ankles and only remembered her injured calf when she cringed.

"Shit. Maizie..."

"Fine. I'm fine. Don't stop. Please God..." She lifted one foot free and opened wide, grabbed his head and pulled his face to her pussy.

Gray smiled even as he drew his tongue from the opening

at her sex up to her clit. She moaned loud with the feel of his mouth on her and so he did it again. It was most likely the virus that made her so bold, but he didn't care. He liked it. A lot.

The tops of her inner thighs were wet, her curls glistening, and Gray slipped his finger between her swollen flesh, finding the tight slick entrance. Her muscles pulsed, gripped his finger and welcomed a second, her cream hot on the back of his knuckles. She was on fire, so needy he fought to take things slow, to please her before he gave in and fucked her so hard she'd scream his name. Every primal instinct inside him hammered his brain, so he could hardly think, barely see straight.

He spread the hood of her lips from her clit, flicking the plump nub with his tongue, making her body quiver even as her pussy milked his fingers. Her hips rocked against him, riding his hand, driving his fingers deeper. He arched his fingers inside her, curved along her channel to find the spot that made her head fall back, her eyes close and her hips set a frantic pace.

Her hand fisted the hair at the back of his head. "There. Right there. Yes."

He latched onto her clit, sucked and toyed, pulling the juicy flesh into his mouth, coaxing the small spasm trembling through her muscles into a full-on orgasm.

"Gray..." She fell back. He caught her, his fingers still pumping her pussy, his mouth still suckling her clit until her hips slowed, her hand in his hair went slack and the last spasm of her sex fluttered around his fingers.

Dear Lord he wanted her to come again. He leaned in, mouth open, gaze flicking up to her face. The back of her shoulders leaned against the wall, her body angled out to him where his arm still held her around her ass. Maizie's eyes were closed, her face flush, chest rising and falling with deep breaths. She needed a moment to recover.

Gray couldn't resist one last playful bite on her pussy as he pulled his fingers out of her. She squirmed a little, made a soft laugh.

She was utterly pliant to his touch, not even opening her eyes when he stood and removed her bra. He tossed it over the glass wall then turned and set the temperature for the shower. It'd turn on when the water in the pipes had warmed enough. The process took less than two minutes.

He stood shielding her from the sudden rush of hot water that would come. She had yet to open her eyes or let her pretty smile falter. He stared at her, the pale creaminess of her skin, the delicate features of her face. Long reddish eyelashes, nearly translucent, shadowed almost-there freckles high on her cheeks. Lips so soft that rose petals couldn't compare, bowed with a smile that flipped his heart, made him happy to be a man. When had Granny's Little Red become such an enchanting woman?

His gaze dropped to her breasts rising toward him with her slowing breaths. He reached out to one, his finger tracing along the outside curve, bringing a rush of tiny goose bumps shivering over her body. Her smile brightened but her eyes remained closed.

He feathered a single finger up to the darker flesh of her areola. The skin reacted like a delicate flower, puckering at his touch, her nipple growing, defining, hardening. His hand opened on her without thought, fingers squeezing gently, catching the hard nub. His heart picked up a beat, blood rushing to his cock, muscles tightening.

There was nothing like the feel of a woman's breast so perfect, so sensual, he had to feel it in his mouth. Gray slipped his free arm around her waist, his hand sliding down to cup her ass. He pulled her close. His cock twitched against her, the wet hairs of her pussy teasing him. He bent over her, flicking his tongue over her nipple, hard as a cherry pit.

Grrr... He'd like to squeeze his teeth on that sweet pebble of flesh, to bite and nibble. Gentleness wasn't easy, but he didn't want to hurt her. He knew he'd failed when she gasped, flinched away. He stopped instantly and met her gaze. There was laughter in her forest-green eyes that set his worry at ease.

"Not so hard."

He growled his apology as he kissed her breast, then drew as much as he could into his mouth, careful not to pull too hard. The puckered flesh of her nipple felt wonderful on his tongue and he swirled around it, reveling in the sensation. She arched into him, pressing her body flush against his, from her ribs to her sex. Gray pressed back, his arms wrapped tight around her.

A soft beep warned him before perfectly warm water sprayed from three walls and overhead. His body shielded her but she flinched anyway.

"Wow, that feels good," she said.

Gray released her, stepped back, allowing more of the steaming water to patter over her body. He reached for his sea sponge in the silver basket suctioned to the back wall and showed it to her.

"You mind? It's almost new." It was still a little stiff, but the water would soften it enough. "I have washcloths if you'd rather..."

She laughed. "I just had your penis in my mouth. I think I can handle your bath sponge on my back."

The image of her lips wrapped around his hard cock flashed through his head. He hooked his hand behind her neck, pulled, bringing her mouth to his. He had to feel those soft lips again, somewhere, anywhere on his body.

Her surprise only lasted an instant and she kissed him back, just as needy. He felt her hands on his hips, her nails digging in, not hard but enough to send a jolt of painful pleasure racing through his system. Her tongue flicked against his, traced the roof of his mouth then darted away. He chased with his own, gathering her body to his as he did.

The quick movement sent her off balance, forced her to put too much weight on her injured leg. She grimaced, breaking the kiss as she stumbled against him. Gray caught her, practically lifting her off her feet.

"Shit. I'm sorry. I... Dammit." He set her down, waited for her to find a comfortable footing. "This isn't me. It's just that you smell so perfect, and you feel... I..."

She laughed, holding his shoulders. "I know exactly what you mean. Really. Everything just feels so right, so good, with you. I swear I've never been like this, but I have to admit, it's kinda great."

Tension rippled off his shoulders with her smile. He held out the sponge, let it fill with water, wrung it out and did it again until it was soft and heavy in his hand. He filled it with soap, squeezed until it was white with suds, then turned Maizie around so the water cascaded over her long hair and down her back.

She leaned her head into the spray, running her hands through her hair, eyes closed, as Gray smoothed the soapy sponge down her neck and over the swells of her breasts. He washed her, every luscious feminine inch of her. He touched her in places he'd likely miss while making love to her and he enjoyed every minute of it. He even washed her hair, something he'd never done before and very much wanted to do again.

When he'd finished and had rinsed the last shimmer of shampoo from her hair, smoothed the last bubble of soap off the round of her ass, she turned and took the sponge from the basket where he'd put it.

She squeezed, soapy white lather bubbling out between her fingers. She smiled. "We still taking turns?"

Chapter Nine

"There mwap mwap mwap you know, Maizie."

Maizie could only make out half of what Gray was saying under the towel while he dried her hair. She could definitely get used to this kind of service. Not to mention the service she'd just gotten in the shower.

In fact...

She dropped the towel she'd used to dry her body and reached for his hands, turning to face him. Her thoughts must have shown on her face. The moment their eyes met, he allowed the last ends of her hair to slip from his grip beneath the towel—forgotten—his gaze drifting to her naked breasts and lower.

You'd think he'd never seen her naked the way he looked at her. Lips parted, eyes intense, muscles tight. She felt beautiful, sexy.

"We need to talk, Maizie. I mean it." There was a hint of guilt in his voice, if not in his eyes. Why? Was this about him stealing her mother's locket? What else? It's why she'd come. Maybe he'd figured it out. But she didn't want to ruin the moment with explanations or excuses. Her mother's locket was the last thing on her mind right now.

His gaze hadn't risen above her chest, and the look in his eyes was not the look of a man hoping for stimulating conversation. She stepped closer, her hands going to the towel snagged around his hips. She tugged and the fuzzy warm fabric parted then slipped to the floor.

His stiff cock sprang up to meet her. *Yeah, he's all about talking.* She wrapped her fingers around the thick shaft, loving the girth of it. Smaller than a rolling pin, thicker than the handle of a bat, enough to fill her but not ruin her.

Gawd, she wanted to know what he'd feel like inside her. Just the thought of it sent a wash of wet heat through her sex. She stroked him, feeling the velvety ridges, the smooth lip of the head then down again. She arched her back so the plump head of his cock pressed into her belly as she stroked him.

He groaned, the sound vibrating low in his chest. His hips rocked with her, coaxing her to continue, to stroke faster. She tightened her grip, followed his quicker pace and found herself caressing her sex against his leg. Her hand to his hip, trying to remember not to dig her nails too deep, she leaned in to kiss the hard muscles of his chest.

Small trickles of water streamed down his chest from his hair, wetting her lips. His skin was hot, a beautiful sun-kissed bronze and so smooth she had to know the feel of it on her tongue. He was clean from the shower but the smallest sheen of sweat had started to form. Salty, earthy and subtly sweet, just the way he smelled.

She found his nipple with her lips, the little pucker of dark rosy flesh, its tiny nub erect, excited. She teased her tongue over it, flicked and sucked and kissed—and bit. Gray's breath caught with a hiss, a wash of goose bumps traveling over his skin. His cock pulsed in her hand.

He grabbed her arms, pulled his hips back enough so she'd let him go. "Jeezus, you drive me to distraction."

"This is a good thing." She reached for him, but he kept her back.

He laughed, playful, genuine. "It's a very good thing, but I want to talk."

She sighed, as dramatic as she could. "Is it always going to be about what *you* want?" She allowed a smile to quirk the corner of her mouth.

"What? No. I..." The poor man hadn't come completely. His hard-on was so stiff she could probably blow him from across the room. It was a ruthless tease. She didn't care. She'd make it up to him if he'd just stop yackin'.

He caught her smirk, his brow creased, a determined frown darkening his face. "Absolutely."

Gray scooped her up, cradling her against his warm chest, and stormed from the bathroom toward his bed. His muscular body practically vibrated with power. He was healthy, excited. She'd deliberately teased his lust, dared him. Could she handle the consequences?

As though he'd sensed her concern, he paused at the side of his bed and looked at her. He smiled, kissed her forehead so tenderly her worries vanished. "You okay?"

She nodded, squirming in his arms, her hand cupping the back of his head to pull his mouth to hers. His lips were firm and took control of the kiss in an instant. His tongue traced along the slit of her mouth and she opened for him. He entered her mouth as he lowered her to the bed, lying half beside her and half on top of her.

His heavy leg draped over hers, his foot working to push her knees apart. She pumped her hips, pressing into the coarse hairs on his leg. Gawd, she was so horny any part of him would do.

Braced on an elbow, he kissed her, taking her lips, drawing on her tongue, exploring her mouth. His free hand felt its way down her neck to her chest. She arched for him, his hand opening wide, squeezing her breast, massaging. His fingers flicked the pebbled nub of her nipple, pinching it, and a fast jolt of pain and pleasure zinged through her, made her gasp. Her hand went to his, held it there, helped him squeeze.

Gray looked to her breast and guided her hand to fondle herself on her own. He watched, his hips pressing the hard shaft of his cock along her side, his flesh hot against her, rocking as her touches made her body respond. She squeezed, offering her breast to him. He took it hungrily, the sultry heat of his mouth flooding through her. His arm wrapped around her waist, turning her, pulling her closer so his cock pumped against her belly.

"Gray...please..." The hard feel of him was such exquisite torture. She wanted him inside her, she wanted him everywhere. Heat washed through her, slicked her sex, made it hard to breathe, hard to think. Her body burned, skin tingling, mind dizzy with need.

He loosened his hold, slipping his hand over her belly through the curls of her mons. Warm trickles seeped between the lips of her sex to wet her thighs. His finger slipped through her folds, smooth and easy.

"Fuck, Maizie, you get so wet." His rich voice vibrated against her chest, her nipple held at his mouth. "Is that just for me? Tell me all this cream is just for me."

"It's you." She tried not to gasp, not to squeal as his finger dove inside her, curling instantly to stroke her G-spot. "You do this to me."

Her hips bucked against his hand as a second finger filled her and a third made it tight. Maizie grabbed his wrist, helped his hand fuck her pussy harder, faster.

"Jeezus..." He panted, shifted his weight, his mouth going

to her neck as he nudged his hips between her thighs. "I have to feel that hot cream on my cock. I want it buried up to my balls."

His fingers pulled out of her and for a half second she nearly couldn't breathe from the loss. Then the smooth fat head of his cock pressed against her and the world went white hot behind her eyes.

She pushed her head back in the pillow, lifted her hips trying to coax him deeper. But he pulled out and moan of protest exploded from her on reflex.

Gray pushed up, balancing on his knees and one hand. She opened her eyes to see him watching as he gripped his cock, teasing the head along her pussy. His smile was wicked and sexy as hell, his hand rubbing the head through her slick folds, from her clit all the way down to her anus.

She held her breath when he pressed there, her muscles pulsed a fresh flood of heat, drenching her. His cock, shiny from her cream, slick and wet, nearly slipped in. A part of her wanted it. *Really* wanted it. But she wanted him to fill her sex more. "Gray..."

She didn't have to ask twice. One solid thrust and his stiff shaft drove deep into her pussy, filling her fast, robbing of her thought and breath. She opened her mouth to scream, but no sound came out, half a heartbeat later her lungs gasped for air.

Gray held her behind her knees, pressing her legs back. The position angled her pussy upward and he moved closer on his knees to fit the full length of his cock as deep as her body could allow.

"Oh...yes..." The feel of him so deep, touching places inside her that hadn't been touched in...she couldn't remember how long. Sweet satisfaction swelled in the core of her body. Eyes closed, her hands fumbled blind for him, found his knees on either side, worked up to his thighs and squeezed.

His hips pumped, fucking her faster, driving deep so his balls slapped against her ass. "You're so tight. I can feel you squeezing my cock."

She flexed her Kegel muscles.

Gray hissed. "Jeezus." He rammed his cock deep and then again. "Touch yourself, Maizie. Show me what you like."

Maizie didn't think twice. She'd never been so hot, needed so much, nothing was too personal. Inhibitions didn't exist. All she wanted was to satiate this hunger, and everything they did felt inexplicably good and made her desire more intense, more urgent.

He growled, watching her, his excitement making him harder, pumping her body faster. Maizie wanted to keep her eyes open to see his handsome face gripped with passion. But she could hardly think past the feel of him inside her, past the hum of her skin, the thunder of her heart, the delicious friction in her sex.

Her mind wrapped itself in the dizzying sensations. His hard cock pushing through the sensitive walls inside her, each thrust filling her perfectly, building an exquisite pressure, every fiber of her body wanting more.

Her heart pounded, muscles milking his body, her fingers teasing her clit, bringing rise to another swirl of needy pressure that enhanced the first and made her muscles clench.

"Yesss..." Gray's pace doubled, the force of his thrusts rocking the bed.

Maizie's breath seized, her head pressed back, her hips bucking up to his, frantic, as the pressure crested, then gushed through her body liquid hot, breathless and wet. She screamed, fisting her toes, pushing her hips hard against his, muscles pulsing.

Gray pushed back, rode her orgasm and then started driving toward his own. His cock was still hard and stiff as steel, his pace selfish, impatient and perfect. In seconds the pressure had built inside her again, her pussy so sensitive and ready. She could feel his orgasm coming, the way his cock filled her, buried deep inside her, fast and hungry. Just when he'd brought them both to the very crest of pleasure, he pulled out.

He grabbed his cock, stroking madly, as his other hand finished off her pussy. Her gasp of shock was more a scream and she watched him climax, bringing herself a half second later. The erotic sight of his hand pumping his stiff cock, his cream spurting warm over her belly, was all she needed to send her spiraling over the edge.

She relaxed back into the pillow, boneless, riding the waves of pleasure rippling through her. Gray collapsed beside her. After a minute spent catching his breath, he grabbed a tissue to wipe the come from her belly.

She smiled. "By the way. I'm on the pill."

"Shit. I forgot."

"What do you mean?"

He kissed the back of her neck. "Nothing. Never mind."

She remembered purring when he gathered her to him, feeling the warmth of his body, the strength in his arms. She couldn't fight the thick blanket of sleep overtaking her. She didn't even try.

"Double the eggs and bacon, Greta. Mr. Lupo has a guest. A female guest."

Maizie jolted straight up, expecting to see Annette carrying on a conversation at the foot of the bed. There was no one there.

"Nooo. Overnight?" The other woman spoke in a thick Spanish accent.

"*Sí!*" Hands clapped excitedly. "I think she's the one," Annette said.

"Oh, *dios mio*. It's been too long." The woman put three slices of bacon with the others, each one sizzling as it touched the skillet. "It's a wonder he didn't shake down the house taking her."

Ah! Rude. Maizie smiled, glancing at the sleeping Mr. Lupo beside her. "But true."

Wait. How was she hearing them from the kitchen? "Intercom," she said to herself. In a house this big, they were probably as necessary as doors.

"Greta," Annette warned. "Mr. Lupo's sexual liaisons—or lack thereof—are none of our business." A moment's pause followed by dueling giggles.

"Dissin' the boss, eh?" Maizie tsked. "No wonder he left the thing on." She looked around, trying to locate the box, or maybe a speaker on the wall. Whatever. She slipped out of bed, carefully moving Gray's arm from around her belly. Rag-doll limp, the man was dead to the world.

She reached over and brushed a thick wave of hair from over his eye. He turned his head and rubbed his face into her pillow, fluffed it, tucked his hand underneath, then stilled. Sexy *and* adorable.

"Whoof," she said, smiling.

Maizie tiptoed into the bathroom and found her torn bloodied clothes where they'd left them last night. The shirt and sweats were garbage, but she could salvage the bra and panties.

"Miss Lynn and de others know?" the cook asked.

"No...er...I don't think so," Annette said.

Maizie padded back into the bedroom. She'd need clothes if she meant to go downstairs for some of that food. The smell of bacon was making her mouth water. Her stomach growled. She clamped a hand to her belly and went to the armoire.

"Dress shirts. Surprise." All long sleeved, all linen, some with folded collars, some with short mandarin collars, but no two alike. "Decisions. Decisions."

She snagged a plain white shirt, pleated, with a stylish wrinkled look and shoved her arms through the sleeves. "Very cool."

She pulled the collar over her nose and inhaled. It smelled like flowery detergent, but underneath, woven into the fabric was the sweet, earthy smell of Gray. Odd that a washing hadn't removed his scent completely. She'd suggest a better detergent. Or not, if she planned on wearing any more of his shirts.

A final deep whiff and she wandered around the room looking for the intercom while she buttoned. The shirt was big on her, brushing her mid-thigh, with sleeves an inch past her hands.

"Perfect fit." Gray's smooth voice made her jump. She spun to catch him lying back, propped on his elbows, watching her. He wore that same I'd-like-some-of-that look on his face from last night with a sexy lopsided grin to top it off.

Her cheeks warmed. She laughed. "You like it? I figure it'll make up for the T-shirt you ruined last night."

"Your T-shirt was already torn."

"It covered the important parts."

"And bloodied."

"But still wearable in a pinch."

"You said I could tear it. In fact, you enjoyed it."

"Fine. You want me to take this off?"

He sat straight, eyes wide. "Yes."

She laughed at his eagerness. "Later. I smell food. Aren't you hungry?"

"Always." He winked.

Maizie blushed again. The man could melt icebergs with those eyes and that voice. "Good. Me too. I think your intercom's broken, though. I could hear people in the kitchen but I don't think they can hear me. Where's the speaker?"

"No speaker." Gray reached for the phone next to the bed and held it for her to see. "Through the phones."

Maizie blinked at the receiver in his hand. "But I heard Annette and Greta."

"My cook."

"Whatever. I've never met her, but I know her name. Why? Because I heard them talking. How did I hear them talking if there's no speaker? I can smell that bacon like it's in the room...and the eggs and toast. She's squeezing oranges right now." There was a reasonable explanation. There had to be. But something about saying it all aloud made her heart race, her words rush, as the realization sank in.

"Okay. Let's talk." Gray put away the phone then held a hand out to her. "Come here. I want to explain—"

"Can we just forget about that for now? I already know. That's why I came." Maizie waved the gesture away from the end of the bed. Did he think she was joking? She was hearing through walls, through floors. Now was not the time to discuss a theft he committed twenty-one years ago.

Gray's hand dropped. He blinked. "You know?"

Ugh. Did he really think Granny wouldn't have told her about the locket? About him being at the accident? What else could put that guilty glint in his eyes, the soft regret in his voice?

"You may be *friends* with Granny, but I'm blood," she said. "I know about the locket. Okay? I'm not pissed. I'm not happy you stole it, or that you waited twenty-one years to give it back. But I'm not pissed. Okay, maybe a little. But that's not what made me come here last night."

"Then what?" Gray sat with one knee bent on the bed and the other dangling over the edge, covers at his waist.

"What? What made me come here? I...had some questions. About the accident. About that night."

He shrugged, his face darkening with his sobering mood. "So ask. I've got nothing to hide."

Was that attitude? He was giving her attitude, now? "No?"

"No. I'm not a thief...*Little Red.*" He made the nickname sound like an insult.

She matched his scowl. "Don't call me that."

Gray shook his head, threw back the covers and stormed past her to the bathroom. His beautiful body, tan and muscled. "You're a child. *Their* child."

He returned, wearing a gray silk robe, the lapels and sash a lighter shade. "Next time you come to a man's house accusing him, get your damn facts straight."

She propped her hands on her hips. "Correct me if I'm wrong, but didn't you give Granny my mother's locket yesterday? A locket you *found* at the site of their fatal accident? A locket you've kept for twenty-one years?"

He turned on her. The movement so fast she dropped her arms, losing the cocky stance. "Yes. I found the fucking locket at the scene of an accident. My *wife's* fatal accident."

"What?" She couldn't breathe. "Fatal? But I thought she just moved away."

"No." Gray straightened and seemed to reel in some of his anger. "She's the reason I was there. I didn't give a damn about your parents. They'd killed her. Mowed her down like a...a..." He made a frustrated growl and turned, walking to the turret windows off the sitting room.

"What are you talking about? We didn't hit anyone. We hit a wolf." Her own words sent a shiver down her spine, made Gray's shoulders tense as he stared out the windows. She knew, but she didn't want to.

Memories flooded back. "We were driving to pick up Granny. My parents were happy but...I wasn't. I didn't want to leave my forest."

"*My* forest," Gray said.

Maizie barely heard. "Daddy had just gotten a promotion. We'd be moving..."

Gray knotted his arms over his chest. "They were trespassing in *our* forest. Mine and Donna's."

"It was dark and raining. We took the shortcut."

"They were driving too fast," Gray said.

"The wolf, it jumped out of nowhere."

"*She* had every right to run in her woods."

"My parents couldn't stop. They tried..."

"Not hard enough."

"Daddy jerked the wheel. We went over the side. Mommy was screaming, Daddy too. And then those eyes, cold green, heartless eyes..." Her gaze focused on Gray's back. "The wolf. The wolf that caused my parents' death. It was your wife. Your wife was a wolf. A werewolf."

158

His voice was soft and cold. "And I've gone and mated with her killer's child."

"But there's no such thing as—"

Gray turned, anger etching his expression. "As what? A werewolf? Stop lying to yourself, Maizie. You've been doing it long enough. What do you think attacked you last night? What do you think I am?"

She flinched. He was so angry. No. It wasn't anger glistening in his eyes, it was guilt...and blame. "Ohmygod, you blame my parents for your wife's death. You blame me."

Gray dropped his gaze, his expression softening. "No. You were just in the car. She was dead. You weren't."

"Yes, you do. You blame me, just like I blamed her..." Gray met Maizie's gaze, but he didn't stop her from continuing the thought. "All this time, you couldn't stand the sight of me. Made Granny keep me away. Stick to the path, Maizie. Stay away from that part of the forest. Beware of the big bad...wolf."

"Maizie..."

A knock at the door stopped the conversation cold.

"Mr. Lupo?" Annette was quiet on the other side for a moment. "Mr. Lupo, I have a message for Ms. Hood. I've also brought breakfast."

"Come in," Maizie said when it was clear Gray wouldn't respond. He stood stoic, feet planted, his back to the windows, his arms folded over his stomach.

Annette opened the door, juggling a bed tray, her bright smile vanishing when it met Gray's dark glower. "Oh. I'm sorry. I've interrupted—"

"No. It's fine. We're..." Maizie glanced at Gray, "...finished. We're done." She looked back to Annette hovering half-in, half-out of the room.

"What's the message, Annette?" Gray asked.

One hand under the tray, she pushed up her glasses then grabbed the tray again. "Oh. Yes. Green Acres Nursing Home called. They'd tried to reach Ms. Hood and when they couldn't they called here. Apparently Ester had a small health scare."

"What?" Maizie's heart stopped.

"Oh, no, no," Annette hurried. "She's fine. It was just a scare. They took her to the hospital last night and released her this morning. She should be back at the home by now."

This morning? To the hospital and back already? "What time is it?"

"It's nearly four," Annette said.

"Four? PM?" Maizie watched her nod. "That's not possible. I slept more than fourteen hours?" She looked at Gray.

His gaze remained fixed on Annette, silent, his brows tight, jaw stiff. It wasn't until Maizie spoke again that he flicked his attention to her.

"I have to go."

"Where?" he said.

"Where do you think? I have to make sure my grandmother's okay." She went to the bathroom and grabbed her sneakers. They were speckled with blood, but it wouldn't affect how well they'd protect her feet.

"Annette told you she's fine."

Maizie came out hopping, struggling into one shoe and then the other. "I have to check for myself."

"So call Green Acres. You can use the phone here."

"I'll call from the cottage. I want to shower before I go in to see her anyway."

"Shower here."

"I don't have any clothes."

"What you're wearing is fine." He slid his hands into the pockets of his robe. Shrugged. "Or I'll send Annette out to buy you something more suitable. Whatever you need."

Why was he making this so difficult? He should want her gone as badly as she wanted to go. Except that she didn't really want to leave him. Gawd, so much had changed so fast. Everything had gotten screwed up and twisted. She wanted him as much as she had twenty minutes ago.

But how could she stay when he obviously hadn't worked out his feelings about her part in the accident? How could she stay when she hadn't worked out how she felt about his part in her parents' death?

"You have to stay, Maizie."

"I really don't." She focused her gaze on the opened door. She couldn't bear to look at him. She couldn't risk seeing that look in his eyes—anger, blame, hate. She'd rather never look at him again.

"It's not safe," he said. "You don't understand—"

"No. *You* don't understand." She closed her eyes, emotions clogging her throat. She wouldn't cry. She wouldn't. "I don't have time for this shit. I told myself I didn't have time for a romantic relationship from the start. I told Granny. I've already neglected the shop. And now I've neglected Granny. That's enough. I don't have time for this. I don't have time for you."

She ran. It wasn't mature, it wasn't brave, but it was the only thing she could do. She had to get away, get some distance from all those feelings, the memories, the confusion of what she thought she knew, what she thought she wanted. She had to get some distance from him.

By the time she reached the cottage she'd made herself sick. She'd run the whole way and gotten a stitch in her side, and her stomach was tying itself into knots.

She went in the backdoor. She'd left it unlocked last night. "I just need to eat something."

In the kitchen all she found were a few cans of diet soda and two jars of peanut butter. She leaned against the counter, soda beside her, and ate. It was the best peanut butter *ever*. She looked at the label after every few bites. "It's not even name brand."

She finished the jar in minutes, scraping the spoon on the bottom to get every speck of creamy brown heaven. When she could see through the clear bottom, she tossed the empty jar in the trash and had the other opened before she realized what she was doing.

"Crap. I should just spread it directly on my ass." She scooped the spoon in three more times, then finally set the jar down and backed away. When she reached the steps her stomach growled, then cramped. She winced and after a few seconds the pain subsided.

She jogged up to her bedroom and grabbed her cell phone from her purse. She had Green Acres on speed dial. "Hi. This is Maizie Hood. I'm calling to check on—"

"Maizie, hi. This is Clare, from the front desk. Your grandmother is fine. She had a little angina attack last night, but they checked her out at the hospital and she's already back. She's sleeping now. I can tell her you called."

"Thanks, Clare. Tell her I'll be in tonight."

"You bet."

Maizie snapped the phone closed, tossed it to the bed and snatched her fuzzy robe from the rocking chair as she passed. Her stomach rumbled again and she winced through the twinge of a cramp. "An entire jar of peanut butter in one sitting does *not* do the body good."

162

She went to the bathroom and pulled the cream shower curtain from the old clawfoot tub. She turned on the hot water, let it run. A shower would make her feel like herself again.

Although last night's shower had made her feel better than herself, better than she had in years. Even with the injuries, she'd never felt so good, so turned-on, so alive. Was it Gray or something else?

Naked in front of the medicine cabinet mirror, Maizie eyed the bite on her shoulder. Two little puncture wounds and twin runs of red dots. She turned, peering over her shoulder. The back was a little worse, some scabbing but still remarkably healed. She put her foot on the toilet seat and checked her calf. The bite was nearly healed just like her shoulder.

A cramp made her grab her stomach, she winced, bending a bit to take the pain. It passed, but the intensity was obviously increasing. What was wrong with her?

Maizie shook her head, put her foot down. "Ugh. You're fine. This isn't some horror flick or fairy tale."

More likely Gray had some sort of curative agent in his water to keep the animals on the preserve healthy. Yeah, that made more sense than her turning into a... She wouldn't dignify the thought.

Maizie stepped into the tub, adjusted the water temperature, closed the curtain and pulled the lever for the shower. Warm water cascaded over her body, washing away every touch, every kiss Gray had left on her. Too bad it couldn't wash away the hot memories of his body pounding into hers.

Or the craving for him to do it again.

Chapter Ten

"Who did it?" Gray stood at the edge of the pool, arms folded tight across his chest. "Which one of you mutts committed suicide last night?"

Lynn raised her head to turn to the other cheek, one eye squinting at Gray. She was on her belly, topless, tanning in the late-afternoon sun. "What are you grumbling about?"

"Who sank teeth?" His hands fisted tight under his arms, thoughts of them squeezing around one of their necks flashing through his mind. Dammit, this wasn't like him, but when it came to Maizie his priorities changed.

Rick shrugged from the back end of the diving board. "What difference does it make? It's what you wanted. What we all needed." He took three long strides, bounced once then angled headfirst into the pool.

"What's done is done." Joy sipped her iced tea then set it on the table between her and Lynn before finding her place in the romance novel she held. "I'm sure it was an accident, sweetheart. There's nothing to be done about it now."

"An accident? She fall into someone's open mouth?" Gray didn't need to be told. He was positive he knew which one of them would dare touch her.

He dropped his arms, striding along the pool to loom over Lynn. "Where is he?"

Lynn lifted her head again, squinting. "Who?"

"Your dead mate," Gray said. "At least he will be once I get my hands on him."

"It wasn't Shawn."

"Bullshit." He'd had to pry the mutt's jaws off Maizie. Being new, Shawn had the least control and the least respect for the pack. Gray looked to the house, saw the curtains in Lynn's bedroom window flutter closed. Coward. Without a word he headed for the glass doors, murder in his mind.

"Gray, no. No! He didn't do it. I swear," Lynn screamed behind him. He knew she'd gotten up, was chasing after him. "Rick! Rick, stop him. He'll kill him."

Rick scaled the metal ladder at the end of the pool just as Gray neared. He foolishly stepped in front of him, hands up, as though that would even slow him down.

The newcomer would die. Someone had to pay for turning Maizie, for forcing him to face a fact he'd been working twenty-one years to avoid. Maizie was his mate. She'd always been his mate. His marriage to Donna should never have been. She'd deserved better. By the time Rick pushed against his chest, Gray's whirling thoughts, his heavy guilt had weakened the foundation of his rage.

"Uncle Gray, it wasn't Shawn," Rick said. "He got excited and chased after her when she ran. He's a new wolf, still learning control. But we stopped him. We had him back under control. He wasn't the one who bit her."

"Then who?" He was yelling now, his voice so close to a roar his throat protested, growing sore. "Who did it?"

Rick shook his head, looked away then back, chin high, eyes defiant. "It was me. Okay? I did it. I turned her. I told you I would if you didn't."

Anger, pain, guilt and remorse churned into a furious storm inside him. Gray exploded, shoving at Rick's chest, sending him backward several feet. The younger man caught himself, landing on the balls of his feet, ready to fight if he had to.

"C'mon, boy." Gray spoke through his teeth. "We end this today. Take the pack or get out."

His body tight, Rick snarled at Gray, edging forward a little, but not attacking. Rick was born a werewolf and stronger because of it, but Gray was older and turned by his late wife, the strongest among them. She'd chosen him to be alpha, sensing the natural strength within him. It would be a battle, but Gray had rage on his side.

"No. Stop it." Shelly scrambled out of the sunken hot tub and raced to the other side of the pool. "Ricky, if you lose you'll have to leave. You can't fight for alpha and then go back to subordinate."

"Stay out of this, Shelly. I didn't challenge him. He challenged me. I can't be cast out for defending myself. I'll handle this."

"Uncle Gray, please. It wasn't Ricky."

The hairs at the scruff of Gray's neck bristled, his muscles tight, instinct pumping a heady mix of adrenaline through his body. "Disobeying my order is a challenge. And I accept."

"That's how you're going to play it?" Rick asked, disgust thickening his tone.

"I did it." Shelly jumped between them and shoved Gray's shoulders. "You hear me? I did it. I disobeyed. I turned her. Not Ricky. Not Shawn. Me."

"Shut up, Shelly."

Gray blinked, the fast shift of emotion fogging his brain.

"You? Why?"

Shelly huffed, tears glistening in her bluer-than-blue eyes. She stepped back, dropping her gaze. For a minute she looked every bit the teenager she appeared to be, despite her true age and the way her curves filled her brown and pink string bikini. "I wanted things to be *normal.* I wanted us to be a normal family. Like it was before Aunt Donna..."

Gray stroked her cheek. "How does turning Maizie make us normal, honey?"

"It was an accident," Lynn said, walking up beside them, her black bikini top now tied in place. Joy followed close behind. "Okay, I admit Shawn got a little out of control, but when Maizie started to run he just couldn't keep a hold on his instinct. Well you know how it is. The chase, the prey's fear flavoring the air. With him losing it, Shelly got a little overexcited."

Joy joined them, slipped an arm around her granddaughter. "The twins are still young, Gray. Their wolf instincts get the better of them sometimes."

"I didn't lose control, Gram." Shelly shrugged out of the one-arm embrace. "And it wasn't an accident. I wanted to turn her."

Gray's muscles knotted across his shoulders, a dull throb thumping in his head. He loved his niece, but she was becoming every bit as complicated as all the other females he'd known. "Shelly, honey, explain to me exactly why you wanted to turn Maizie Hood into one of us."

"Because I love my family and I want my pack to stay together. You know she's the one, but you love your precious guilt so much you couldn't let it go and take her. And I'm too young to marry some stupid old dog because you couldn't take a mate and keep this pack alive."

"Never would've happened," Gray said, his anger simmering.

"It would. You can't disobey the laws of wolves, Uncle Gray. They won't let you," Shelly said. "Either some self-appointed stud would eventually come sniffin' around and challenge you, or Rick would take a mate and they'd see him as the strongest mated pair and challenge him. Neither worked for me, so I did what I thought would be best for everyone. Including you, Uncle Gray."

Gray snorted, shook his head, looking from one set of eyes to the next. "That's what you've all been thinking? You're worried some asshole's going to come in here and fight me for all of you?"

They didn't answer. Finally Joy spoke up. "You're family, Gray. I know you and Donna weren't natural mates, but she truly cared for you. You were so strong. A born leader." She stepped in front of him, cupped his face, loving, maternal.

"You made your marriage work even when it was clear the bond wasn't there. But since we lost her, you haven't even tried to find your true mate. And when you pushed the Hood girl away too, we worried you'd never take a mate." Her hands dropped to his chest. "We don't want to lose you. Losing Donna was hard enough."

"No one is losing anyone." They'd have to kill him before he let someone separate him from Donna's family—from *his* family.

"Right. Thanks to me," Shelly said. All eyes riveted on her. "I did what you couldn't, or wouldn't. Maizie Hood's your true mate. We all know it. You're just squeamish about turning her because of some twisted loyalty to Aunt Donna. She shouldn't have turned you. You weren't meant for her, but her death led you to the person you *were* meant for. Now you have her."

"I don't have anything." Rather than admit his guilt, he'd

allowed Maizie to believe he blamed her for the accident. Now she was out there alone, her body changing. She was too angry with him to let him help. He didn't deserve her.

"She'll be back," Joy said. "She's pack now. Pack always finds their way home."

"Only if they want to." Gray turned and stormed back to the house, Maizie's sad, wounded eyes flashing through his thoughts. Jeezus, he'd been an ass to let her leave like that.

He could fix this. He'd grab a quick shower, throw on some fresh clothes and go find her. He could explain why he'd spent the past twenty-one years blaming his loneliness and domestic imprisonment on a child.

Yeah. Then I'll tell her it was my fault Donna ran off that night. Gray set the water temperature for the shower. *Hell, if it weren't for me her parents would still be alive. And last night never would've happened.*

No. No matter how hard he tried or how much he thought he should, he couldn't regret last night. It had been too perfect.

The warning beep sounded. A half second later the front, sides and top showerheads burst with steaming water. He stepped in, bent his head back and let the water cascade over his head and body.

Images of Maizie bombarded his thoughts, those pretty green eyes, the way they wrinkled at the corners when she smiled at him and turned a shade darker when she was angry. He could almost feel the soft touch of her kiss and her cloak of red hair slipping through his fingers.

The feel of her firm round breasts squeezing in his palms, the fast pucker of her nipples. His hand smoothing over her belly, slipping between her thighs to her hot wet sex.

Jeezus, she was amazing in bed. She didn't just show up, she joined in, giving as good as she got.

His thoughts shifted, purposely remembering her eyes peering up at him with her pink lips wrapped around his cock. Her mouth was so hot and moist, his cock sliding through those soft lips, sucking him back in again and again.

Gray put his hand where her mouth had been, stroking his shaft. He was hard as stone with just the memory of her mouth on him. His balls tight, he brought his free hand to fondle them. A steady thrum of pleasure rippled through his body, his balls rolling through his fingers, muscles pulling the sac tighter. He gripped his shaft harder, pumping over the head and back, rocking his hips.

Thoughts and memories slipped through his mind, coming to the forefront then receding while another image took its place. Maizie, her ripe body pinned beneath him, his hard shaft slamming into her pussy, so tight and wet, rocking up to meet him. The walls of her sex squeezed around him, the sensitive head of his cock pushing through the muscles the same way it pushed through his hand now.

No. Not the same. His imagination wasn't that good. He looked at his hand gripping his cock, water pattering over his fingers, keeping the taut flesh slick as he stroked. But what he felt was Maizie's pussy squeezing him, her hot cream wetting his balls, her ass slamming into him as he pumped.

"What the fuck?" He stopped, his hands dropping, leaving his cock to wag in front of him. A heartbeat passed, and when the invisible muscles suddenly squeezed around him, he nearly came.

"Jeezus..." He pushed his hips forward, just as he would if Maizie's pussy was there to beg him in. Hot moist walls hugged around his cock, stroking him, holding tight as he pulled back. He braced his hands on the shower walls, watching his hard penis as he drove his hips into thin air, but felt the unmistakable sensation of a woman's pussy—Maizie's sex—give way.

He pumped again, and then again. He couldn't help it. The sensation was too good. Waves of pleasure rippled through his body with each thrust, humming over his skin, building in the tightening sac of his balls.

Gray didn't have a clue how this was happening, what was happening, but then he didn't really care. He rocked his hips, thrust his cock into nothing, but felt the welcoming squeeze of Maizie's pussy. He held tight to the showerheads on either wall, braced his feet and let the strange phenomenon take him over.

His head lolled back, the warm water of the shower enveloping him as he fucked his invisible Maizie harder, faster. Thoughts of her supple breasts pressed into his palms filled his mind, her nipples squeezed between his fingers. The feel of her lips on his, the sweet taste of her mouth, her skin, as he drove himself deeper inside her.

"Maizie..."

"Gray..." She wanted him—now. The gentle thrum of shower water was a poor substitute. It massaged along her body, trickling over her nipples and wetting between her thighs, but it was little more than a tease.

Gawd, he'd crushed her earlier with those accusing pale blue eyes and that cold heartless silence. How dare he blame her? Losing his wife was clearly difficult, but she'd lost her parents. Did he have a clue how hard that was for a seven-year-old girl?

She'd blamed that wolf, all wolves, for years. Now she knew it was his wife who'd raced out in front of their car. It was an accident, and she suspected Gray understood that too, but the randomness of it all was so hard to accept. She'd spent so many years pointing a finger, needing to blame someone for the injustice. Would it have been any different for Gray?

The realization left her numb. His cold eyes left her aching. She didn't want to want him, to feel his warm arms around her, his mouth on her breast, the teasing draw on her nipple. She wanted to stay mad at him, but she'd seen the guilt in his eyes and knew the power of it. She'd felt the same kind of gnawing guilt—that Granny had wasted her golden years raising her. She'd do anything to escape that feeling. Even blame someone else for it if she could.

Gray was caught in the same heartbreaking trap of guilt and blame as she was. But at least in his arms Maizie had found relief. A sense that there was a reason behind it all, a reason her parents died on that forest road—his forest. It linked them forever and always. She wanted that feeling now. She wanted him.

Maizie closed her eyes, imagined his hand tracing over her skin. She mimicked the picture in her mind with her own hand, feathering over her collarbone, down her chest to her breast. She cupped herself, her fingers finding the hard pucker of her nipples, squeezing as she slid her other hand between her thighs.

The thought of him had her pussy hot and wet. He looked older than her, but only by a few years. She knew now it was probably much more. His shoulder-length hair with its distinguished silvery gray color, his face showing the light creases of wisdom and age, made his virile body all the more surprising. He had the endurance and flexibility of a man half his age, but the control of a seasoned pro.

The memory of him standing naked before her flashed through her mind. His fit body like a soccer player, thick muscled legs, ripped stomach, defined pecs and arms like cannons. He was built for speed, endurance and power. And he'd used it all to fuck her senseless, make her scream his name.

Maizie leaned against the wall, the shower curtain molding over her back and down her legs to the tub. She dipped her fingers into her sex, curling inside, trying to find the spot Gray had found again and again.

She caught her bottom lip between her teeth, pumping her fingers in and out of her pussy, imagining the feel of his fat cock ramming deep inside her, filling her. Maizie pinched her nipple, the nub hard and sensitive between her fingers.

"Damn it, Gray. I want you."

Maizie gasped, pushing to her tiptoes with a sudden hard thrust between her thighs. All at once her pussy was filled to the brim, her fingers still buried deep inside her. She pulled her hand away but the sensation didn't change. Staring wide eyed at the dark red thatch of hair between her legs, her brain dizzied with the first rush of panic. But then a slow withdrawal pulled a toe-curling tingle through her body and panic gave way to desire.

Her hands fisted the shower curtain as the invisible shaft plowed deep into her again. "Oh God..." Just the way Gray's thick cock had pounded into her last night, stretching her muscles, an exquisitely tight fit.

The thrusts jarred her body an instant before the warm moist feel of a mouth covered her breasts. One for each breast, suckling them, firm tongues flicking the hardened nipples, teeth scraping, teasing, sending electric jolts tingling along her skin.

Maizie closed her eyes, her head leaned back against the wall. She bucked her hips, riding the rhythm of Gray's invisible cock, pressure building deep inside her, a need winding tighter and tighter.

How was it happening? It felt so real. Was it? Could he really do this? She should be scared, but it felt too good, imagining his kiss, his firm lips on hers, the quick dart of his tongue into her mouth, the gentle scrape of his teeth. She could feel it and she wanted more. She remembered how he'd gasped when she teased his nipple and wished she could do it again.

She licked her lips and felt the firm wrinkled skin of his nipple, the little hardened nub. She bit, gentle, then drew it into her mouth.

Gray gasped, the draw on his nipple pulling the muscles in his groin tight. Damn, he'd liked it when she'd done that last night and liked it even more as he imagined it now. It felt real.

He thrust his hips, keeping the rhythm, his balls slapping against his thighs, imagining himself slapping against her ass. He'd come like this, fucking thin air, feeling he was fucking Maizie. He could feel her breast in his palm, squeezing the supple flesh, loving the way it molded in his grip. He felt her lips on his, her tongue teasing his mouth even as another zing of pleasure shot from his nipple to his cock.

Her pussy muscles squeezed and pulsed around him, building the pressure in his balls, driving him fast toward the ragged edge of release. Jeezus, he wanted to fuck her inside and out, everywhere, every way. Gray thought of the firm round of her ass and instantly felt the smooth skin on his palm. He squeezed, the muscles taut, he imagined his fingers slipping around to the crease between her cheeks, sliding further to the tight hole of her anus.

Would she want this? Would she allow it? Screw it, this was his fantasy and he wanted it so bad he could actually feel his finger slip through the tight barrier.

"No...yesss..." The strange mix of pain and pleasure rolled her eyes back. Maizie panted, the overfull sensation in her ass melding with the fullness of her pussy. She rocked her hips, her anus slicked, and the rhythm suddenly came easy. Uncomfortable tightness gave way to luscious dueling strokes, muscles tingling with sensations she'd never known possible.

She reached for the curtain rod, desperate to ground herself against the fast whirl of need building inside her, shaking her thighs, flexing her pussy, slicking her ass. She would come this way. Nothing touching her, but feeling utterly consumed with sensation.

"Oh God..." Her mouth gaped, hips bucking, legs wide. The promise of release was coming hard and fast.

Gray's jaw clenched, his hands gripped tight on the showerheads, his cock pumping hard. Hot wet pussy muscles hugged around him, pulsed against his cock teasing him closer and closer to the edge. His finger pushed deep in her ass, feeling the virgin muscles give way to him.

She was close. He could feel it.

And so was he.

But she was just a figment of his mind.

This was all in her mind, wasn't it? The feel of him, the undeniable pleasure, the coming release.

She didn't care.

He didn't care. He'd lasted as long as he could, longer than he needed since he had no one to please but himself. But those invisible muscles squeezed, begged him to hold on. His phantom Maizie demanding he last just a little longer. Every instinct inside him promised her pleasure, her release, would make his all the more mind-blowing.

Muscles coaxed him faster and faster. She was coming.

Maizie's breath seized, her body froze, allowing the invisible cock's frantic pace to pound her over the edge. Sweet release, coming hard and fast, rolled through her muscles, the force of it trembling through her knees. Her body hummed, skin hot, heart hammering in her ears.

"Yes. Yes!" Alone in the house she screamed the words with abandon, reeling in the uninhibited orgasm. She was panting, trying to catch her breath, but her phantom Gray's pace never faltered, his thrusts coming harder and harder.

His cock thickened. He was coming.

Not a second longer. The needy pussy milked his last thread of control and Gray let go. The hard rush of pleasure, of pent-up denial, nearly swept him away. A wash of heat stormed through his body, rocked through his mind. His hips pumped his cock, shooting his creamy white come on the back wall of the shower.

"Oh, yeah. Fuck. Me. Yeah!" He rammed his cock again and again, bucking his hips until every last drop of his load emptied out of him. Then he slumped between the showerheads—boneless, exhausted, satiated.

"Wow." Maizie stumbled under the spray of water turned cold, doing her best to stand on rubbery legs while she washed away the sticky results of her orgasm. Her breasts were tender, her pussy sore, as though she'd actually just been fucked—and good.

It didn't make sense, wasn't possible, but then again neither were werewolves. Gawd, what was wrong with her? How much time had she wasted masturbating in the shower, fantasizing about Gray? All the while, poor Granny struggled through the trauma of a near-death experience alone.

Was she worried, wondering why her Little Red wasn't at her side? How would Maizie explain about the strange allure she felt for Gray Lupo despite their macabre connection? How would she explain about the attack, the sex, the werewolves? What would she say?

"You've been bitten." Granny pushed up in bed as the door to her suite drifted closed behind Maizie. Her withered hand trembled, gesturing for Maizie to come closer.

Maizie shook off her surprise and strode across the room. She took her hand. "I'm fine, Gran. It's just a scratch. You're the one I'm worried about. I'm so sorry I wasn't here when they took you to the hospital."

"Bah! Never mind that. Fieldtrip. The hospital has the best pound cake on Thursday nights."

"Gran—"

"How'd it happen? Why? Did he explain everything? The book says the first time's the hardest." Her eyes wide, back straight, Granny was the most lucid Maizie had seen her in years, and she didn't have a clue what she was talking about. "It'll hurt, y'know, the first time."

"What will hurt? Explain about what?"

"About... Maizie, dear, where is he?"

"Who?"

"Gray Lupo, of course. You don't know any other werewolves, do you?" Her tone made it clear she was joking, but when Maizie didn't answer, Granny drew her own conclusions.

Voices in the hall pulled Maizie's attention. Geez, why were they talking so loud? She could hear the nurse talking to Mr. Peterman in the hallway like they were both in the room. And who was pounding on the piano? Had they put a microphone inside the baby grand? Of course they'd need a microphone on the piano to be heard over the pots and pans being slammed around in the kitchen. God, why was it so noisy at Green Acres today? How could anyone think—

"So you've met the whole family then," Granny said, adjusting the flowered quilt covering her from the waist down.

"What?" Maizie snapped her attention back to her grandmother.

"Gray's family," she said. "Joy's a nice-enough lady and the twins are polite, but I can't say I like that Lynn too much. Always trying to get into Gray's drawers. He's a widower, for heaven's sake, and her brother-in-law."

"You knew? About all of them? All this time?" Someone flushed a toilet, the sound of swishing water echoed through Maizie's head.

"Why, yes, dear. So did you. I've told you about my beautiful silver wolf hundreds of times." Her brow wrinkled, her voice taking on that careful tone people use with small children and the mentally unstable. "How did you think he got the violets in the vase and cleaned out the gutters?"

Someone yelled "bingo" and Maizie glanced around the room for the speaker. There was no one, though several people voiced their congratulations to Millie, whoever that was. "I...I thought you were..."

"One brick shy of a full load?"

"Yeah." Although now she was wondering the same thing about herself. "I mean, I thought it was one of your spells."

Maizie collapsed into the bedside chair, resisting the urge to cup her hands over her ears. What was happening? Pain twisted her stomach, made her cross her arms over her belly instead, holding tight. It was the first cramp since her shower, but it seemed to hurt twice as bad. She grimaced, rode the pain, waiting for it to subside.

"It's starting already," Granny said with a nod to Maizie's belly.

"What?" Maizie squirmed in her seat. The pain dulled but still hadn't completely gone.

"The change. The change is starting. Good gravy, he really didn't explain anything?"

"Gran—"

"Well, dear, I'm sorry. But you shouldn't have let him turn you without asking a few questions. You wouldn't hop into bed without discovering the important things about a man first, would you?"

Important things like he blamed her for his wife's death and that he was the very thing she'd spent her life despising? *Apparently, I would.*

"How did you know I'd been bitten?" A sly subject change. Maizie hoped Granny wouldn't push her to admit *all* the careless things she'd done last night.

"I can see it in your eyes." Granny leaned toward Maizie, staring at her eyes but not into them. "They have that wild look. Quick, larger pupils, like you see everything."

Maizie wasn't sure about that. At the moment she was too busy noticing how the dull pain in her stomach had spread to her legs and arms. Her muscles ached as though they'd been sorely overworked. And the racket of the nursing home was becoming damn near deafening.

"You smell like him too."

"What?"

"You must have noticed it. It's such a wonderful smell, like earth and trees and wind. I can smell that on you now. But that's normal for werewolves."

"Werewolves..." Maizie still couldn't fully wrap her brain around it. "Gran, how do you know about all this?"

Granny opened the drawer of her nightstand and pulled out an old leather-backed book. She handed it to Maizie. "Gray gave it to me years ago when your grand-dad passed. He offered to take me into his pack. Tells you everything. I can't believe he didn't at least warn you about the first change."

"It wasn't Gray."

"What? Then who? What happened?" Granny's face paled.

"Don't worry. I'm sure Gray took care of it. He took care of me. But then we got distracted." He was too busy fucking her blind to tell her she'd been turned into a werewolf. "And then I just...I didn't stick around."

"Well, I can't imagine what could possibly distract him from something so important. What..." Her cheeks flushed. "Oh. Yes, well... A highly amorous nature is normal too."

"It tells you that in here?" Maizie read the cover. "*The Wolf Curse* by Gervase of Tilbury, in the year of our Lord twelve-hundred and fourteen."

"Some of it's bullshit, of course."

"Gran." The woman hardly ever swore which made the rare occasions all the more surprising.

"They were afraid of their own shadows back then. And it's not a curse. It's a virus. You come down with the full-blown disease first, like chickenpox, before your body creates antibodies to control it. After that you can change back and forth at will. The rest of the book is fairly accurate, I'm told. Pack law, instinct, tradition. You should read it before things progress too far."

"Great." She felt like crap, achy, sick to her stomach, overwhelmed by all manner of noises, and now she had homework. Maizie shivered, her skin tingling. She checked her arm to make sure it only *felt* like ants crawling all over her. "I have to get home."

"Yes, dear. I heartily agree. Read the book or find Gray. Your choice, Little Red."

Something told her the time for choices had just run out.

Chapter Eleven

Her body was trying to turn itself inside out...through her bellybutton.

Maizie snuggled tighter into a ball on the couch, tugging the blanket under her chin. The cottage was full of shadows, the sun nearly set. The temperature on the hummingbird thermometer suctioned to the window read eighty-two degrees, but Maizie was shivering so hard her teeth chattered.

This was worse than the time she'd caught the flu and had to be hospitalized for a day and a half while the worst of it passed. They'd been afraid she might die. What did that say about her chances now?

Another shard of pain tore through her abdomen, like a chainsaw slicing her from navel to neck. She screamed, but the sound was hoarse, the last half hour had ruined her voice. She should've called Gray. But what could he have done except watch? She'd already thrown up until there was nothing left inside her. No one needed to see that.

Her body convulsed, every muscle pulled tight then stretched apart. The blanket flew across the living room, falling behind the chair in the corner. Dear God, she was freezing, even as sweat dripped from her chin and nose. She couldn't stop shivering and when another wave of pain raked through her body she found herself writhing on the floor.

Her hair was sopping wet, long strands clinging to her face, stuck to her neck and dripping little puddles on the floor. She pushed up, locked her elbows then rested there for a second trying to find a moment's peace. Her body wouldn't have it.

"Ohmygod, ohmygod. Something's happening." She collapsed.

If it was possible to survive every bone in her body being broken simultaneously and rearranged, muscles ripping from tendons, organs shifting, cartilage growing, stretching her skin—if it was possible to survive her own autopsy—Maizie now knew what it would feel like.

Her mouth opened on a voiceless wail as she watched her fingers shrink, the bones in her arm pulling back, reshaping. She could feel each thick hair poke through her skin like fat needles forcing their way through the smaller follicles.

She screamed again when the cartilage of her nose crumbled and reshaped, stretching her flesh, her jaw thrusting out, teeth sharpening, ripping her gums as they grew. But the sound wasn't her own, or at least none she'd ever heard herself make before. It was a crazed, high-pitched screech that hollowed toward the end.

Her spine arched one way then the other, bones breaking along her back, reshaping, pushing beneath the sensitive flesh above her ass.

"No. Please...a tail." Tears stained her face, but she couldn't feel the moisture through the fur. Her legs transformed just as her arms had, the pain just as excruciating.

And then...finally it stopped.

Maizie lay motionless on the floor next to the living room couch. Her eyes closed, she panted, trying hard to catch her breath. The pain had lasted a lifetime. It took several minutes to trust it wasn't coming back.

She licked her lips, except she didn't have any. Teeth, long and sharp, scraped along her tongue. She licked again and nearly touched the top of her nose. The fur was rough against her tongue, salty from sweat and tears.

She opened her eyes, almost crossed them trying to see the long muzzle where her nose had been. Something scurried along the foundation of the house. She listened and felt her ears turn. She shook her head at the strange sensation and got to her feet, shaky at first, the center of balance so different from two feet to four. Her shorts were crumpled around her back feet, and what was left of her T-shirt still hung around her neck.

She tried her best to paw the torn fabric and managed to catch her claw in the collar and rip it the rest of the way. She made a mental note to be naked next time this happened. The thought stopped her for a second. She knew there'd be a next time.

Free, she shook herself. *Yuck.* It was too weird. Her thick heavy fur slid her skin back and forth on her neck. A shudder traveled from her shoulders over her back and down her tail.

The tail. She'd almost forgotten. Maizie twisted, trying to see her ass, but when she turned, her backside followed. She circled again, catching only a glimpse of reddish fur and maybe a hint of strawberry blonde at the tip. She couldn't be sure. If she could just get a better look.

Shoot, how do you work a tail? She tried wagging it as she circled around but that took more coordination than she'd mastered at the moment. She kept trying to see though, circling and straining, straining and circling, but she couldn't quite catch her... *Oh God, I'm chasing my tail.*

She stopped, thankful no one had seen her. *I'm an intelligent humanish-being. I can figure this out. Now, if I want to see myself I—*

Something was in the flowers right outside the sunroom. Maizie lifted her head and sniffed. *Deer. And it's upwind. I could catch it if I...*

No. Wait. She was thinking of something else a minute ago. What was it?

Her butt smacked against the couch and then again. But she hadn't moved her butt. She curled her neck around toward her rump and saw a flash of strawberry blonde fur swing out at the tip of her tail. *I'm wagging my tail. Cool. How?*

The instant she thought about it though, her tail stopped. *Shoot.* She'd only gotten a quick look. She wanted to see more. *That's it!* She'd been trying to think of a way to see herself without running around in circles. *A mirror.*

Sheesh, what was the matter with her? Why couldn't she keep a straight thought in her head? Maizie turned and headed for the stairs, amazed how quick and easy she moved now that she had four feet to climb with instead of two.

There were so many scents, so many sounds, even everyday things captivated her curiosity. It was all she could do not to sniff in the wastebasket when she went into the bathroom.

She nudged the door with her nose so she could see herself in the full-length mirror behind it. But when the reflection showed a tall, rusty-brown wolf, she panicked. The hairs down her back to her haunches bristled, a snarl vibrated her jowls, bared her teeth. The rust-colored wolf snarled right back, mimicking her low crouch, baring its teeth.

She could fight or run. This was her den. She wasn't running anywhere.

Maizie leapt at the wolf and the wolf leapt at her. They collided hard, a spider-web crack shattering where their heads

185

met. Maizie stumbled back, shook her head and saw the rust-brown wolf do the same. She snorted, and so did her reflection.

Ugh. What was she thinking? No. The problem was she wasn't thinking. She was acting on instinct, wolf instinct. It was more powerful than anything she'd felt as a human and surprisingly hard to ignore. She'd have to keep that in mind as best she could.

Maizie took a better look at herself. She made a big wolf, probably normal for werewolves, but scary big for a natural wolf. Her fur had a darker cast than her normal hair except for the strawberry blonde on the tips of her ears and tail, which she could now see if she bent around at the right angle.

Her eyes were the same green they'd always been, but the shape was different, more almond-like, longer. Maybe that's why her vision seemed clearer.

Holy cow, it was hot. Her mouth lolled open as she watched, her tongue flopping out to the side. She panted, stopped herself, and then did it anyway. It cooled her and it was better than drinking out of the toilet which was another horrifying urge pounding through her brain. She had to get out of the cottage before she did something completely gross.

Maizie nudged the door open with her nose and jogged down the stairs. Her heart beat faster at just the thought of open air, free space to run, a forest to explore. She wound through the living room into the sunroom then out the back door. The screen door smacked closed against the wood frame behind her, giving her a start, but she kept moving.

The sun was below the horizon, its soft glow fading fast. Beyond the threshold to the forest, it was as good as full night, and Maizie could see perfectly. No wonder she hadn't been able to escape Gray's family last night. She'd been running blind while they'd toyed with her. *Jerks.*

She pushed the thought away, allowing the night to steal her focus. The forest was alive before her, not just teeming with a billion heartbeats but with colors and scents and sounds. So many things were endlessly fascinating, the army of ants marching in streaming lines carrying bark and leaves and bug carcasses.

The pungent odor of a skunk that'd passed by hours ago took her one way before the trail of a groundhog and her young turned her around.

An owl called to its mate overhead and a bat swooped so low she tried to jump and catch it. A crop of purple wood violets scented the air in one spot and a patch of bunchberries had her stomach growling in another. She could actually taste sweet tree sap on her muzzle and the bitter flavor of fox spray by accident.

Somewhere deep in the forest, a buck scraped his antlers on a tree and three does in season stirred, waiting for his arrival. Maizie's heart raced, her muscles jittery, anxious for the hunt. If she chased them they'd run. She probably couldn't catch them, but it didn't matter. They'd run.

The thought entered her mind and her body obeyed. She sliced through the forest with a speed and grace that defied reason, defied gravity. She knew things, where the log she couldn't see lay across her path up ahead, how low the thorny limbs of a branch dangled in the darkness, which stones to hit across the stream that wouldn't topple her into the water.

She knew when to veer to the left, duck to the right or change direction to save time in the long run. The forest spoke to her, told her its secrets, welcomed her into its fold. Nature, the forest, the plants and animals, they were parts of the whole and so was she.

The deer were beyond a thicket five hundred yards away,

grazing on the sparse grass of the forest floor. They hadn't smelled her approaching downwind or heard her running with stealth, keeping to the soft earth and plants. She slowed, scented the wind, pinpointing their exact location without ever seeing them.

Yes. They were there, a yearling and two older does. Two were late in their cycle, the third was primed for mating. All this came to Maizie on the air, but there was something else, something familiar but out of place.

Cranberry apple walnut tart. She'd brought three for Granny yesterday. The scent was unique, but diluted by distance. Granny must have the screen in her window and the tarts nearby. Maizie wanted to see Gran and so she turned from the deer to go to her. That simple. That uncomplicated. Her wolf instinct made decisions easy but something in the back of her mind niggled that easy wasn't the same as best.

It was too difficult to think about now. Maizie was lost in the fast rush of sensation, floating through the forest, her leg muscles pumping like the pistons of a finely tuned engine. One with the forest, she weaved and jumped, turned to the left, veered to the right, moving seamlessly through the dark woods. It was like nothing she'd ever known and she never wanted it to end. But when she broke through the line of the forest into the backyard of Green Acres Nursing Home, everything changed.

Head low, she loped along the shadows, weaving her way to the edge of the building. The glass doors along the back wall of the home were all closed, but the corner lights inside cast a soft honey glow and lit the recreation room enough Maizie could see the group of people gathered around a TV. She crept out from the corner, the light inside and the dark of night making her virtually invisible.

Maizie looked for a familiar face, worried her wolf brain

wouldn't know her grandmother when she saw her. She glanced at the elderly men sleeping in twin recliners and paused only a minute to study the features of the woman between them knitting. There was a woman in the far rocking chair reading beneath one of the corner lamps and another sitting on a love seat hand in hand with a tender-looking elderly man. These two were the only ones of the group who seemed to be watching the exuberant TV evangelist. But Maizie didn't recognize them. She didn't recognize any of them.

Granny, where are you? Maizie's brain was fuzzy, filled with intoxicating scents and sounds, with the instincts of her wolf-half. There was just too much, too many distractions. But she knew what Granny looked like, didn't she? Yes. She remembered her, the way she made Maizie feel, what she meant to her. None of these people were Granny.

Maizie turned and jogged along the building, avoiding the cast of light spilling from the windows. She followed the edge around corners, into the alcoves and out again. She finally made it to the back of the building where four windows were spaced evenly along the façade. The first overlooked the backyard, but the forest edged close to the last three. *Granny's suite.*

The light from Granny's room cast a wash of light into the forest, illuminating a matching rectangle of foliage. Maizie circled out to the edge of the light, careful not to be seen.

Granny's lace curtains were drawn, but the heavy toile drapes were pulled back to the sides, exposing the room to anyone who cared to see.

Granny. Maizie knew her instantly. The old woman sat in her hospital-style bed, the top section angled up so she could watch TV. A remote control in one hand, she held a fork in the other, poised over a cranberry apple walnut tart waiting on a rolling tray table over the bed. Her feet wiggled a happy rhythm under the blanket, her mouth curled in a half smile, still working on her last bite.

She was happy and Maizie's muscles relaxed, releasing a tension she hadn't noticed before. Granny was safe and cared for in case this transformation didn't reverse itself. Maizie shuddered at the thought.

She wasn't stuck like this, was she? The old stories always had some poor hapless sap who'd gotten himself bitten returning to his human form. Reclaiming his life was a struggle, but he always tried, always wallowed in denial.

Of course most often he didn't succeed and wound up transforming at the worst possible moment. The villagers would storm and the hapless sap would mindlessly attack some innocent child, giving good reason for his brutal death.

Maizie shuddered again and made a mental note to stop watching so many horror flicks. She'd be fine. This couldn't possibly be a permanent state and villagers hardly ever stormed these days.

Granny took another dainty bite of tart, her smile broadening as the pastry passed her lips. She leaned her head back, dancing her fork in the air like a conductor. Maizie never realized how long and lovely Granny's hair was. Like a blanket of fine white snow, it lay in a shimmering sheet down her back to her bum. White curls pooled around her hips, tiny wisps tickling her cheeks.

Gawd, she meant the world to Maizie. Why hadn't she got one last hug, one last feathery kiss? She wanted to hear Granny's voice, to feel her soft hand smoothing over her cheek, telling her life was more than loss and heartache. She wanted to go to her now.

Maizie took a step, her front paws and head bathed in the

light from Granny's room. She stopped, instinct warring with human want. She couldn't. The fear was too great. Her wolf-half wasn't ready to trust humans, even the ones she loved.

She backed up, stealing into the shadows again. *Another time.* If she stayed this way, Maizie would keep trying to overcome the scream of her wolf instincts. But for now, even if the worst happened—furry wolf parts forever, rampaging villagers, whatever—Maizie knew Granny was safe.

A knock sounded at Granny's door and riveted Maizie's attention.

"Come in," Granny said, the words more sung than stated.

The door opened and a dark-haired man poked his head through the crack. "Hey, Mom. Were mwap sleeping?"

"Riddly?" Granny's hand dropped to the bed, fork, remote and MTV forgotten. "No...no. I'm mwap. Is that mwap, Riddly?"

Maizie's wolf brain struggled with the words. *Daddy?* Maizie edged forward, light touching her toes and muzzle. The man smiled, stepped in and closed the door behind him.

"How's my mwap girl?" Handsome, sophisticated in his tailored business suit, the man was familiar, but Maizie wasn't sure why. He was thickly built, like a tall wrestler, with broad shoulders, a squared jaw and a prominent Romanic nose. He was graying at the temples, the dull color all the more noticeable against the sheer blackness of his neatly trimmed hair.

He kept his right hand hidden behind him as he came across the room to Granny. When he reached her bedside, he leaned in and kissed her forehead then offered the bouquet of white roses he was hiding.

Maizie snorted. They were beautiful, but they weren't Granny's favorite. *Violets.* Granny would do anything for a handful of violets. Maizie's thoughts were proven by Granny's placating expression.

"Oh, mwap mwap, dear. They're mwap. Could you mwap them in mwap mwap me? There's a mwap in the mwap mwap." Granny shook her fork toward the bathroom door.

"Sure, Mom."

That man was not Riddly Hood. Maizie's father never would've brought his mother the wrong flowers. A strange vibration hummed in her chest, a low growl filled her ears. It took a second to realize the growl was coming from inside her, anger manifesting in her new wolf form. She liked it.

The moment the strange imposter left the room, Granny fumbled at her chest. She found her locket and worked hard to open it. A wide sentimental grin filled her face, a sadness pinching the corner of her eyes as she gazed at the pictures inside.

"I, ah, brought mwap papers we mwap about," the man said from the bathroom.

Granny hurried to close the locket, fisting it in her hand before he strolled back into the room, vase overflowing with roses. He paused for a moment, his gaze studying her face then dropping to her hands at her chest. His expression darkened, his smile suddenly more stiff, forced.

"What'ya mwap there, Mom?"

"Mwap nothing, mwap." But the phony Riddly's attention was riveted. He set the vase on Granny's nightstand and reached for her hands.

The growl vibrating through Maizie grew louder. She took another bold step into the light.

Granny giggled. Let him open her hands. "Just mwap mwap locket. The picture's so old. You hardly look like yourself. And look at little Maizie. Barely five years old."

The man studied the pictures, his thick black brows wrinkled tight over his dark eyes. But then he smiled, closed the locket and placed it gently on her chest. "That picture mwap mwap ages ago. I looked mwap a different person mwap then."

Granny nodded, her smile bright. "Still handsome mwap mwap, though."

"Thanks, Mom." The man slipped a hand into the breast pocket of his suit and pulled out a thin stack of papers folded long-ways. He set them on the tray next to Granny's tart then placed a thick fancy pen beside them.

"Mwap I miss mwap top twenty mwap?" He nodded toward the TV.

"Mwap on sixteen. Sit, sit, mwap a little mwap mwap with mwap old mwap," Granny said.

"Old." He scoffed. "You'll mwap mwap us all." He pulled the storage bench from around the end of her bed then dragged one of the high-backed chairs closer. He dropped into it with a casualness that belied his sophisticated attire and propped his expensive leather-shoed feet on the bench.

What were the papers he talked about, the ones sitting conspicuously on Granny's tray? And who the hell was he anyway? There was something familiar about him, but her wolf brain wouldn't make the connection. It didn't matter. Everything inside Maizie told her she needed to get him away from Granny. Even her wolf-half agreed.

She backed into the shadows again, jogging toward the end of the building. Maybe she could find a door propped open or slip in behind someone else. She had to get to Granny, protect her, despite her instinctive fear of humans.

She edged along the building, skirting the pockets of light as best she could. She turned a final corner where the forest and grass ended. Her toes edged against the wide expanse of blacktop. Before her, the parking lot of Green Acres Nursing Home stretched between her and the front door.

The forest encircled Green Acres on three sides, leaving the front façade and the parking lot exposed. The lot was lit like daylight by three enormous lights placed just right to keep shadows at bay. Beyond the parking lot, directly across from the nursing home, cars whizzed by on a busy two-lane road, and on the other side of that, the night evaporated in the glow of human encroachment. A restaurant, a grocery store, a gas station and more—the edge of civilization on one side, acres and acres of forest behind her. Maizie wanted to turn back so badly her muscles ached from the restraint.

Granny. She needed her and Maizie took a tentative step. The black ground was warm on her pads, still holding the heat from a sunny day. She moved farther, her gaze fixed on the glass entrance. Inside she could see the front desk and a familiar face seated behind it. What was her name?

It didn't matter. She wouldn't recognize Maizie like this anyway. Maizie kept moving slow and steady. She stayed low to the ground, crouched, trying to be smaller, less noticeable. It was pointless, she knew, she was utterly exposed.

A car door slammed and Maizie froze, heart pounding. Her gaze darted over the parking lot, five cars. Her ears twitched, she sniffed. Nothing. Muscles tensed, wanting to run, but she didn't move.

"Maizie?"

She knew that voice, deep and rich, soothing like...

"It's mwap...Gray. Mwap it easy, mwap mwap?"

Gray? Maizie followed the voice with her eyes. She found him standing next to a long black car parked by the forest on the other side. She watched him, his hands low, out from his body as though he meant to seem less threatening. Her instincts weren't buying it.

She sniffed again and picked up only a hint of his scent when the wind shifted around, bouncing off the building. Mmmm...she knew that smell, earth and plants, the forest, but there was more. A hint of sweetness, human cologne. Maizie's wolf-half balked at the odor, edging backward.

"No. Wait." He stopped moving. "I mwap help. Let mwap mwap with you."

Maizie knew the words, but couldn't wrap her wolf brain around their meaning. He was human. She didn't trust humans. She moved another step back.

"Jeezus, you mwap mwap beautiful animal. I know mwap, scared and you're mwap mwap mwap half of mwap mwap saying, but mwap mwap be mwap mwap running mwap alone."

Maizie took another step back. Why was she even out in the open like this? Where was she going? She couldn't remember. It didn't matter. She had to get away. She had to run, her instincts demanded it and they were too hard to ignore.

She turned, but something about the human stopped her. She looked back and saw his face contorting, changing shape. He stripped out of his shirt, popping buttons, throwing the remains to the ground. He moved to his pants, working his buckle and zipper even as he toed off his shoes. He was naked in seconds, his body shrinking, skin rolling as though his bones moved and reshaped beneath the flesh.

Thick silvery fur sprouted over his shoulders, rippled down his chest to his belly, hiding his penis and balls in an instant. He fell forward, his arms and legs changing to paws before they touched the ground. Just like that he was a wolf.

He snorted with a hard shake of his head, pausing as though he needed a moment to recoup. Then his pale blue wolf eyes focused on her and he sauntered forward. Maizie's muscles twitched, the urge to run screaming loud in her head.

Yes, he was a wolf, but he was a male wolf. The apprehension remained, only the reasons for it had changed. This wasn't her territory and she knew with a shift of the wind it was his. She'd detected his scent all over the forest. This place belonged to him and his pack. She was an outsider. If she were male, she'd likely already be dead. As a female there were choices—for him, not her.

He could attack, deciding he had enough females in his pack and dominating another wasn't worth the trouble. Or he could take her now, possess her, claim her as his own. Either way, Maizie would have little to say in the matter. He was at least six inches taller at the shoulder and a solid fifty pounds heavier. His decision would be absolute.

A warm shudder tickled under her fur down her back. Even in wolf form the thought of him taking her was an erotic temptation. But until she knew his intentions, complete passivity could be fatal.

Maizie lowered her shoulders, her ears pinned back against her head. She growled, bared her teeth. Gray stopped his slow approach, his pale eyes fixed on her, judging her intentions just as she judged his.

He was too far away, his body language ambivalent. She'd have to allow him closer to be sure, close enough to strike. She couldn't take that chance. Her wolf-half wouldn't allow it.

Maizie spun, springing off her powerful back legs, pumping her front legs to propel her forward, away from the male aggressor. She didn't know where she was going. It didn't matter as long as she got away.

Her nails clawed at the blacktop, slipping when they couldn't dig in. Gray's nails clattered behind her, giving chase without hesitation. She glanced back, saw his body eating the distance between them, his pale blue eyes alight with fury. He'd overtake her in seconds.

Panic clogged her throat, hammered through her heart, pumped her legs harder, faster. She shifted her attention forward, ready to throw herself into the run.

Lights. Blinding. Two brilliant orbs barreling toward her. Thunder rumbled behind them, vibrating through her brain. Maizie gasped, a sharp high-pitched yip. She tried to stop, throwing her weight backward, her paws scrambling to slow her momentum.

Gray's heavy body collided with her, unable to shift speed and direction any better than she. The impact knocked the air from her lungs, both of them tumbling off the blacktop onto soft grass. Maizie found her center and stopped her roll just in time to pull her nose out of the way of the minivan rolling up the driveway.

Twisting hard, throwing her head and neck, Maizie got her feet under her. Adrenaline surged through her body, giving her a dizzying high while she puzzled what to do next. Where was the male? Nothing mattered more.

A low growl turned her around, the sound so visceral it vibrated through her flesh and bone, stuttering the beat of her heart. She peered into the forest, trying hard to pinpoint the sound. Full dark made for a night blacker than pitch, even for her enhanced wolf eyesight. Straining, she managed to catch a subtle shift of movement behind a cluster of trees and focused her gaze as the soft glow of pale blue eyes broke the curtain of black.

Gray's silvery fur caught the light. The chase was on.

Chapter Twelve

He'd saved her life, knocking her out of the way when her animal instincts froze in the headlights. Normally that should have earned him some points but Gray knew Maizie's fevered wolf brain wasn't up to the logic. Once her body manufactured enough antibodies to break her fever, she'd shift back to human form. Unfortunately, there was no way for Gray to know how long that would take.

Maizie crouched, ears pinned back, belly nearly touching the grass. She bared her teeth, growled at him, warning she'd fight or run if he dared to approach. Protecting her until her fever broke wasn't going to be easy this way. They were animals now. No way to communicate except the way nature intended for the species. At least in that respect, Maizie was capable. She was more wolf than human for the time being.

Gray snorted with a hard shake of his head and stepped from the shadows. Maizie edged back, her brilliant green eyes fixed on him. She snarled, her voice louder.

Gray had the feeling she was more ready to run than fight if the opportunity arose. He couldn't read her mind or her his, but they sensed each other, understood each other's wants, desires and needs. A natural phenomenon created by an enhancement of the normal five.

With a small whimper, a submissive sigh, Gray lowered himself to the forest floor. On his belly, he edged closer, head cocked to the side, eyes downcast as much as possible. *I'm not going to hurt you.*

Maizie straightened, not completely but enough he knew she understood. Ears perked, her head twisted one way, then the other before she gave a curious yip. *What do you want?*

Gray continued the submissive approach, not really answering. *I'm not going to hurt you. I'm not going to hurt you.* He was almost to her, but Maizie was becoming antsy.

Her heart beat so hard he could see the subtle vibration of her fur. Her feet shifted, finding the best footing to launch into a run at a moment's notice. Fear seasoned her body chemistry, the scent seeping through her pores, a bitter taste on the air. It was a risk for her to let him get too near. She'd know he could overpower her in seconds.

She stepped back, gave another yip, but this one was harder, laced with warning. *What the* hell *do you want? Stay away. I* will *bring you down.*

Another whimper, Gray edged closer. *I'm not going to hurt you.* Just a few more feet and he'd be close enough to strike.

Maizie was smart, evolution affording her centuries of knowledge, the instinct that enabled the weaker sex to survive the demands of the stronger. And Maizie was functioning on almost pure instinct.

She barked—sharp, angry—her feet dancing her backward, her tail swished once, quick. She started a low growl. *I won't be dominated. I won't be killed. I'll fight...if I have to.*

Gray didn't buy it. She was so frightened he practically choked on the scent of it. Her feet fidgeted, her muscles rolling tight under her fur. She was ready to bolt, to run at his slightest distraction. He wouldn't be distracted.

In a straight-on foot race, Gray knew he could smoke Maizie's smaller stride, but through the twists and turns of a forest run, her smaller size would turn to an advantage. He had to get closer before she took off or he might never catch her.

He called her bluff, throwing up one of his own. Gray rose, not to his full height but enough that he met her eye to eye. He bared his teeth, his growl deeper, louder, more visceral than hers. *Move and I'll end you here—now. My forest. My pack. I decide. Don't move. Let me nearer.*

Jeezus, she was beautiful. To his wolf-half she was as alluring a female as she was a woman to his human-half. Fear sparked in the jewel green of her eyes, but underneath they still managed to captivate him with their curiosity and intelligence—with her sheer defiance.

She was brave, strong, fast and smart. She was everything a male could want in a mate, in the mother of his offspring. Despite her fear and her angry warnings, she wanted his dominance. He could smell it. She wanted him to take her. He was alpha, bravest, strongest, fastest and smartest, everything a female could want in a mate, in the sire of her brood.

Maizie froze to the spot at his show of dominance, her scent thickening the air. She cowered slightly, despite her arousal, believing his threat even as her heat reached across the cool night and enveloped him.

Her musky aroma, more tangy than normal, tickled his nose, stirred his primal body. It wasn't the scent of the natural estrus that preceded ovulation, but Maizie's human-half allowed her sexual excitement without the biological inducement. Combined with everything else she offered, Gray's tight leash on his animal instincts pulled hard on his muscles. A mental shake knocked thoughts of mounting her to the darker recesses of his brain.

Gray held his tall crouch and crept closer, his gaze locked with hers, willing her not to move. He got within feet of her. One more step and he'd be near enough to lunge, to pin her, assert his authority as alpha and earn her compliance. It was the only way to protect her in her wild state.

Maizie was having none of it. She waited, dancing on her feet, a split second of Gray's overconfidence, and she spun, ran. She'd waited too long though, and Gray was able to give chase only seconds behind. In minutes her size, her swift maneuverability, increased the distance between them. Gray thundered on, trusting experience and human strategy would level the field.

The forest was black, the moon and stars no match for the thick canopy of leaves. The air streaked through his fur, the sound of his heart, his steady breaths and the rhythmic beat of his paws echoed around him. Maizie darted toward a barricade of low hanging branches, slipping beneath with ease. Gray's taller body scraped through, the stubborn branches digging into his thick fur, a few breaking through, scratching his skin.

Up ahead she scrambled beneath a fallen tree, making it to the other side in seconds. The trunk was too low for Gray to follow her path and the branches were too thick to jump. Without breaking his stride he swerved, running toward the enormous clump of earth and roots. It ate up precious seconds, but Gray drove harder, faster, made it around and caught the swish of blonde fur dashing between the trees in the darkness. He closed the distance.

She was running wild and panicked. Gray kept his head, his human unfevered mind becoming his only advantage. He ran wide to the right, scaring her to turn left. Then a few minutes later he turned and ran close along her left to frighten her to the right. He herded her toward the quarry lake while she was too crazed to realize.

A thick brier patch lay off to the right. Maizie turned and headed straight for it before Gray could cut her off. She barreled through, head low, her smaller body slicing between the prickly branches and thorns to the other side. Too wide to go around, too tall to jump, Gray had no choice.

He kept her in his sight, focused, determined, driving headlong into the scratchy wall of brush. He didn't fit. The tiny thorns couldn't penetrate his thick fur, but his face was vulnerable. He closed his eyes to slits and kept his head as low as he dared without losing sight of Maizie. It wasn't enough.

The sharp pricks cut along his muzzle, tore at the corners of his eyes. He didn't care. For the first time in forty-three years both halves of his soul united, human and wolf, wanting the same thing—Maizie Hood. He wouldn't let her get away and when he broke through on the other side, a heady wash of relief rippled through him.

Gray knew this forest like he knew his backyard. They were almost there, on the high side of the lake where the ground dropped five stories to the water below. His only fear was that Maizie might skirt along the edge before he could come around to stop her and his chance at cornering her would be lost.

He had to drive her straight to the edge and trust her instincts would stop her before she plunged over the bluff, but not warn her before it was too late to change course. Maizie glanced over her shoulder at him. Her fine-tuned muscles pounded her paws into the ground, propelling her faster.

Her eyes widened for a moment, a cloud of panic wafting up from her fur to tell him her thoughts.

She wasn't thinking. She was just running. This would work. The quarry ledge came up on her fast. Gray watched, several strides behind.

She yipped, her weight shifting to her hindquarters, her

feet scraping backward as her momentum skidded her to the edge. Paws clawed the dirt, turning her so her ass swung around and slipped over. Back claws dug at the cliff wall, front paws spread her toes wide, desperate to hold on. But she was slipping.

Gray lunged, caught the scruff of her neck. He managed to stop her fall. To pull her up he had to get his feet under him and use brute strength.

He saved her...again. It earned him nothing.

The instant Maizie was back on solid footing she snapped at him, catching him under the jaw, drawing blood. Gray snarled, pain stinging through his mind, trying his already haggard patience. He rammed her, his broad chest colliding into her shoulder, driving her back. She stumbled, a tiny yip squeezing out with her breath.

Lightning fast he jumped at her, his big jaws clamping under her neck, catching her jugular between his teeth. He dropped on her, his heavy body crushing her beneath him, her underbelly exposed. Utterly at his mercy, she stilled.

He held her there, catching his breath, reeling back instinct, reining in his control. Her life coursed between his jaws and he growled low, the sound rumbling through his chest, communicating his conditions for his mercy. *I am alpha. My forest. My pack. I decide. You will obey.*

Maizie squirmed suddenly, her tail thrashing the ground. *I will not be dominated. I will not—*

Gray pressed down on her, squeezed his jaw. His tooth broke her skin. A small trickle of blood wet his tongue and sent a zing of primal thoughts storming through his brain: *hunt, catch, devour.* His eyes rolled back, his jaw tightening ever so slightly. He fought the euphoric reaction and felt Maizie go quiet beneath him.

His growl vibrated off her again, echoing back through his own body. *I am alpha. My forest. My pack. I decide. You will obey.*

Maizie whimpered, her tail tucking toward her upturned legs. *Mercy. I submit.*

Minutes ticked by as Gray held her beneath him, forcing her continued submission. She was warm against him, her body gripped by the fever. Still, he liked the feel of her there, chest to chest, her heart pounding so hard the rhythm thumped through his body.

Maizie whimpered, relaxing despite her vulnerable position. She wagged her tail, her long pink tongue lapping out, trying to placate him with kisses. She couldn't reach his face with his mouth on her neck, but the gesture was more than enough.

Gray released his hold, but kept her pinned and Maizie was quick to thank him with long licks to his muzzle, cleaning the wound she'd made under his jaw. Her hot tongue warmed through the short hairs of his face, her body radiating heat. He should lead her back to the mansion where she could rest but he liked the feel of her caresses, the wild smell of her fur, the thick aroma of her sex.

No. She needed rest. She needed protection. The *last* thing she needed was his cock buried deep inside her. Gray got to his feet, careful not to put any further pressure on her smaller body.

Maizie twisted and churned, turning from her back until she got her feet under her. She went to him instantly, lapping at his face, her tail tight between her legs, her body low, submissive.

Her actions spoke volumes. *I am with you. I accept you as dominant. I am yours.* It was the wolf in her that was so submissive. As a human woman, Maizie's sociological beliefs would no doubt bring the abject passivity to a screeching halt. For the moment though, Gray found her eagerness an erotic temptation. The feel of her, the smell of her, the want in her, it was a ruthless tease on his tired wolf brain. His body went tight with need.

As much as he wanted to mount her and ram himself inside, he wouldn't. To take her now would be to take advantage of someone under the influence of drugs or alcohol. Gray stepped back and snapped at her to stop the toadying. *Enough.*

Maizie jumped out of reach, her entire demeanor changing. She gave a delicate snort and a hard swish of her tail. *Absolutely.*

Gray could only blink in surprise—staring. She'd been acting?

Maizie had been doing as she must to assure him she was no threat. Mission accomplished, her natural independent nature stiffened her spine. The fever must have begun to break. He hadn't expected the virus to work through her so quickly. She was stronger than he imagined, in body, mind and spirit. But then he shouldn't have been surprised. It was part of what he loved about her.

Minute by minute, day by day, she showed herself a perfect match for him. *Donna, forgive me.* It was hard to deny.

Gray shook his head, pushed his shoulder into her as he passed, pointing her body in the right direction. *Follow.*

Maizie bit his tail when it went by. *Not yet.*

Gray spun, a twinge of pain itching up his spine. Maizie's tongue flopped, her jaw working hard trying to get the tuft of his tail hair out of her mouth. She shook her head, the last of it floating to the ground.

Those green-as-alder eyes focused on him, the look unmistakable. *Claim me.* A low rumble vibrated from the thick fleece of her chest, a purr so alluring it pulled his cock from the pocket of his fur. *Claim me.*

No. Not here. Not like this. Gray stiffened. His refusal standing.

Maizie licked his muzzle, her tongue warm, not as hot as before. Her long lapping kisses caressed his cheek, cleaned the blood from the brier scratches at his eyes. She pushed the side of her face into his neck, rubbing her body along his, heading for his tail.

Gray's muscles pulled tight, Maizie's high tail drawing closer. His heart hammered, his breaths ragged. *Damn*, she smelled good. She smelled like sex.

She shifted her hips when she knew her ass was at his nose, flicking her tail over his eyes. *Claim me.*

Without warning his wolf blood rampaged through his body, primal need surging through his brain. *Maizie. Take her. Claim her.*

The thoughts were stilted, frenzied. She'd pushed him too damn far. Gray spun, sunk his teeth into the thick fur of her ass, his paws clawing at her, drawing her around to his hard waiting cock.

She pressed her tail flat against her side, exposing her sex to him. Pushing against him Maizie wiggled, encouraging him to follow through. Gray closed his eyes, his mouth full of her fur, his nose and mind swimming in her scent, her taste. His breath panted out of him, his heart thundering. He needed a moment to find the ragged thread of control. *Not like this.*

His hips pressed into her, his cock burrowing deep in her wet fur, but missing her sex. Gray released his hold, pushing off her, jogging a few feet away. He turned back to see her collapse to the ground.

She rolled to her side, curling and stretching, squirming as though trying to find some measure of relief. She came to her belly, those enchanting green eyes focusing on him, hungry, needy. *Claim me.*

Gray snorted and took another step back. *Not like this.*

Maizie fell back, resigned, her head resting on the forest floor. Her side rose and fell with several heavy breaths before her fur rolled along her body in a way that could only mean her change had begun.

Gray watched, helpless. Returning to human form wouldn't be as painful as the initial shift, but it would still hurt. It would always hurt a little, but nothing like these first times. There was nothing he could do for her.

He tried to keep a sympathetic thought in his head as he watched the fur recede from her body, her paws return to hands and feet, her tail shrink, her teats reshape to womanly breasts. He tried, but she'd pushed him so damn far. Staring at her lying on her belly, panting in the aftermath of her change, he wanted her as much as he had a moment before.

Her long fiery red hair cloaked her back, ass plump and smooth, her pussy thatch wet and glistening. His wolf cock twitched, his mind filled with thoughts of driving it deep between the rounds of her ass. He snorted and stepped closer, he couldn't stay away. He'd tried.

Her fever had broken. The virus had passed through her system and her body had adapted to its effect. Maizie's mind was her own again, but he had claim to her body. He felt driven to stake that claim now.

He sniffed her first, the wild scent of her fur was fading, the sweet aroma of her flesh growing strong in its place. The effect on him was the same, pulling the muscles in his body. He licked her, from the back of her upper thigh to the firm round of her ass.

Maizie groaned, her hips rising to meet his caress. Her pussy lips spread, the scent of her arousal hitting him full force. His tail swished, his cock wagged hard and stiff. He raised up to his hind legs, mounted her, pawing along her back with only a passing thought not to mar her tender flesh with his claws.

He could take her this way. He was tall enough, his cock long and thick enough. But the thought of her protesting, forcing him to stop, was more than he could endure.

Gray closed his eyes, forced his beast to recede to the darkness, called up all that was human inside him. His paws reshaped to hands and fingers holding her sides. His back legs lengthened and he had to adjust so he stayed on his knees, holding himself against her.

For the second time in his life, his cock held its erection throughout the shift, its moist head turning velvet smooth, tickling in the wet hairs of her pussy. He shoved his hips forward, plunging deep inside her. He couldn't wait a second longer.

Like a blast of hot air, heat shot up his cock and over his body at the feel of her around him, tingling along his skin and pulling his balls so tight it fisted his toes. He clenched his jaw, bit back on the too-tempting call of release. He wanted more— so much more.

His thighs trembled as Maizie pushed up to her hands and knees, locked her elbows, arched her back. "Yessss..."

Her voice was hoarse, but Gray recognized the low purr of wolf, how the virus had permanently altered the tone, made it richer, sexier. He pulled his hips, drawing his cock back through the rippling tight squeeze of her pussy walls. His skin hummed with the feel of it, that delicious pressure building, tempting him to give in, to tumble into a wash of release. *Not yet.* He drove himself into her again, so the slap of their bodies vibrated deep in his groin.

She pushed back, forcing him deeper. Her inner walls squeezed, milking every last inch of him, pulling a shuddering tingle from nerve endings all through his body. Gray watched as his hard shaft slid wet and shiny from between her folds, the erotic sight zinging through his mind and body. He slid his hands to her ass cheeks, squeezed, pulled them apart for a better view.

The sweet hole of her anus winked at him as he drove his cock into her pussy again. He licked a finger, wet the opening and shuddered at how easily he slid it inside. The tight squeeze of her ass on his finger made his cock twitch inside her, made her muscles answer with a hard draw of their own that jolted up his cock and seared through his body like lightning.

Maizie gasped. "That's it. That's it. Like I dreamed you did in the shower."

Gray flicked his gaze to Maizie's face, etched with concentrated pleasure. The invisible shower-Maizie had been his dream. Was it possible she'd felt him the way he'd felt her? Could they be that connected—that destined? Maybe. Possibly. If they were true life mates. But what would that make Donna?

His hard-on softened. He didn't want to think about it. Not now. Gray thrust his hips, pumping his cock until her hungry muscles made him so stiff he nearly came. He didn't want to think about Donna. He had Maizie in his arms, her wet pussy, her sexy ass. He wanted to fuck her senseless, he'd wanted to from the start.

He pulled out and bent to her anus. He licked and kissed, thrusting his tongue into the tight opening as his fingers pumped her pussy. Maizie writhed against him, keeping the fast rhythm until her anus was as slick and ready for him as her sex.

Gray drew himself up to her, guided the head of his cock as he held her ass cheek. He pushed, felt the sweet resistance and allowed Maizie to bring him inside her. She pressed back against him and Gray's cock slipped through, smooth and easy, muscles so tight he gasped at the surge of pleasure, raising the hairs all over his body.

She moaned loud and the sound reverberated along his cock, made him pump when he wanted to hold still. Jeezus, she drove him wild. He reached around and found her clit. He stroked her, using her own cream to keep his fingers wet. She wiggled against him as he pumped, her muscles squeezing tight, pushing him toward the edge, swelling the need inside him. So close, so close, the coming release pulling his balls, humming through his thighs and tugging his gut.

Not a moment too soon Maizie threw her head back, her body driving hard against him. His balls were drenched in her come. Her clit pulsed with another orgasm, her ass muscles throbbed around his cock with a third. She was coming all at once, her clit, her pussy and her ass.

"Maizie…" There was no holding back. Her orgasm pulled him over the edge so fast he couldn't breathe. His body worked on its own, pounding into her. If she'd asked now he couldn't have stopped. He was out of mind, out of body, lost to the whirl of sensation.

Something inside him gave way, heat rumbled over him like a summer storm, rolling through his muscles, massaging his balls, sucking the come from his cock so he felt utterly undone.

He collapsed onto her and she collapsed to the ground.

Maizie winced at Gray's soft cock sliding out of her bum, her sex still pulsing and flexing with after-waves. Gawd, she'd never come like that in her life.

She pushed up to her elbows and Gray shifted off her, his lips trailing soft kisses across her back. She shuddered, her belly quivering. Everything he did seemed so intense, affecting her mentally and physically. She felt him everywhere, sensed him, more tonight than before. Something had changed. She felt marked by him. The werewolf blood coursing through her veins forged a connection between them. Or strengthened one that had already been there.

He sat up, his leg touching her thigh, and scooped a handful of her hair off her back. She heard him inhale, knew he held her hair to his nose, and then she remembered the way his nostrils had flared when she asked if he blamed her for his wife's death.

Anger burned down her spine, stiffened her shoulders. She twisted, pushing up to sit, not caring how the movement yanked her hair from his grip.

She looked at him.

He smiled.

She slapped him hard, hard enough he nearly fell over. When his head snapped back to her, his glower was set in deep lines across his forehead, his lips tight.

"What the hell was that for?"

"What did you turn me into?" Her anger was a bit misdirected, she knew. Gray hadn't done this to her. He'd only blamed her for his wife's death then screwed her senseless anyway. She couldn't really complain since it was obvious she'd wanted it as much as he had. That didn't make her any less pissed about it or make the slap any less satisfying.

"I'm sorry. But I didn't infect you." He rubbed the red

211

handprint she'd left on his face. "It shouldn't have happened. If I could fix it, I would. Believe me."

"Fix it? Yeah. Because you're all about doing what's right. Like blaming me for the accident that killed my parents...and your wife."

"I'm sorry for that too."

Maizie's jaw snapped shut. She blinked. She hadn't expected him to admit to it. "Then why did you? I mean, if that's really the way you feel, what was all...*this* about." She gestured to their naked bodies and the crush of grass where they'd had sex.

He raked a hand through his mop of silvery hair, grunted and pushed to his feet. She tried not to notice the way his muscles rolled under his skin, the tempting bundle between his legs. Would he say tonight was a mistake? She might agree, but it hadn't felt that way. She pulled her knees to her chest, hugging her arms around them, feeling small and vulnerable.

He stared out over the cliff, hands propped on his hips. "It was easy blaming your parents and you for Donna's death. They were dead, and you were just a kid."

The moonlight silhouetted his body in a blue-white light, made her breath shudder to look at him.

"I don't know why," he said. "It didn't bring her back. It didn't change a damn thing. But until you walked into my forest, I didn't really give a shit."

"So how'd I change things?"

His shoulders shook with a silent laugh, though when he spoke there was no sound of it in his voice. He knotted his arms under his chest. "By being everything to me that I couldn't be for her. Jeezus, I had no idea. I mean, I knew it was harder for her. She was born a werewolf, her instincts were stronger. She *needed* to find a life mate, *her* life mate, and I just wanted to be married to her. After she infected me it was too late. I'd made a mistake. But I was just too damn stubborn to admit it."

"A lot of people consider honoring your wedding vows a good thing."

"I wasn't honoring the damn vows. At least not the spirit of them. Not the way she needed." His head lowered, she couldn't be sure, but she thought he'd closed his eyes. "Our marriage was killing her. She was dying of loneliness lying right next to me. If I had understood better..."

He shook his head, raising his gaze. "I was just pissed as hell that our marriage was failing. I loved her. I know she loved me, but there was something missing, something she needed. When she tried to find it with another man I..." He shrugged. "I lost it. We had a blowout fight. Damn it, I hated what I'd driven her to, hated I couldn't be what she needed. So when she ran...I let her go."

"That was twenty-one years ago, Gray. Maybe you're remembering it wrong."

He turned his chin to his shoulder, looking back at her. "I remember like it was yesterday. I remember because I feel the bond with you I could never forge with her. Your family took my wife from me, but gave me my life mate. So, tell me, should I thank them, or curse them...or both?"

She swallowed hard not knowing if she wanted to smile or cry. She wanted to go to him but the muscles in her arms and legs still trembled from everything they'd endured.

He came to her on one knee. "Don't try to get up. Your body needs to rest. It's still sort of in a state of flux."

She'd protest except she could feel he was right. "Whatever you do, Gray, you should start by letting yourself off the hook. It was an accident."

He snorted, a short sardonic laugh. "That's just one explanation, according to your grandmother. An accident, yeah, but predestined too."

"You mean like fate?"

"Like a goddamn fairy tale."

Chapter Thirteen

Maizie knew Annette was there before she opened her eyes. Her Opium perfume filled the room. It was hard for Maizie to breathe without coating her nose or the back of her throat with the scent.

She pushed up to one elbow, trying to clean the waxy perfume taste off the roof of her mouth with her tongue and blinked the sleep from her eyes. "Morning."

Annette froze, a pair of jeans half folded in her hands. Her gaze flicked to Maizie from the foot of Gray's bed. A genuine smile stretched her small face. "Good morning. Actually, it's afternoon."

Crap. Not again. Maizie noticed the empty pillow beside her. "How'd I get here?"

"Mr. Lupo carried you here last night. After you, uh, passed out." Her little cheeks flushed. Chin down she glanced at Maizie from beneath long lashes then quickly returned her gaze to the clothes. She folded them onto the storage bench.

Maizie thought about that for a minute, pushing up to sit, sheet clutched to her naked chest. She remembered being with Gray at the quarry, his confessions, his admission of their strange, intimate connection.

He'd knelt beside her when she couldn't get up and then...nothing. "He carried me the whole way? Wow."

Annette's thin brows rose above the big frames of her glasses, her nod quick and happy. "Mr. Lupo said you passed right out. I don't think he minded. In fact I'd lay odds he quite enjoyed holding you so close. Certainly looked that way this morning."

The small woman laughed, her toothy smile bright. She clasped her hands at her chest and for a second Maizie expected her to rub them together with an eager glee.

"This morning? So he was here earlier with me?" Maizie tried not to read too much into the fact she needed someone else to confirm her bed partners.

"Of course. He had a hard time letting you go, but he had a, ah, business meeting."

A warm tingle filled Maizie's belly. He'd held her all night. She remembered the warm feel of him now, the safety of his arms, the strength, the tenderness. Gawd, she liked the way he seemed to treasure her. She liked the way she treasured him. Things were good.

Maizie shoved the snarl of bed-hair back from her face and fought the goofy grin threatening to control her mouth. They were destined for each other, like a real-life fairy tale.

Annette chattered on. "He made sure I knew to get you fresh clothes and something to eat and whatever else you might need. The jeans, T-shirt and undergarments here are for you. I guessed your size, but I'm pretty good at it. There's a peanut butter sandwich and glass of milk when you're ready." She gestured to the nightstand. "Mr. Lupo thought you'd like it, but if you'd rather—"

"No." Maizie glanced at the silver tray and plate cover, smiling. "It's, uhm, perfect. It's absolutely perfect."

Annette chuckled again, her shoulders high. "It is, isn't it? He's so romantic."

Okay, now her giddiness over Maizie's love life was starting to get weird. "Wow, you're really *close* to your boss, huh?"

"Oh, yes. He's just so, well, he's just so wonderful."

"Yeah. Exactly how close are the two of you?"

"He means the world to me." She shrugged, wrinkling the clean line of her high-buttoned blouse for a moment. "I love him."

"Really? I see." So why was she so happy to find Maizie in his bed? *Twisted.*

Not that it really mattered. Annette was cute and tiny, early thirties, sweet with her mousy brown hair pulled to a bun, big glasses and tight-buttoned librarian look. She had pretty brown eyes and a decent B-cup figure, shapely legs in comfortable low-heeled shoes, and if she was really competition for Gray's affection, she'd be the one naked in his bed. Still...

"So, uhm..." Maizie tried to think of a discreet way to word her question—and failed. "You two ever have sex?"

She was exhausted, her body felt like it'd been drawn and quartered, and her powerful bond with Gray had turned her brain to mush. She didn't have the brain cells to spare beating around the bush, and going by the way the rest of the family behaved, it seemed a legitimate question.

Annette's brow scrunched. "No. Of course not. I could never...blah..." A hard shudder shook her from head to toe. She looked as though she was going to be sick.

"Geez, don't hold back. Tell me how you really feel." Maizie's offense at the woman's repulsion was too messed-up to think about.

Annette's gaze flicked to Maizie. "No. It's not that. I love him. I do. Just not in *that* way."

"Okay, I'm lost."

Annette laughed. "Sorry. You see, I've known Gray, Mr. Lupo, nearly my whole life. It'd be like sleeping with my father."

Maizie's cheeks warmed. That certainly explained Annette's shudder. Gray didn't look old enough to be her father, unless you factored in the werewolf thing. Did he really age that slowly? "How'd you meet?"

Her hands laced together in front of her, very proper. Annette came around the end of the bed and leaned her hip against the edge of the mattress. "He rescued me."

Of course he did.

"My father, my biological father, was an abusive man," Annette said. "And things only got worse after my mother died of cancer. I was six when Gray found me. He'd just been walking past my house and heard my father attacking me—"

"Attacking?"

"The abuse was...sexual."

"God, I'm sorry." Maizie suddenly wanted to hug her.

Annette shrugged. "It was a long time ago and Gray got me out of there that same day. He just stormed into the house, walked right into the bedroom and threw my father off me, across the room. Told him he was taking me someplace safe and if he ever tried to contact either of us he'd kill him. I think he would've killed him right there if it weren't for me watching."

"That's horrible, Annette. I'm glad Gray was there for you."

She nodded, her fingers absently toying with a thread on the comforter. "We never heard from him again. He didn't even file a police report. Just sort of...disappeared."

That last statement made Maizie's blood run cold. She ignored it. Too many potential skeletons in that closet. Besides, this wasn't the movies. Being a werewolf didn't automatically make you a killer. Even if the guy had it coming.

"Gray's taken care of me ever since. He and Donna were like my parents. When their marriage started going bad, I was terrified, but I knew staying together was destroying them both."

"You knew Donna?"

Annette nodded again and inched closer alongside the bed. "She was a really great lady. Beautiful sandy brown hair, green eyes and a warm smile. They loved each other, but they were never at ease together. Y'know what I mean? Like they didn't quite...match."

"Yeah." She knew exactly what Annette meant by a match. Like the way she felt with Gray, as though they were two halves of the same puzzle. A perfect fit.

"That's why I was so happy when he brought you home." Annette inched closer toward Maizie. "He's never brought anyone home before. And when I caught him smiling...I knew."

Maizie's belly fluttered. Gawd, she was in deep. She didn't care. It was exactly where she wanted to be.

"He's a good man. He deserves to be happy. And now he has you. You're one of them, one of the family." Annette repositioned herself for the last time, now directly beside Maizie. "I'd do anything to switch places with you."

"I thought you said you didn't think of Gray that way."

"I don't. He's not my type. I meant switch places with you in the family, in the pack."

Maizie's heart skipped. "You know?"

"What?" Annette laughed. "That you're all werewolves? Of course."

"And you're not creeped out? You're not afraid?" Maizie remembered her struggle to believe, to come to terms with the truth.

219

"No. They're like my family and you will be too, except..." Annette sulked, her shoulders drooped. "I'm not really *one* of them. I'm still full human."

"And you want to be like them—I mean us?"

Annette caught her bottom lip between her teeth, her gaze downcast. She nodded.

"But Gray won't turn you?" Maizie guessed.

"No. He says he won't ever bite anyone to turn them. He was bitten, not born like his wife and the rest of them. But since they weren't true life mates his experience has been...hard. He can't imagine anyone would choose the life. It's not that he doesn't want me to be one of them, he just can't bring himself to do it."

"What about Lynn and Rick and the others?"

Annette kept her gaze fixed on Maizie's outstretched legs, her hand finding Maizie's knee through the cover. She squeezed, her thumb massaging the side. "They keep putting me off. But I was thinking, since you've adapted to the virus you could probably pass it along already. We could make it fun."

A warm musky scent tickled Maizie's nose and stirred her body. Annette was aroused...for her. Keener werewolf senses made the air seem ripe with the woman's growing excitement. Annette's idea of fun was becoming abundantly clear.

"Uhm, Annette." A nervous laugh bubbled out of Maizie. She squirmed, feeling the familiar rush of heat to her sex. "I'm really flattered, but I don't swing that way. Not that you're not...I mean you are, you're really...that is, I've just never...well, I've always...I like guys."

Annette pulled her glasses from her face with one hand, the other still warm on Maizie's knee. She tossed them to the nightstand so they clamored over the silver tray. Those pretty mousy brown eyes locked on Maizie, the mouse having turned to a lioness in heat. "How do you know if you've never tried?"

She reached up and pulled the pins from her hair, letting it tumble down silky smooth past her shoulders. She shook her head and Maizie's breath caught, her sex muscles flexed. The woman was attractive. There was no arguing that.

Whoa! What was wrong with her? She'd turned into a sex maniac. Maizie pushed at the mattress with her free hand, tried to scoot away. "Listen, I'm not like this. I mean you're really...but I can't..."

"Don't worry. There's nothing wrong with you. Werewolves have heightened senses, increased appetites. In all things." She started to unbutton her blouse, exposing the sweet lacy bra underneath. "Besides, even though the virus is neutralized, your body is still adjusting. I did some research. You'll be horny as hell for a few weeks. Like I said, Gray's not my type, but we do share similar tastes."

"Oh, please don't bob your eyebrows like that," Maizie said. "It's disturbing on so many levels."

She tilted her head to the side, her lashes seeming longer, thicker, as they shadowed her cheek. "Haven't you ever wondered what it's like to be with a woman? It's not like touching yourself. Every woman's different, but we're enough alike I know what feels good for both of us."

It was Maizie's turn to shudder, but it wasn't repulsion rippling down her back, pooling between her thighs. It was lust. *Shoot.* Her gaze dropped to that pretty lace bra, to the swells of flesh peeking over the edges. She licked her lips, her mouth suddenly dry.

"We can go slow. We'll take turns." Annette's hand slid farther up Maizie's leg, slipping to the side to trace the inside of her thigh.

Maizie's breath caught and Annette stopped, but not before Maizie's legs opened a half inch on reflex. "Turns?"

"Uh-huh." Annette nodded, her gaze shifting from her hand, warm and heavy against Maizie's inner thigh, to her face and back again. "You can go first. Whatever you do to me, I'll do to you. That way nothing gets done to you that you don't want."

"But I don't really want to—"

Annette's expression stopped Maizie's words in her throat. Hurt, disbelief, maybe a bit of both, either way she was right. Part of Maizie was curious and another part was just plain horny. The sudden flood of heat between her thighs was proof of it.

Maizie's belly quivered, her heart racing, anticipation tingling along her skin. "I don't know what to do."

Annette's massage began again, slow, firm, erotic. Maizie felt herself inch closer, so Annette's fingers rubbed wickedly close to her pussy. "You're a beautiful woman, Maizie, with a great body. Honestly, I'd love to touch you anywhere—everywhere. So wherever you want to touch me is perfect."

Annette's gaze dropped to Maizie's hand clutching the sheet to her chest. "You do have amazing breasts. Mine aren't as big, but my skin's soft. You can touch them. See for yourself."

Maizie swallowed hard, stared at the small mounds beneath white lace. She reached out and Annette arched toward her. Her fingers brushed along the strap, tracing down to the lace that made a waving line along one breast to the center. She barely touched Annette's flesh, but goose bumps rose, blanketing her chest, and her breath caught.

Emboldened, Maizie opened her hand, pressed her palm to Annette's chest, felt her heart racing beneath. Annette's breaths were coming fast and shallow as Maizie cupped her hand, slid lower, took the whole of her breast into her palm. The weight, the warmth, the supple feel of her, she was woman, she was divine and Maizie's body hummed to life.

She squeezed, gently, her thumb massaging over the hard pebble of flesh at the tip. She caught Annette's nipple, pinched and rolled it between her thumb and finger. Annette moaned, her eyes closed, her back arching her firmer into Maizie's grip.

Maizie's own breasts ached for attention, her erect nipples rasping against the sheet. Her heart hammered in her chest, her pussy flexing, needy and ready. She slid her fingers under Annette's bra strap, pushed it off her shoulder and slipped her hand underneath.

Like rose petals, Annette's skin was satiny soft, even where she was hard, puckered and velvety. A zing of heat tingled over Maizie's body, shooting straight to her sex, opening her legs to Annette's persistent caress. Annette's hand slipped to the apex of Maizie's thighs, expertly stroking her pussy through the sheet. Her juices soaked through in seconds, molding the sheet to her so the details of her pussy were palpable.

The feel of a woman's breast in her hand was sinfully erotic, so new, so soft, so sensitive to her touch, Maizie wanted more. She leaned in, cupping underneath, offering up the excited nipple to her mouth. Maizie flicked her tongue, tasting the powder-sweet flesh.

Annette gasped then thrust her breasts toward Maizie, her body begging for more. Maizie opened her lips and suckled Annette into her mouth. The addictive texture rippled over her tongue, hard and soft at once. Maizie's gut clenched, tightening muscles low on her body.

Annette's breast filled her mouth, molded to the squeeze of her hand, warm, supple. She caught the nipple with her teeth, gave a small nibble that made Annette gasp, then pulled back.

Annette licked her lips, her eyes fluttering open to meet

Maizie's. "God, that felt good. I want to do the same for you."

She reached for the sheet still fisted at her neck. Maizie let go, allowing it to slip to her lap, exposing her naked breasts.

"You're so beautiful, Maizie," Annette said, her gaze fixed on the hard nipple of one breast. She didn't hesitate, reaching out to her, smoothing her hand over the sloping contours.

Her small hand cupped underneath, held the weight of her. Maizie had never been with a man whose hands were as small and delicate as Annette's. The difference was oddly exciting. Her soft palm, her slender fingers, the perfect mix of pressure and gentleness only a woman could know, Maizie found herself pressing into Annette's touch.

Even as Annette's hand kept a delicious rhythm on Maizie's sex, she leaned in and took her breast into her mouth. Maizie gasped at the moist suction, tingles racing over her skin, heat flooding through her body. Her tongue toyed with Maizie's hard straining nipple, flicking and swirling, drawing it in.

Maizie's sex muscles flexed, aching to be filled. She braced her hands into the mattress on either side of her hips, unable to deny the pleasure Annette stroked through her. The overly sweet smell of her perfume, her long hair tickling her belly, her skin silky smooth, the sensations were maddening.

Maizie looked down for a moment and watched the sweet feminine face pressed to her breast. Her little ear with its silver hoop earring, her smooth skin and pouty lips. She watched Annette's tongue toy with her nipple, noticed her long mascara-covered lashes shadowing her cheek. She was a woman. The sight was all wrong and all the more erotic.

Maizie's brain spun with a heated mix of sensation and reason, but it wasn't natural. Not for her.

Her body had a mind of its own, wanting anything, everything, recognizing satisfaction in any form. But Maizie's brain couldn't allow it, couldn't let go of instinctive preferences.

"No." Maizie's voice was barely there, her breath hot and panting. "Stop. I can't. Annette, stop."

Annette drew back from her breast, her fingers still caressing Maizie's pussy. She licked her lips, her eyes hooded. She drew close to Maizie's lips. "But you like it." Her voice was husky, her lips brushing Maizie's. "I can tell you like it."

"Yes. I like it, but not...not this way. This...this... No, no, this isn't...me. *Shit.*" Annette kept stroking her, Maizie's hips pressing toward her touch despite herself. She couldn't think.

"Annette..." Maizie grabbed her wrist, pulled her hand from her sex. "Please. Stop."

Annette straightened, blinked. Her brows creased, her bottom lip pouting, she avoided Maizie's eyes. "Sorry. I thought you were liking it. I didn't mean to force you."

"You didn't force me," Maizie said, fighting to catch her breath, to calm the pound of her heart, the need storming through her body. "I should've stopped you sooner. Maybe it's the virus. But I'm with Gray. Not even sure what that means, but I can feel it and this...this is wrong. Not just because you're a woman, but..."

"Oh. I hadn't thought about that. Shoot." Annette's eyes stretched wide and hopeful. "Will you at least bite me? We don't have to have sex for you to turn me."

Maizie couldn't help the smile tugging at her mouth. What an odd world she'd fallen into. "I'm sorry, but I can't. Not now. I'm not sure how I feel about being...what I am. I don't feel right condemning you to the same fate until I do."

Annette's hopeful smile faltered, but after a deep breath she forced it brighter, though the expression still wasn't convincing. "I understand. You and Gray are a lot alike, I kind of figured. Maybe in a few weeks or months you'll change your mind."

"Maybe." Maizie smiled, hating the disappointment edging Annette's tone.

"Thanks." Annette's smile flickered as though she fought to keep it on her lips. She stepped back, fixing her bra, slipping into her blouse. "I'd say I'm sorry about trying to seduce you, but I'm not. I love Gray, but I had to try. I know how you feel though, so you don't have to worry about it happening again."

Maizie's cheeks warmed. She pulled the sheet to her neck and smiled. "Okay."

Annette grabbed her glasses and twisted her hair into a bun as she left. "Gray won't be back from his meeting with Mr. Cadwick for another hour or more. So if you need anything use the intercom. Some of us don't have super-werewolf hearing," she said, teasing as she closed the door behind her.

Ravenous, Maizie devoured the triple-decker peanut butter sandwich and downed the tall glass of milk before she even considered a shower. She took her time under the hot water, memories flashing through her mind. They were skewed through the eyes of her wolf-half, cloudy and ominous as though something about them was important. She couldn't put her finger on it, though. She'd dried her hair and finished dressing before it hit her.

"Cadwick." The memory crystallized in her mind the moment she said his name. Those papers, what were they? Maizie's gut told her they were nothing good. Annette had said Gray was meeting with Cadwick now. If she could reach Gray maybe he could use his business connection to get the wolf of a man to leave Granny and her land alone.

Maizie raced to the phone on the opposite side of the bed. The intercom buzzed and buzzed, but no one picked up. She couldn't wait. She had to find a way to contact Gray before his meeting was over, a cell phone or pager number—something.

She ran full-out down the long halls, her footfalls echoing off the high ceilings and paneled walls. She found the enormous staircase leading to the foyer and took the steps three at a time. Tall entry doors in front of her, archway to parlors and living rooms to the right, Maizie turned to the wide double wood doors at her left.

She'd seen Annette emerge from this room the first day Gray had brought her to the mansion. She'd glimpsed bookshelves and thick carpeting behind her through the open door and a large oak desk. Had to be his home office.

She knocked first. No answer. She knocked harder, pounded, still no answer. Maizie tried the door. It clicked open and she slipped inside.

The desk she'd seen through the open door was the smaller of the two. Stacks of papers, open file folders and sticky notes covered the top, chaotic organization. Maizie guessed the desk belonged to Annette. There was a large flat-screen monitor in one corner that matched the one in the corner of the other, larger desk.

Maizie glanced at the larger sleek wood desk, neat and tidy with its dark leather desk set. She could almost see Gray sitting behind it, scowling as he scribbled notes or sent out important emails to one of his high-powered connections.

Her belly quivered, a smile pinching her cheeks. She tore her thoughts from silvery hair and hard muscles with decided effort. She circled around Annette's desk and searched for an address book or a speed-dial button on the phone. There had to be some quick easy way for Annette to contact Gray.

Maizie reached for the phone in the opposite corner from the computer monitor when something on the desk caught her eye. An open letter, paper clipped to its envelope, the golden letterhead glinting in a stream of sunlight. She recognized the name, Judge Charles Woodsmen, from Granny's Green Acres phone bill. The nursing home tracked both incoming and outgoing calls for security reasons.

She hadn't thought anything of it at the time, figuring the guy was humping for reelection votes or something. Was it just a coincidence he knew Gray? She scanned the letter.

Gray,

Enclosed are the papers and procedures we discussed for gaining guardianship of Ester Hood. I spoke with her over the phone and I don't foresee a problem supporting an argument for mental incompetence, provided there are no family members to protest your filing. Should such a dispute arise, I will of course fully examine their argument. In the meantime, as you surmised, you will retain full control of the holdings. All sales and transfers undertaken during this time will not be easily overturned. I hope this information is of use to you.

I look forward to our game on Sunday. I've got a new seven-iron I'm dying to try out.

Sincerely,

Chuck

Judge Charles Woodsmen

District Judge

Pittsburgh County Courts

Maizie couldn't breathe. She swallowed hard, her heart pounding in her ears. She'd been right all along. Gray was after Granny's land.

"What's this?" Anthony Cadwick took the stack of papers from Gray, glancing every few minutes back to the crowd of reporters milling around the spot of his soon-to-be riverside restaurant.

"A copy of an amendment from the township zoning board, stating that the sale of property will be kept to a two-acre maximum for residential, eight acres for commercial. Passed at last night's meeting. Unanimously."

Cadwick pinched his fat cigar between his fingers and yanked it from his mouth. His gaze slid to Gray, brows tight. "Ya don't say. When's this get filed?"

"Monday." Gray loved the smell of defeat in the afternoon. "Goes into effect in sixty days."

Cadwick grunted, scanning the papers. "That's fast."

"People want to keep a lid on growth. Keep the community quaint. Rural." Of course they didn't realize they wanted to control growth until Gray had pointed it out to them. Once he told them about Cadwick's plans for superstores and parking lots, his battle had been won.

"Buncha tree huggers like you. No wonder you like it there." He shoved the papers back at Gray, crumpling them into his chest.

Gray rolled the documents then held them in his hand at his side, the other hand slipped into the front pocket of his slacks. Cadwick's sore-loser display only made the victory all the sweeter. "Glide's a quiet town. Good people. I've made friends." *Several of them sitting on the zoning board.* "Yeah, I like it there."

Cadwick shoved his cigar back between his teeth and turned to stare at the reporters hammering his PR man with questions. "Look at 'em. Wettin' their panties about my riverboat casino. Not one question about the restaurant or the twenty other businesses that'll benefit from the boat docking here."

Cadwick made his voice high, mocking. "How's Mr. Cadwick gonna have a riverboat casino when the state won't pass the gambling laws?" He snorted. "Idiots. Always two steps behind. Do I look like a man who doesn't consider every contingency? Do they think I got to where I am—that I built my business—by being stupid?"

He turned to Gray, pinching the cigar out of his mouth again. His eyes narrowed, a telling grin pulling the corner of his mouth. "What about you, Lupo? Do you think I got to where I am without thinking ahead? Without planning for state laws, politicians and township zoning boards?"

Gray's jaw tightened, his fist squeezing the worthless documents. He'd been afraid of this. Cadwick must've gotten Granny to sign. It's the only way he could have beaten the system, had the sale grandfathered in. *Damn it, when had he done it?* Gray had checked on her yesterday.

Cadwick wouldn't be able to resell the land, but that wouldn't stop him from developing it himself. Even if Gray could close the loophole, it'd be too late. His beast roared inside his head, angry, frustrated. But he kept his face an empty mask. He wouldn't give Cadwick the satisfaction.

Cadwick laughed, chewed on the end of his cigar. "Just like old times, huh, Lupo? You always took a little too long to figure things out. Hell, even Donna got tired of waiting around for you to realize you were losing her. Though, God knows why she was with you to begin with. You didn't deserve her."

His expression sobered, Cadwick gazed out over the river. "If she had belonged to me, she'd have never gotten away."

Tension rippled along Gray's back, pulled his muscles into a tight knot. His hands fisted so hard he knew there'd be half moons in his palms from his nails. Cadwick had guts talking to him about Donna. Even after all these years. Did he think Gray didn't know?

A low growl rumbled in his chest. He couldn't help it. When he spoke the deep resonance made his voice sound deadly. "My *wife* was never something to be possessed or kept. Maybe if we...if *I* had remembered that, she'd still be around. She wouldn't have gone away."

Chapter Fourteen

"What'd he say when you asked him about the letter?"

Maizie shrugged. "I didn't ask. I just left."

Cherri sprinkled the final bit of flour into the churning mixer. "'Course not. Why give Mr. Tall-dark-and-wonderful the opportunity to explain? I mean, he's pretty much perfect. Gorgeous, smart, rich, romantic. Gorgeous—"

"You said gorgeous twice."

Cherri looked at her. "Yeah. I know."

Maizie rolled her eyes. "No one's perfect."

"He does a pretty good imitation."

The smell of licorice tickled Maizie's nose. "Too much anise," she said with a nod to the mixer.

"You haven't even tasted it."

"Trust me." She hadn't told Cherri about Mr. Wonderful's other attributes, like his ability to turn women into sex-crazed werewolves who could smell anise and creamed panties at a hundred yards—among other things.

Granted, he wasn't the one who'd turned her, but still, she didn't want to hear Cherri come up with any more excuses for the man. She'd tell her eventually. Probably.

"I just can't believe I was right all along. I let my hormones get in the way of my brain. Dammit." She thrashed a rubber spatula through the bowl of butter-cream icing she held, taking out her frustration. "And poor Granny. How am I going to break this to her?"

"She really likes him, huh?" Cherri dipped a spoon in the cookie batter and cringed when she tasted it.

"She adores Gray. It'll crush her when she finds out he was just being nice to get her land."

"I'm surprised how well *you're* taking it." Cherri added more flour and sugar to the batter. "I mean if I thought the love of my life was just using me to nail a real-estate deal I'd bawl my eyes out."

Maizie didn't mention she'd cried the whole way back through the forest from Gray's house and more than half the drive in from the cottage. She felt as though it was a piece of her heart he'd conspired to steal away with those papers, not just her grandmother's land. Except Granny still had her land, Maizie couldn't say as much for her heart.

She was done crying. "What I can't figure out is this other guy…Cadwick. He made a full-court press to get me to call him if Granny decided to sell. Then I saw him with Granny last night. He had papers with him. They looked official. But I don't know if he's working with Gray or if the two of them are competition."

"You think Cadwick's the guy who was tricking your Granny into thinking he was your dad?" Cherri dipped a fresh spoon into the tweaked batter. She tasted it. A smile flickered across her lips.

"I guess. When I told Gray about Granny thinking Dad was telling her to sell, he seemed genuinely surprised." Maizie stood and plopped a spatula full of icing onto the sheet cake on her prep-table.

"Probably because he was surprised," Cherri said behind her. "I've met Gray, Maizie. He didn't set off any of my jerk alarms. Just ask him about the letter. See what he says."

Maizie shook her head, spreading the icing as though it was paint on a clean canvas. "What could he possibly say? He used his connections to find a way to steal Granny's land. Does it matter whether he went through with it or not?"

"That depends on you."

Maizie glanced over her shoulder. "On whether I think he would've used it if things didn't work with us?"

"On whether you're so scared of your feelings for him, you'll use any excuse to run away from them."

Maizie turned back to her cake with an exasperated sigh. "Don't start that crap again. I don't have any deep-seated emotional scars from my parents' death that affect my views on relationships."

"You mean any scars you're aware of." Cherri came over and leaned a hip against Maizie's prep-table, still nibbling the last bit of batter from her spoon. "Most crazy people have no idea they're crazy."

"I am not crazy."

"That you're aware."

Maizie slanted a look at her. "Cherri..."

"Okay, okay, you're not crazy." She waited a half beat. "But you do have issues."

Maizie grunted and rolled her eyes. Gawd, she hated it when Cherri played armchair psychologist. She honestly believed the one lone psych course she'd taken in college qualified her to diagnose everything from passive aggression to emotional transference.

Maizie picked up the spatula and went back to her icing.

Cherri caught the subtle telltale signs of Maizie tuning her out. "Just listen. What's the one thing you always say you remember about your parents right before the accident?"

Maizie really didn't want to do this. It was an annoying, quasi-amusing distraction, but in the end she'd still have to figure out what to do about Gray. "I don't know, Cherri. Let's drop it, okay?"

"No, wait. Every time you talk about the accident, you remember how happy they were. And then it was all taken away. Your dad got too *distracted* by his *happiness*. And so now you avoid happiness to keep the same thing from happening to you."

"They were just laughing, Cherri. Joking. My dad looked at my mom for a second. That's how most accidents happen. The driver looks away, gets *distracted*, for whatever reason."

"Exactly."

"So if it had been his coffee cup spilling or his cell phone ringing, you're saying I'd avoid relationships with people who have coffee in the car or talk on their cells while driving?"

"Maybe."

Maizie couldn't help but laugh. "That's messed up, Cherri. Don't quit your day job, 'kay?"

"I'm serious." Cherri pushed at her glasses with her knuckle. "Okay, fine. Maybe that's simplifying it a bit. But you have to admit there's a pattern here."

"Oh yeah?" Maizie covered the last inch of chocolate cake with ivory icing then grabbed the blue piping bag.

"As long as I've known you, nothing gets in your way. Nothing distracts you...especially men. You date, but most times it's just a physical thing. Y'know, something to take the edge off, sexually."

"You make me sound like such a lady."

Cherri ignored her comment, pushing her hairnet off her brow. "Every once in a while someone with a little more going on upstairs comes along. He makes you laugh, makes you a little bit happy and then...*BAM.* You dump him. You make up some lame excuse about being too busy taking care of the shop and your grandmother and not wanting to be *distracted...*"

"Okay, one—I *am* busy. And two—none of this has anything to do with Gray trying to steal my grandmother's land."

"Yu-huh. Name one guy who's ever affected you the way Gray Lupo does. One guy who's made you smile just thinking about him, who's had more in common with you, who's made you feel even half of what you feel when you're with him."

Maizie didn't say a word. She couldn't. There had never been anyone like Gray in her life. Cherri was right. But Maizie kept her focus on decorating the sheet cake.

"Face it, girl, you're wiggin' out and it's got nothing to do with real estate."

Maizie slammed the piping bag on the prep-table, blue icing squirting out in an arch to the floor. "The letter was there, Cherri. On his desk. Nothing ambiguous about it. At some point he'd planned how he could steal the land."

"But you don't know why. Maybe he was trying to help."

"Help? How? By taking the one thing she loves almost as much as me?" Maizie's voice rumbled in her chest. Tension roiled through her belly, her heart beating faster and faster like a thing gone wild.

She swallowed hard, tamped down the first stirrings of her wolf. When she spoke again, her voice was calm, controlled. "Fine. You think I'm jumping to conclusions? You think I'm just trying to avoid some...some...guy?"

Maizie reached back, untying her apron. She yanked it over her head and crumpled it onto the prep-table. "I'll ask him. Happy? And when it turns out he's got no legitimate excuse, I'll be back here with a big fat I-told-you-so."

"And if he has a good excuse?"

Maizie's jaw tightened. She pressed her lips into a flat line, breathing through her nose. She didn't want to think about it. She was already too close to the edge with Gray, too close to falling head over heels. If he gave her even the smallest reason to admire him, he'd own her heart completely. She'd have no control, no chance to protect herself if something happened to take it all away.

She shook her head and turned toward the door. "I'll be back."

"I'm so sorry, Maizie. He went out for a run with the others about an hour ago. There's no way for me to contact him. Honest." Annette stood in the marbled foyer of the Lupo mansion, wringing her hands.

Shoot. If Maizie hadn't stopped off at her apartment to shower and spend two hours choosing the perfect outfit before driving the forty-five minutes to Gray's mansion she might have caught them.

"Do you know which way they went?" In her wolf form she could probably track the pack and catch up with them. Unfortunately, Maizie hadn't figured out how to switch back and forth yet. Wasn't completely convinced she could.

"I'm not certain, but they usually work their way down to your grandmother's cottage. Gray's always kept an eye on her.

It's sort of become part of their normal route."

I bet. "Thanks, Annette. I'll drive around and wait there. Maybe I'll catch them before they head back." Maizie turned to leave, but Annette's words stopped her.

"He loves you. You know that, right?"

Maizie glanced over her shoulder. "I don't know anything."

"Wolves mate for life, Maizie. Even though you're his true life mate it took a lot for him to let go of his bond with Donna. It went against everything he is, but he did it for you. For both of you. To give you the soul-deep connection you both need."

Maizie shook her head. "Like I said, until I see Gray, until I talk to him...I don't know anything."

It was full dark by the time Maizie got to the cottage. There was a limo parked out front, empty. *Gray.* Who else? He'd likely ordered the car be left for a comfortable ride back home. The lights were off in the cottage, the door dead-bolted from the inside. She hadn't used that lock in years. Wasn't even sure she still had the key.

The hairs at the nape of her neck bristled, invisible fingers thrummed down her spine. Maizie ignored the sensation, her mind racing with what she'd say when she saw him. After trying two wrong keys she found the right one and opened the door.

"Hello?" Her muscles coiled, she peered into the pitch-black living room, ready for anything. She could hardly breathe.

But she could see. Being a werewolf had perks. Maizie forced herself to relax, trust her body. Her night vision was incredible once she chose to believe it. And what she could hear and smell filled in where her vision left holes. Her heightened awareness was still too new though, constantly feeding her information. Everyone who'd been in the house the last few months left scents behind. She struggled to sort through smells and sounds, tell old from new, familiar from foreign.

The downstairs was lifeless, filled with deep shadows and the yawning silence of night. She closed the door behind her, a soft click when the latch snapped into place. The floorboards above creaked, made her shift her gaze upward.

Gray would likely want to stay in Granny's good graces just in case seducing Maizie didn't work out the way he planned. And what better way to charm Granny then to offer up another old trinket she'd forgotten about.

Maizie could feel in her bones he was near. He was probably up there sifting through Granny's boxed-up belongings looking for more memories to ply her with. At least this one wouldn't be taken from a death scene.

Moment by moment Maizie worked to harden her heart, prepare for the painful truth. What excuse could he have for that letter? Her chest pinched. Anxiety tightened the muscles across her shoulders. What would it mean for her now that she was a werewolf? Would she have to stay with Gray and the pack regardless? Would she have to leave? Neither option offered her comfort.

She took the steps, rounding the first landing as the swooshing sound of leather shoes scraping over a hardwood floor reached her ears. Leather fringed the scent of sweet male cologne, mixing to create a fragrance that was expressly masculine, unmistakably extravagant.

Maizie wasn't purposely quiet, but the slightest breath seemed to echo like a gale wind in the silence. She reached the top of the landing on the balls of her feet, sidestepping the old floorboards she knew would squeak.

She glanced to the right at the dark wood door of Granny's

room, then to the left at the matching door of her own room. The bathroom door was directly in front of her and not even a sliver of light showed underneath. Why hadn't Gray turned on any lights?

A small gasp and the tiny click of a door being closed made her look toward Granny's room. He'd been watching her. The tension knot across her shoulders tightened, anger boiling away caution and reason.

Maizie cleared the distance to the door in three quick strides, turning the knob so hard and fast the cheap lock broke with a little snap. A split second passed for Maizie to consider why the door had been locked to begin with. She threw open the door.

Light from the tall dusk-to-dawn lamp out front streamed through the side window, creating contours of light and darkness across the wood floor. The room was empty expect for the bed and several boxes stacked in the far corner. The closet doors were gone. The space had once been so full with Granny's things, doors had just gotten in the way. Now the closet stood empty and dark.

Maizie stepped into the room, her senses flaring, her gaze searching for Gray. Someone's panicked breaths filled the dark silence, fear sweetened the air. It wasn't Gray.

No sooner had the thought formed in her mind than a hand latched around her upper arm and the door swung shut behind her. A hard yank stumbled her backward into Anthony Cadwick's big chest.

"Where is it?"

She gasped. Cool steel pressed against her neck, the sharp point of his knife pricking her skin. She hissed against the pain. Her heart stuttered. "No. Don't. Please."

He kept his mouth close to her ear, his voice a low

grumble. His breath warmed the side of her face, moist and rank with fear. "How'd you get in without it tearing your throat out?"

Maizie worked fast to get her surprise behind her, to slow the gallop of her heart. She tried to think, to understand what was happening. "What are you doing here? This is private—"

"This dump's mine now, so shut up about the trespassing shit. Who cares? I gotta get out of here, and if you made it in, that means I can make it out." Anthony pushed her forward, his fingers digging into her arm, leading her to the window.

"What do you mean you own this place? Granny—" She stumbled, but Anthony kept pushing her forward. Before she could finish her sentence, they reached the window.

He leaned their shoulders against the frame, their bodies angled to face the door across the room, her body in front of his like a shield. His gaze darted over the front yard, the driveway and into the darkness of the forest. His rapid-fire pulse hummed through his chest into her back. He was desperate, near crazed with fear.

"What's going on, Anthony?"

His grip tightened around her arm. "Did you see it?"

"See what?"

"The wolf. A big silver son of a bitch."

Relief washed over Maizie like a warm blanket. Gray was here. How had she missed him? She must've slipped inside before he'd gotten a chance to stop her. But where was he now? What had he done to cause a man like Cadwick to behave like a frightened rabbit? "I didn't see anything. What happened?"

"It chased me, that's what happened. The fucker tried to kill me. Barely made it inside. Can't say as much for Frank."

"Frank?"

"My driver. The thing chased him off into the woods. God knows what happened to him." Anthony's whole body shuddered against hers. "I think I heard him scream. Shit, this is bad."

Maizie remembered the deadbolt on the front door. Frank didn't make it inside because Anthony hadn't let him in. Of all the things Gray might be, he wasn't a killer, but Anthony didn't know that. In his mind, he'd sacrificed another human being to save himself. And he was good with it.

Her stomach roiled at the thought. She squirmed, but Cadwick pressed the knife, drawing a warm trickle of blood. She winced, the tiny stream raced down her neck, hot against her skin. "He won't hurt you, Anthony. Just let me go."

"Right. You didn't see the size of its teeth."

The better to eat your selfish heart out with, you bastard. Maizie had had enough. She grabbed his wrist, pulled his knife-wielding hand from her neck and stepped out of his hold. He didn't seem to notice. She wasn't sure if he'd let her go or if she was just that much stronger than him now.

"You're being ridiculous. Letting your imagination get the best of you." She went to the door and flicked the light switch. "Pull yourself together and tell me why you think you own my grandmother's property."

The room flooded with light. Anthony squinted, though the enormous black pupils in his eyes showed his panic. He raced past her to the light switch, slammed into the wall and clawed at it until the room went dark again.

"No lights, no lights. It'll come back." He was panting, leaning his side and face against the wall. "Those eyes. God damn, I'll never forget those big pale eyes."

The better to see lying swindlers like you. She folded her arms across her belly. "Fine. But I want answers. Why are you here? And what did you mean you own this place?"

Anthony swallowed loud enough for her to hear. He turned, pivoting on his shoulder against the wall. His head leaned back, his chest swelling and falling with deep breaths as he dug into his breast pocket. He pulled out a small stack of neatly folded papers. "Ester signed the deed last night. The house, the land...it's all mine."

He held the papers out to Maizie and she took them. Even in the dark she could read the word "deed" perfectly. Below it, typed along the lines provided, was the address of the cottage.

"That's not possible. Granny would never—"

"She'll do whatever her little boy tells her to do," Anthony said, his voice steadier, edged with a smug humor.

Maizie snapped her gaze to him. "So you *were* the one pretending to be my dad."

He pushed up along the wall, got his feet under him. He tugged the hem of his suit jacket, straightened his tie and smoothed his shirt. "Nobody's going to believe the old lady didn't know who I was. Can't swing a dead cat around here without hitting a magazine or newspaper with my face on it. It's just business."

"It's not business." She hated how her emotions thinned her voice. She swallowed. Calmed herself. "It's trickery. It's theft. It's taking advantage of an old woman who misses her son. It's...despicable."

The insults seemed to put Anthony in his right mind, as though the normalcy and familiarity of it calmed his fear. He shoved off the wall and sauntered past her, snatching the papers back as he went. "It's also a timely turn of events for you."

"Excuse me?"

"What with your loan application rejected, I'd imagine the income from the sale will come in handy."

She hadn't heard from the bank yet. No one knew she'd even applied. Without the loan she wasn't sure she could manage everything, the business, her rent, Green Acres, the taxes on the cottage...food. How could he know?

Anthony turned, catching her gaze. "I paid a fair price, Ms. Hood. More than fair. She couldn't have gotten a better deal. And with your financial situation, you really can't be choosy."

"I didn't want to sell."

He shrugged. "Another poor business decision. Lucky for you, your grandmother has provided the means to save your business."

"I didn't want to sell." How had this happened? She'd let herself get distracted, let her heart cloud her focus. Granny counted on her, Cherri and Bob counted on her. She thought she could do it all, take care of everything all by herself if she just kept focused. She'd failed.

A shrill howl pierced the night. Cadwick's whole body flinched. He crouched as though something might swoop down and snatch him. "You hear that?"

Maizie nodded, the sharp tang of Anthony's fear infusing the air. She couldn't care less. He'd won. He'd beaten her.

Anthony snagged her arm again, pulling her in front of him, knife to her throat. Apparently he hadn't realized how easily she'd escaped him before. Maizie didn't bother to try this time. Gawd, she'd made a mess of things.

"You're gonna show me how to get out of here the same way you got in." He pushed her toward the door and Maizie stumbled into step.

Anthony dropped the knife level with her kidney as they

passed through the bedroom doorway. His hand slid to her shoulder, keeping the distance between them at arm's length. They crept down the stairs, Anthony's fingers digging in at the slightest sound.

Maizie jerked her shoulder, made him lose his grip, but she didn't try to escape before he latched on again. She knew she could if she wanted to. That was enough. She was more desperate for time than freedom.

She stopped at the bottom of the stairs. Anthony leaned over her shoulder to look into the kitchen then the other way into the living room.

"My grandmother will be devastated once she realizes you tricked her into selling."

"Ssshh. It'll hear you," he whispered. "Probably hears us thinkin'. I've never seen ears that big."

The better to hear your lies, you heartless coward. Maizie jerked her shoulder and Anthony lost his grip again. She spun around, leaning out of reach of his groping hand. "Granny didn't know what she was doing when she signed it. You had no right."

"Ssshhh...ssshhh..." His eyes wide, Cadwick pressed a finger to his lips, then tried to cover her mouth.

Maizie flinched away. "Stop it."

"Then keep your voice down." He went to the door, palms flat, peering through the arched window at the top.

"What can I do to get my grandmother's property back? How official have things gotten?"

Cadwick glanced over his shoulder, his dark brows tight. "She signed the deed." He turned his attention back through the window. "It's done. I'm taking it to the courthouse Monday."

"You mean the papers in your pocket are the originals?"

Could it really be that easy?

He looked at her again, eyes narrowing. "Whatever you're thinking, Red, you can forget it. I've waited too long to get one over on Gray Lupo. I'm not turning back now."

She heard something scratching and flicked her gaze toward the door. It was soft, like a padded foot in the gravel driveway. She could barely hear it. She looked back to Cadwick, still staring as though he might read her mind. He hadn't heard anything at all.

The pack was outside. She could sense them—now that she knew to try. Maizie exhaled a breath she hadn't realized she was holding. She wasn't alone. She closed her eyes for a minute, opening her mind to them. A deep breath brought the scents of the pack into her body, the musk of their fur, the earthy smell of the forest, the wild tang of their breath.

"What's with you?" Cadwick said, and Maizie opened her eyes.

He straightened, turning his back to the door, studying her. "You look like...like you just got hugged or something."

She couldn't stop her smile if she'd wanted to. "I can't let you leave here with those papers, Tony."

His glower deepened. "It's Anthony and I don't know how you're gonna stop me, Little Red."

The door suddenly shook with a loud boom. They both jumped and turned in time to see the wolf charge again. His huge face snapped at the window, drool splattering the glass. His eyes flashed for an instant, big and furious, before he fell out of sight below the window.

"Shit." Cadwick grabbed Maizie's hand, yanked her along behind him. "Back door. Let's go."

Maizie could've pulled free, could've broken his arm if she

wanted. She didn't. She wanted those papers, so she went with him through the living room into the sunroom to the back door.

Cadwick crouched as he passed along the wall of windows, watching the darkness as he went. He pulled Maizie in front of him when he reached the door, slipped his arm around her waist and opened the lock.

"Go," he said.

"What if that thing's out there?" She knew he wasn't. Ricky was still out front with Shelly and Joy. There was only one wolf waiting in back. But Cadwick didn't know that.

"Guess we'll find out. Now, go." He brandished the knife at her and Maizie stumbled backward, narrowly avoiding the sharp point. She pushed through the door and made it beyond the arbor before Cadwick followed.

Movement to her left caught both their attention, a flash of blonde-tipped fur among the moonlit flowers. Poor Lynn, her dye job didn't transfer forms the same.

A low growl raised the hairs at the back of her neck and had Cadwick scampering up beside Maizie. "You hear that?"

Maizie nodded, allowing Cadwick to cower behind her again. He held her above the elbows, using her body to shield against whatever watched from the high flowers.

"Christ, what kind of fucking beasts does Lupo keep in these woods?" He squinted into the darkness. "Not that it matters. They'll all be roadkill once I get through with this land."

Lynn's growl went primal. She leapt from a patch of towering sunflowers, teeth bared. Cadwick's girlish squeal deafened Maizie's ears a split second before he pushed her into Lynn's path.

It was too late for Lynn to stop. Her heavy furred body

slammed into Maizie, chest to chest, knocking her off her feet, driving the air from her lungs. Maizie's head smacked the patio brick, starbursts lit her eyes.

Lynn writhed on top of her, trying to find her footing. Her long wolf legs and sharp bones poked Maizie's stomach as she launched into the chase. She followed Cadwick's trail through the flowers in the opposite direction, her blonde-tipped fur disappearing in the thick foliage.

Shaking off the dizziness, Maizie followed, leaves and stems sticking to her clothes, smacking her face despite the shield of her hands. She broke through the edge of the garden at the corner of the house, already angling her body for the turn and nearly toppled over Gray before she could stop.

She threw her weight backward, landing hard on her ass, her feet sliding into Cadwick's outstretched legs. He lay spread eagled on his back, Gray's snarling face inches from his, one thick paw pressing his chest.

Maizie scrambled backward, got to her feet before Cadwick's wide frightened eyes found her.

"Help me. Please. Help me." His voice was breathy, panicked.

Lynn gave a hard snort from a few feet away, her tail snapping once against her rump. As if on cue, Ricky, Shelly, Joy and Shawn jogged around from the front of the house, forming a circle around Maizie, Gray and the pleading Cadwick.

Maizie threw a glance at Shawn, his darker fur and larger body a nice contrast with Lynn's. He rubbed his muzzle along her neck, taking his place at her side. He was new to the pack, new to being a werewolf, but he seemed to fit seamlessly. Could it be that way for Maizie? Could she forgive and forget?

She stepped nearer to Gray, his low growl vibrating the silvery fur along his back. She dug her fingers in, closing her eyes at the luscious feel of his fleece. His scent filled her lungs, wild, earthy forest and the barest hint of sweet male cologne. Gray leaned into her touch, the shift almost imperceptible, but enough to send a warm shiver straight through Maizie, from her head to her toes.

She dropped her gaze to Cadwick. "Give me the deed."

Chapter Fifteen

"You knew?" Maizie stared, dumbfounded by her grandmother's cheek-pinching grin.

"Of course, dear," Granny said. "How else would I know to crazy up my answers when the judge called?"

"Then why didn't you go through with it?"

Granny gave a nod toward Gray beside her. "Lost his nerve."

Gray's stoic face flushed, the tightness around his eyes softening as well as the lines across his forehead. A smile flickered across his lips, but he spoke before it took control. "It was a last resort, and not a pleasant one."

Maizie leaned back in her chair, folding her arms under her chest. "Especially if Granny decided she wanted to sell."

Gray's brows creased. "That was never her wish."

"If it was? I mean, after you'd gotten control over *everything*. What if she decided she wanted to sell?" She wasn't sure why she was testing him. She just had to be sure, had to hear it from his own lips.

Gray's pale blue eyes narrowed, his expression questioning. He leaned forward, elbows on his knees. "The guardianship was a ruse, Maizie. A line of defense against rash decisions."

"Doesn't answer the question."

"You're really asking?" Gray shook his head and pushed back, his lean body tall in the chair. He looked away, talking more to himself than Maizie. "Of course you're asking. She's your grandmother. You should."

His gaze darted out over the plush lawn of Green Acres backyard. Nearly an acre of manicured grass dotted with trees and flower gardens, and edged by the forest. They'd snagged a comfortable set of wicker chairs under a giant white ash. The limbs, thick with leaves, let the sun dapple through around them.

Gray's handsome, sharp-boned face darkened, yet there was no anger in his eyes. He'd worn his normal Armani blazer and slacks, lightweight, dark charcoal gray, with a white crewneck shirt underneath, business casual, sexy as hell. His thick silver-gray hair matched perfectly, curling just below his collar, a striking contrast with the glacier blue of his eyes.

He looked back to her and it was all Maizie could do not to gasp at the impact of those eyes. "Had it come to it. Yes, I would've taken control of Ester's holdings. I would've kept her from selling until I could be sure the decision was sound, sure she knew what she was doing, and why."

"And if she was?"

His gaze locked with hers, his expression unflinching. "I would've followed her wishes."

Was it enough? Maizie caught her bottom lip between her teeth, looked away. She couldn't allow his sexy good looks, his sweet, wild aroma, or the memories of his hard body pressed to hers cloud her mind. She couldn't let her hormones distract her again until she was sure.

"It was my idea, Little Red." Granny reached her hand out to Maizie's, so soft and frail Maizie hardly felt it. She relaxed the tight knot of her arms and took Granny's hand.

"With my spells I can't always be sure what's real and what's not," Granny said. "I didn't want to bother you. You were already so busy with the bakery. So I asked Gray to watch out for me, even though I knew it made him uncomfortable. He agreed. He's a good man, dear."

Maizie studied Granny's adorable weathered face, sky blue eyes peering from beneath soft wrinkled lids, wisdom sparking in their depths. Granny trusted him, loved him even, it meant everything.

She swung her gaze back to Gray, his brow creased, worry glazing his pale eyes. She smiled. She couldn't help it. "He's a very good man."

Relief washed over his face, relaxing the muscles along his brow, the stiffness of his mouth. He dropped his gaze, his cheeks turning a shade pinker.

He looked back to her, his eyes intense, earnest. "Ester is beloved to me. But you're part of me, Maizie, a part of my soul. You have been since I held you in my arms that night. You were so young, and I was...a mess. But none of that mattered. The bond was made between us anyway. We're helpless against it. Just took me twenty-one years to admit it."

Maizie reached across the low glass coffee table and Gray took her hand in both of his. "We'll have to work on that stubborn streak."

He laughed and kissed her hand, his gaze sliding up to hers so the pale blue peered beneath long black lashes. "Sounds like fun."

His low voice rumbled through her body, vibrating all the tiny hairs along her skin and sending a liquid hot flood to her sex. She exhaled, her breath shaky, leaning back in her chair when he released her hand. Oh yeah, it was definitely going to be fun.

"Now you're sure that Cadwick fellow won't be coming around anymore?" Granny said.

Gray nodded, still staring at Maizie, his head turning slowly toward Granny, his eyes the last to leave her face. "Yes," he said. "I stopped by his office to see how he was, uh, handling last night's events."

Maizie took her glass of tea from the table, her mouth suddenly gone dry. "What'd he say?"

Gray glanced her way. "He's convinced you're a female Dr. Dolittle and now has a powerful desire to donate money to the Bad Wolf Wild Game Preserve. He said he wants to make sure the animals never have reason to wander from the forest."

Granny laid her hand on his forearm. Her thin fingers squeezed. "Thank you, Gray. I know how difficult it's been for you having to deal with him. I'm so sorry."

Maizie took another sip and set her glass back on the coaster. "I think I'm missing something."

Gray caught her gaze but looked away. "Cadwick, he...he's the man Donna was seeing before the accident."

"Oh, Gray..."

He shook his head. "It was a long time ago. A meaningless affair. It was my fault. I wouldn't listen to what she needed. Wouldn't let her go. I think he really fell for her though. He thinks she left town. Everyone outside the family does. But it seemed to make his issues with me even worse."

"He's a dang fool," Granny said. Both Maizie and Gray looked at her. "Comin' 'round here pretending to be my sweet Riddly. Thinkin' I wouldn't know the difference."

Maizie glanced at Gray and Gray at her. Neither wanted to mention the fact Cadwick had done exactly that.

"Asked me to sign those papers, like I wouldn't know what

they were." She huffed. "Fool. Never even checked how I signed."

It didn't matter, Gray had shredded the documents. "How'd you sign them, Granny?" Maizie asked.

Her smile brightened, cheeks apple-round. "Little Red Hood of course. I told you he was a wolf of a man."

Maizie stood and threw her arms around Granny's neck, pressed a kiss into the soft skin of her cheek. "I love you, Gran. You're a trip."

Granny patted her arm. "Thank you, dear. I may be old, but I ain't stupid."

Gray laughed as Maizie plopped back in her seat. "No, Ester. No one would ever call you stupid."

"Still," Granny said. "That money would've gone a long way to help ends meet, wouldn't it, Little Red?"

Maizie's face warmed. She didn't want Granny worrying about her financial problems. "Cadwick say something to you, Gran?"

"I don't want to be a burden."

"You're not," Gray said. "Maizie's money problems are solved."

"I'm not taking a handout from you, Gray," Maizie said, guessing how his rich-boy mind worked. "I started the business on my own. If it succeeds I want to be able to take full credit. Same if it fails."

"I'm not giving you money."

"You're not?" A part of her had kind of liked the security, even though she'd never take it.

"No. I did, however, cosign a loan." He held up a hand at the hint of her protest. "*I* am not giving you the loan. I simply assured the bank you're good for the money. I know you can make a success of anything you set your mind to, Maizie. I'm just making sure you get the chance."

"Thank you."

"But if I could make a suggestion regarding your one-eyed driver..."

"Bob? He quit," Maizie said. "Got a job driving a city bus."

"Jeezus."

"I know. Great job. Union, perks and everything. Couldn't pass it up. Speaking of jobs..." She checked her watch. "I was supposed to help Cherri ice four hundred and fifty-three cupcakes for the elementary-school open house tomorrow night. I really have to go."

"I'll drive you," Gray said.

Granny took his hand and Maizie's. She squeezed. "It's right the two of you came together. I knew yours would be the kind of soul match people tell stories about. Only out of tragedy could such a love be born. That's what you've found, the kind of love dreamed of in fairy tales."

Maizie fought hard not to roll her eyes. She smiled and kissed Granny's cheek and watched as Gray did the same.

He whispered in her ear, but Maizie could hear as clearly as if he'd whispered in hers. "Thank you, Ester. You're right. She's my Snow White, my Sleeping Beauty and my Dorothy Gale. She couldn't be a better match for me if she'd been plucked from the pages of a storybook."

Granny's grin brightened just a bit and Gray kissed her cheek again. She stared at him as he straightened, but then her gaze focused on something behind him, her eyes went wide.

"Oh dear, I hope he didn't see that."

Maizie and Gray both followed her gaze to a white-haired man fussing around a bird feeder several feet away. He held a fistful of violets in his hands and couldn't seem to stop himself from glancing Granny's way every few seconds.

"You have a suitor, Gran?" Maizie couldn't help the teasing tone in her voice.

"Stop it, Little Red. I had the love of my life already. George is just a...a hobby." She blushed, smoothing fine wisps of hair back toward her bun.

"Cute hobby." Maizie watched George adjust his bowtie and smooth his suspenders over his plaid short-sleeved shirt. She knew it was the thick mane of white hair that had captured her gran's attention. The preference must run in the family.

Granny licked her lips, then pinched her cheeks for a sweet natural blush. "Now run along, the two of you. He won't come over if I've got company and his memory's not what it used to be. He'll forget why he's waiting over there before long."

Gray caught Granny's chin with the crook of his finger, met her gaze. "You're happy?"

Granny smiled. "Yes, my lovely silver wolf. I'm happy being human. But thank you for the offer as always."

Maizie's belly warmed watching him bend to kiss her cheek one more time. "Only for you, my sweet Ester," he said then took Maizie by the hand.

"I love how you are with her." Maizie settled into the deep leather seats of his limo.

"She's a dear friend," Gray said. "Without her Donna's death would've been intolerable."

"Annette said you wouldn't turn her because you were so unhappy with the life you'd been saddled with, you wouldn't commit someone else to the same fate."

"I decided long ago, for Ester I would make an exception if

she truly wished it." Gray slid his hand across the seat to Maizie's. He couldn't be this close and not touch her.

Their fingers laced. Her hand so small in his, he treasured it. "She's always refused. I believed, although she denies it, Ester knew the emotional trials far outweighed the added years. Still, it was all I had to offer."

Maizie's forest-green gaze dropped to their clasped hands. "Is being what we are really so bad?"

The trepidation in her voice touched his heart. He brought her hand to his lips, tasting her sugar-sweet skin as he spoke. "For twenty-one years I couldn't imagine a worse fate."

Her exhale shuddered, her skin warming against his lips. "And now?"

"It was worth every moment to have you as my reward."

Her quick arousal scented the air, filled the private compartment like the most captivating perfume.

He closed his eyes, breathed her in. He'd never get enough of her. How could he? She was his life mate and yet he'd tried for so long to deny she existed. But she did exist and he'd make damn sure she had every reason to stay.

"You know, when I was a teenager all the young lovers went parking on Saturday nights." He tugged her hand, and brought a mischievous grin across Maizie's lips.

"It's Sunday afternoon," she said, following his lead, moving to her knees on the seat. "We're not parked and we're...ah, not alone." She glanced over her shoulder at the solid privacy wall.

"The partition's soundproof." He scooped her around the waist, pulling her to his lap. "Besides, Dave doesn't hear anything he's told not to."

"Now *that's* a good driver." She straddled his legs, pressing the moist heat of her sex to his groin. His hips pressed up into her, he couldn't help it, his hands cupping the soft curve of her waist, holding her to him.

Maizie arched her back, adding her own delicious pressure, her breasts riding high beneath the low neckline of her sundress. Gray's muscles pulled tight, wanting her, needing the feel of her pussy hugging his cock, milking him dry.

She was ready for him, her arousal so thick in the air his wolf-half stirred at her scent. Her desire rolled through him like a physical touch, stirring his body, calling to everything male inside him. They were so connected, too connected. She could undo him—and he'd enjoy it.

His balls tight, his cock pulsed at the thought of driving into her. His mind slowed, blood racing to his cock, making it hard to think beyond sliding his hands beneath that sweet little dress, the silk flesh of her thighs against his palms, the wet heat of her panties—

His phone rang. *Fuck.* "What is it about thoughts of screwing you while I'm in this car that makes that damn phone ring?"

Maizie fell forward, bracing her hands on his shoulders. Her breaths were deep, but still under control. "It might be important."

Gray jerked the small BlackBerry from his breast pocket. "What?"

"Uncle Gray?" Rick said. "You okay? You sound... Oh. Maizie's with you, huh?"

"To the point, Rick." His jaw tight, Gray tried to soften the heat in his voice.

"Yeah, right." His voice held a ring of laughter. "Mom wanted to know if you were bringing Maizie around tonight. Sort of a get-to-know-the-family shindig. Personally I just wanna watch the great alpha wolf go all soft and squishy around his mate."

Gray flicked his gaze to Maizie, her soft kissable lips, her delicate neck and nearly bare shoulders. The way a single red curl lay atop the shelf of her full breast. "Trust me, kid. There's nothing soft and squishy about me right now."

Rick snorted. "No doubt. So? Ya comin' or not? I gotta tell ya, Mom's kind of freaking about Maizie's first impression of her...ya know, now that she's Suzie homemaker and everything with Shawn."

Maizie leaned into him, nestled her little face under his chin and pressed her lips to his neck. Her perfume, the scent of wildflowers with a hint of forest underneath, smoothed through his body like warm brandy. Gray closed his eyes, heat rippling out from the spot her lips touched in fast dizzying waves. She kissed again.

"She's pack now, Uncle Gray," Rick said. "Y'know, family. We'll do right by her. I hope she knows that."

Gray met Maizie's gaze, raised a brow.

She smiled. "All my life it's only been me and Gran. Even after the rough start I had with them, I've never felt so connected to family the way I did when the pack came to help me. I want to be a part of that again. Always."

"Always." He leaned forward, taking her mouth with his, feeling his world click into focus, complete in a way he'd never thought possible.

"Uncle Gray? You there?"

Gray brought the phone back to his ear. "Uhm...I...I'll get back to ya, kid." He thumbed the off button on his cell phone and tossed it to the seat. His arms wrapped around Maizie, his hands sliding down to cup the firm cheeks of her ass.

She gasped when he squeezed, his fingers finding the edge

of her panties, then sliding underneath.

"How much do you like these things?" His lips brushed the downy soft skin of her ear.

"They're hideous."

His laugh rumbled between them, echoing through her body, reverberating back into him. "Good answer."

A quick tug and Gray ripped the crotch, another yank and he ripped the side. He pulled the ruined cloth from under her dress. His gaze dropped to his hand before he tossed the panties to the floor. They were lace and silk, the same milk white as her skin.

Maizie's hands cupped his face, brought his attention back to her. "I want you to know...I love you. And not because of what happened, not because I got infected. I loved you before. I think I've loved you all along. I've been wandering through that forest for years not even knowing what I was searching for. Now I know."

"Now we know." He closed the distance between them, taking her mouth with his. Her gasp stole his breath, her exhale filled his lungs.

Her hands worked his pants, his belt, his zipper. She rose up enough to slide his slacks and briefs to his knees, his cock wagging stiff and eager. She ran her hand over his shaft, sending a mind-numbing jolt shooting through his body. Her fingers laced around the girth of his cock, stroked him as her other hand tucked her hair behind her ear so she could watch.

Gray swallowed, his mouth dry, body tight. He shoved her pretty dress to her hips, exposing the red thatch of pussy hair between her thighs. Her cream glistened in the coarse hairs, her scent stronger now, more maddening.

A growl started low in his chest, a wild need edging closer and closer to the surface. *My mate. Claim her again.*

His hips rocked, following her rhythm as he dipped his fingers into her warm wet curls. Her gasp squeezed his lungs, her pleasure vibrated along his skin so he had to close his eyes to keep from losing control. He felt what she felt. The tight filling sensation of his fingers inside her, how each thrust built that exquisite pressure, spun her closer and closer toward release.

He knew her body's reaction to his touch just as she knew the feel of her hand pumping the sensitive flesh of his cock. Each stroke pulled a tingling string of pleasure from every corner of his being, so undeniable he couldn't still his body. His heart hammered his chest, his beast rolled and growled inside him, wanting more, wanting it all.

He curled his fingers inside her, pulled her to him even as the walls of her pussy hugged around him. When the head of his cock bobbed against her sex and her cream wet over its head, he pulled his fingers out and drove his hard shaft deep inside her.

She rode him fast and wild, the pace frantic, right from the start. The pressure swelled between them, through them, one body feeding the other. Maizie screamed... No, it wasn't a scream. She howled. And a simple understanding crystallized in the most primal recesses of Gray's brain.

She'd claimed *him,* marked him as her mate. Her body held his, her spirit reaching through the connection of their flesh down to his soul and touched him there. His lungs seized, a storm of heat flooded his body, burning every hard-won tether of his control. Release came hard and fast. There was no stopping it, no waiting for her to join him. There was no need.

Maizie's orgasm rocked through him an instant later. Like free falling from a towering cliff, he couldn't breathe. The pleasure was too intense, stimulating every nerve ending in his body so his balls, his muscles, his flesh hummed and quivered with sensation. A pleasure so close to pain he nearly ached with it.

She collapsed against him, the fast beat of her heart like thunder through his chest. Nothing like that had ever happened to him before and he knew nothing like it would ever happen again with anyone else. *Life mate.*

Maizie pushed up to look in his eyes, her arms warm around his neck. "Granny used to warn me the big bad wolf in the forest would gobble me up." She smiled. "I have to tell you. I feel utterly consumed."

Gray kissed her, a quick touch of lips. "Whoever said, Little Red, being gobbled up by a wolf was a bad thing?"

About the Author

To learn more about Alison Paige, please visit www.AlisonPaige.com. Send an email to Alison Paige at Alison@AlisonPaige.com.

Alison Paige is the penname of multipublished author Paige Cuccaro. She writes as Alison Paige when her stories run hot and spicy and as Paige Cuccaro when the fun in the bedroom is more of a sexy simmer. The romance is always key, whether it's between beings of this world or out of this world.

Alison (Paige) lives in Ohio, with her husband, three daughters, three dogs, three cats, a parakeet, and a bearded dragon named Rexy, in an ever-shrinking house. When she's not writing she can be found doing the mom thing with a book in one hand and a notepad and pen in the other.

Ideas come without warning and the best way to stimulate your imagination is to enjoy the imagination of someone else.

GREAT
cheap
fun

Discover eBooks!

THE FASTEST WAY TO GET THE HOTTEST NAMES

Get your favorite authors on your favorite reader, long before they're out in print! Ebooks from Samhain go wherever you go, and work with whatever you carry—Palm, PDF, Mobi, and more.

Lightning Source UK Ltd.
Milton Keynes UK
14 September 2010

159853UK00001B/115/P